DARK ANGEL

DARK ANGEL

SKIN GAME

MAX ALLAN COLLINS

Based on the television series created by

James Cameron and Charles H. Eglee

BALLANTINE BOOKS • NEW YORK

Dark Angel: Skin Game is a work of fiction. Names, places and incidents either are products of the author's imagination or are used fictitiously.

A Del Rey® Book
Published by The Ballantine Publishing Group

TM and copyright © 2003 by Twentieth Century Fox
Film Corporation

All rights reserved under International and Pan-American Copyright Conventions. Published in the United States by The Ballantine Publishing Group, a division of Random House, Inc., New York, and simultaneously in Canada by Random House of Canada Limited, Toronto.

Del Rey is a registered trademark and the Del Rey colophon is a trademark of Random House, Inc.

www.delreydigital.com

ISBN 0-345-45183-X

Cover art and design by Redseal

Manufactured in the United States of America

First Edition: February 2003

10 9 8 7 6 5 4 3 2 1

For BJ Elsner—
Looney lady,
angel of light

MAC & MVC

ACKNOWLEDGMENTS

Once again, my frequent collaborator Matthew V. Clemens—with whom I've written numerous published short stories—helped me here immeasurably. A knowledgeable *Dark Angel* fan, Matt coplotted this tale and created a detailed story treatment from which I could develop *Skin Game*.

My editor Steve Saffel again provided consistently strong support, which included not just rounding up materials, but adding his own creative input.

Both Matt and Steve pitched in to solve numerous problems created when the original concept of this novel—intended to take place early within the second season, as a continuity implant—needed reshaping into a sequel to the final episode of the series.

I would like to thank the creators of *Dark Angel*, James Cameron and Charles Eglee, who provided the story for that episode—"Freak Nation," teleplay by Ira Steven Behn and Rene Echevarria, who also deserve thanks and recognition. Also particularly helpful was Moira Kirland Dekker, the writer of "Designate This," an episode we draw heavily upon here, as well. Thanks too to Debbie Olshan of 20th

Century Fox; Wendy Cheseborough of Lightstorm, and, at Ballantine Books, Gillian Berman, Crystal Velasquez, and Colleen Lindsay.

Matt, Steve, and I hope that *Dark Angel* fans will appreciate this continuation of an innovative series that ended too soon.

"We'll start with a reign of terror.
A few murders here and there."

—DR. JACK GRIFFIN (CLAUDE RAINS)
The Invisible Man (1933)

Chapter One
IMAGER IS EVERYTHING

Like a relentless boxer, rain beat down on the city, first jabbing with sharp needles, then smacking Seattle with huge fat drops that hit like haymakers, the barrage punctuated by the ominous rumble of thunder and the eerie flash of lightning.

An unmarked black car drew to a stop in a rat-infested Sector Three alley, the rain rattling the metal roof like machine-gun fire. Two men in dark suits climbed out, to be instantly drenched, though neither seemed to notice. Each wore a radio earplug with a short microphone bent toward his mouth.

Sage Thompson—the man who'd emerged from the passenger's side—was relieved that the headsets, at least, seemed to be waterproof. In their coat pockets, each man carried one of the new portable thermal imagers that, just this week, had become standard equipment. Thompson— barely six feet, almost skinny at 180 pounds—wondered if water-tightness was among the gizmo's various high-tech bells and whistles.

Water sluiced down the alley in a torrent that seemed to express the sky's anger, eventually bubbling over the edge of a rusty grate maybe ten yards in front of them. Thompson

1

was forced to jump the stream and his feet nearly slid out from under him as he landed and bumped into a triangle of garbage cans, sending them crashing into each other, creating a din that rivaled the storm's, his hands flying wide to help maintain his balance. Then his hands dropped back to his sides, the one holding his flashlight clanging off the imager in his coat pocket, the other moving to make sure his pistol was still secure in its holster on his belt.

The hefty man who'd been driving—Cal Hankins—shone his flashlight in Thompson's face, huffed once, and eased around a dumpster that looked like it hadn't been emptied since before the Pulse. Moving slowly ahead, their flashlights sweeping back and forth over the brick hulk in front of them, the two men finally halted in front of what had once been a mullioned window.

The interior of the six-story brick building—an abandoned warehouse, Thompson surmised—seemed a black hole waiting to devour them without so much as a belch. Next to Thompson, his partner Hankins swept a flashlight through one of the broken panes, painting the rainy night with slow, even strokes. Darkness surrendered only brief glimpses of the huge first-floor room as it swallowed up the light.

"You sure this is the right place?" Hankins asked gruffly.

There was no fear in the man's voice—Thompson sensed only that his partner didn't want his time wasted. At forty, bucket-headed Hankins—the senior partner of the duo—wore his blondish hair in a short brush cut that revealed only a wisp or two of gray. His head rested squarely on his shoulders, without apparent benefit of a neck, and he stood nearly six-three, weighing in (Thompson estimated) at over 230. But the man wasn't merely fat—there was enough gristle and muscle and bone in there to make Hankins formidable.

Still, Thompson knew their boss—that nasty company man, Ames White, a conscienceless yuppie prick if there ever was one—had been all over Hankins about his weight and rode the older guy mercilessly about it. Though he knew better than to ever say it out loud, Thompson considered White the worst boss in his experience—which was saying something.

White was smart, no doubting that, but he had a sarcastic tongue and a whiplash temper that Thompson had witnessed enough times to know he should keep his mouth shut and his head low.

"This is the right place, all right," Thompson said, raising his voice over the battering rain. "Dispatch said the thermal imager team picked up a transgenic in the market in Sector Four."

"This is Sector Three."

"Yeah—they followed him here before they lost him."

Hankins shook his head in disgust. "Then why the fuck ain't *they* lookin' for him, then? What makes us the clean-up crew for their sorry asses?"

These questions were rhetorical, Thompson knew, though they did have answers, the same answer in fact: Ames White.

And Hankins spent much of his time bitching about White, behind the boss's back, of course. But they both knew it was only a matter of time before White found a way to get rid of Hankins . . .

. . . and then Thompson would have to break in a new partner, possibly one even younger than himself. Then he would be the old-timer. The thought made him cringe.

Not exactly a kid at twenty-seven, Thompson was the antithesis of Hankins: the younger man seemed like a long-neck bottle standing next to the pop-top beer can that was his partner. Married to his college sweetheart, Melanie, and with a new baby daughter, Thompson was the antithesis of Hankins in terms of home life, as well: the gristled bulldog had been divorced twice and had three or four kids he never saw and didn't really seem to give a damn about.

This was a partnership made not in Heaven but in Ames White's twisted idea of the right thing to do; and Thompson still hadn't figured out if being partnered with Hankins was a reward—setting him up to step into the older man's shoes—or a punishment—White saddling him with a complainer.

Thompson—in keeping a low profile and, frankly, kissing White's ass—sometimes wondered if their sick, slick boss didn't see through his obsequiousness into the contempt he truly felt.

Hankins took a few steps to the right, Thompson on his heels. Withdrawing the imager from his pocket, Hankins squeezed the trigger and methodically scanned the area around them for the transgenic—nothing.

The new thermal imagers looked like smaller versions of the pre-Pulse radar guns that Thompson had read about in his online history studies. The biggest difference was that instead of having red LED numbers that showed speed, the ass-end readout area of the imagers contained a tiny monitor that showed infrared pictures of any heat source the front end was pointed at. The two men were looking for something with a core temperature of 101.6, the average temperature of transgenics—three degrees higher than humans.

"Fuck it," Hankins sighed, rain streaking down his face like heat-wave perspiration. "Looks like we're going to have to go inside."

"Looks like," Thompson said with a nod.

"We'll split up," Hankins announced.

"Makes us both more vulnerable."

Hankins kissed the air obnoxiously. "You're so sensitive, so vulnerable, even *with* papa bear around."

"Cut it out, man."

Hankins grunted another, deeper sigh. "Sooner we get done with this thankless-ass job, sooner we can get away from this fuckin' monsoon."

"You're right," Thompson admitted, his voice calm even though his guts now seemed to be swimming upstream toward his mouth.

It wasn't that Thompson was a coward. He'd seen action before, plenty of it—even for the post-Pulse world, Seattle was a tough town, and for cops and anybody working security, it was a higher risk job than steeplejack—and he handled the fear and stress just fine. What bothered him was, he didn't think either he or even the rugged Hankins could handle a pissed-off transgenic alone. They weren't human, those transgenics—they were monsters, really.

And Sage Thompson had seen monster movies before—he knew what happened when people split up in such circumstances.

He could tell himself that this was reality, not fantasy; but Seattle in the last few years had turned into a place more ghastly than the imagination of any mere writer or filmmaker could conjure.

Hankins said, "When we find the stairs, I'll head up and start down. You begin down here and work your way up. We'll meet in the middle, agree we didn't find anything, and haul our soggy asses out of here."

"It's a plan," Thompson said with a shrug.

Thompson slipped the imager back into his coat pocket, wiped the rain from his face—a fruitless gesture—and took a couple more steps forward.

The city was the reluctant home to a ton of these shabby old buildings, and they were all around the Emerald City, the structural equivalent of the homeless. Back when the buildings had been constructed in the 1940s and 1950s, they mostly housed factories that built things from scratch, packed them up and shipped them off to the four corners of the world.

But as time went on and the economy eroded around the turn of the century—only to take the devastating hit of the Pulse—many of the buildings stood abandoned, with some then used as warehouse space for other businesses. Each crumbling structure was different, depending on how it had been cannibalized. Thompson knew he might find a floor that was still all offices or one where all the office walls had been demolished to allow for the stacking of larger objects—there was just no way of knowing what lay ahead.

With half a head-turn, Hankins asked, "Ready?"

"Ready," Thompson said, trying to keep a note of confidence in his voice.

Hankins turned all the way now, shined the light in his face yet again. "You okay, kiddo?"

"Yeah."

"You sure?"

"Just get the damn light out of my face."

Grinning, Hankins aimed the flash back into the building. "Yeah, you're okay."

They were stopped outside a broken door, a heavy number that would have made quite a barrier if it had been locked rather than half hanging off its hinges. Both men pulled out their Glock nines and Thompson chambered a round. Hankins, Thompson knew, already had one in the pipe . . . and most likely already had the safety off as well.

Hankins stepped through the door and Thompson watched the older man swing his weapon from side to side, the hand holding the flashlight following suit.

Thompson stepped through the door behind his partner, his arms locked together in the same fashion, his pistol and flashlight simultaneously sweeping the room. Struggling to keep his breathing under control, he was thankful to at least be out of the rain. He could hear it banging on the roof far above him and on the remaining windows on this floor. Carefully, he tuned that out and listened closely for other sounds.

Moving off to the right now, putting himself out in front, Thompson heard Hankins' raspy breathing and suddenly knew that, for all his bluster, his partner fought the same nervousness that wanted to paralyze him. To their left something metallic rattled, and they both swung around, their lights stopping briefly on a rattling soda can, then moving on, both beams settling on a huge brown rat. The rodent froze, but its black eyes were not the least bit intimidated by the lights.

"S'pose that sucker's transgenic?" asked Hankins archly.

Thompson might have laughed—out of nervousness—but his throat felt too dry to pull it off. Letting out a long breath, he went back to checking out the room.

He moved slowly forward, allowing the distance between himself and Hankins to grow, but stayed close enough to cover his partner should the need arise. Halfway across the room, they found a stairwell leading to the second floor. Hankins' flashlight shone up the stairs, his gun still balanced atop his wrist.

Turning his head halfway toward Thompson, he said, "I'm going up."

"Okay. I'll keep at it down here."

"You find anything, let me know immediately."

"Same back at ya," Thompson said. Again he thought about the soggy headset plugged into his ear and hoped the thing had signal enough to get up six flights of stairs.

Hankins headed up the dark stairwell, the steps groaning for a while, but the sound soon getting swallowed by the hammering of rain, which was slanting toward the building, moisture working its way through the loose slats of boarded-up windows.

Thompson watched as Hankins and the light disappeared up the stairs. Shining his flashlight in that direction, he saw scant evidence that Hankins had even been in the building— merely a few wet footprints on the wooden stairs.

Thompson suddenly felt very alone.

Something scrabbled across the floor, just behind him, and

he spun around, the flashlight and gun following in a wobbly arc, rainwater spraying off him like he was a wet hound. The beam of light and Glock settled on what appeared to be the same rat again, only this time the rodent stood on its haunches, and seemed to smile—showing its sharp yellow teeth—and almost appeared to be flipping Thompson off with its raised front paws.

Thompson suppressed the urge to squeeze off a round and end the little bastard, and it took no small amount of will to keep him from pulling the trigger—not just because the creature was a handy surrogate for both Hankins and Ames White, but because it might be helpful to end the distraction of the noise the thing was making.

Only, if the flashlights hadn't alerted the transgenic to their positions, a gunshot most assuredly would . . . and God only knew what Hankins would think if he heard Thompson shooting, moments after the older man headed up the stairs.

Commuting the rat's death sentence to life, Thompson resumed his search of the first floor. He moved carefully, doing his best to stay silent, a couple of times holding the flashlight under an arm as he probed especially shadowy corners with the thermal imager.

"Hankins," he half whispered into the microphone.

No response.

Thompson felt a bead of sweat roll down his cheek, to mingle with the streaks of rain, and he unconsciously found a corner to press himself into as he spoke again, this time louder. *"Hankins."*

This time the response was immediate. "Thompson, would you please shut the hell up? Transgenics from here to Portland can hear you. If you're not in trouble—and it doesn't sound like you are—zip it."

The younger man's face burned as he felt himself blush in the darkness. Seemed that with every shift he spent with Hankins, he found a new reason to hate him. Thompson vowed that once they were out of this building, he would speak up for himself, and finally ask White for a new partner . . . and, failing that, he would simply transfer out of White's unit altogether.

This whole transgenic affair troubled him. He'd been with the program long enough to know that although these human experiments were considered a threat to national security, the transgenics had been engineered to defend this country, after all. So on some level, Thompson felt like his job was to track down and dispose of what might be considered soldiers of his country. He tried not to see it that way, but sometimes it felt exactly like that—particularly when he let himself think a little too much, or on long sleepless nights during which the hypocrisy of his life crawled into his mind like a waking nightmare.

Angrily wiping the sweat from his eyes, Thompson moved deeper into the blackness, punctuating it with sweeps of the flash. At the back of the cavernous space, he found three offices stretching across the rear wall. Two of the doors were completely gone, and the third—its window long gone—hung from one hinge like a stubborn loose rotted tooth, refusing to fall out of a gaping mouth. Of the six panes of glass that had been the top half of the facing walls of the offices, only one remained, a nasty crack running across it diagonally.

Thompson pulled out the thermal imager and slow-scanned the offices without success. Telling himself he was just being careful, he spun in a steady circle, covering the whole first floor again to make sure nothing had skulked in behind him. Except for a few more rats—and what was either the biggest rat he'd ever seen or a small stray cat—the monitor showed nothing.

This left only one thing to do. Since the thermal imager could not see through wood, that meant he still had to check out the offices one at a time.

Letting out his breath slowly, he stepped toward the doorway in the farthest left corner, his pistol and flashlight leading the way. He swept the room quickly once, past the large metal desk, over the peeling wallboard, past the scattered, smashed glass on the floor to the low half wall to his right.

The room was empty.

And he saw no wet footprints on the floor; even the dusty patina of the desktop seemed undisturbed. Still, Thompson played it carefully as he eased around the desk and pointed his gun at the floor behind it.

Nothing.

He let out another breath and felt a little better, and pressed on. His stomach was fluttering, though, and he felt covered in an apprehension as real as his rain-drenched clothes. Middle office, now.

Not only was the door gone off this office, so were the furnishings within: no desk, file cabinets, tables, chairs, nothing but piles of broken glass and fractured wallboard littering the room like the aftermath of a biker party. No transgenics in there either.

Listening intently at the sagging door of the final office, Thompson heard nothing but his own pulse pounding in his ears. Though the whole building smelled of rot and decay—a bouquet emphasized by the night's dampness—the last office seemed to be the nexus of the putrid aroma. The door groaned as he pushed it open.

The desk in this room had been tipped over, its legs sticking out at Thompson, its top facing the back wall. He shoved the door hard, smacking it off the wall, just in case someone . . . something . . . had snugged himself . . . itself . . . back there. . . .

Nothing behind it, though. Swinging the other way, Thompson played his light over the floor and saw nothing but broken glass and other rubble. Slowly, he edged toward the side of the desk and shined the beam behind it, and the light caught something, something made not of wood or steel or glass, but flesh. . . .

There, on the floor, lay the skinned carcass of some sort of animal. The body had obviously been there for some time—even the insects had lost interest in it by now—and Thompson couldn't even make out what it was, between the darkness and decay.

From its size, it at first appeared to him to be a very large dog, or maybe a deer that had wandered into the city; but as the beam crept over the prone form, Thompson realized that what he'd just found was neither deer nor dog.

The body on the floor was that of a man.

Not an animal carcass, but a human corpse.

"Hankins," Thompson said, struggling to keep his voice calm. "Got something."

No response.

The smell of the office oppressive now, threatening to send his dinner scurrying back up his throat, he again hissed, "Hankins."

Finally his partner growled in his ear: "What the fuck is it now, Thompson?"

"Got a body here."

Hankins' voice came back gruffly, unimpressed: "The transgenic?"

"I . . . I don't think so."

"Shit. I knew we couldn't be that fuckin' lucky. Tell me about your catch of the day."

"Office downstairs. Last one on the right. Behind a desk."

Harrumphing, Hankins said, "Jesus, how about a detail that matters? Like is it a man? A woman? Child? What?"

Thompson bit his tongue and kept the obscenity from popping out of his mouth. Discipline, Thompson knew, kept him from being like Hankins, and he wouldn't allow the F word to slip into his reply, no matter how hard it fought to come out. Taking a deep breath and letting it out slowly, he said, "Frankly, I can't tell whether it's male or female . . . probably adult, and I . . . I think it's been skinned."

"What?"

"Skinned," Thompson repeated. "It's a dead body . . . with no skin."

"Goddamn. . . . How fresh *is* that baby?"

How the hell should I know? Thompson wondered, but he said, "Old—there's not even any bugs. Even the smell's died down . . . some."

Hankins sighed in Thompson's ear, then said, "Fuck it then. Move on."

"You don't think finding a dead body is a 'detail' that matters?"

"Sure it is—in the long run. In the short term, we're lookin' for a transgenic tonight."

"Maybe this is the victim of a transgenic."

"Maybe—but we'll let the investigative team figure that out, Sage my boy. If you got a kill that ain't fresh, it's not going to do us any good now . . . and it'll wait until we've cleared the building."

When this becomes somebody's else's job, Thompson thought.

Yet, while he would hate to admit it, Thompson knew that what Hankins said actually made sense. Slowly pulling the flashlight beam off the corpse, Thompson forced himself to turn away and walk out of the office.

He climbed the stairs to the second floor. Even darker than the first, this level had been subdivided into smaller rooms which lined either side of a central corridor that ran the length of the building, starting at the freight elevator that squatted next to the stairwell.

Though a thick layer of dust still covered the floor, this level seemed cleaner than the last, somehow—no debris, no shattered glass. He was just about to go up the stairs to the third floor, when he decided to take the time to double check. He turned and played the beam over the corridor in front of him.

At first glance he hadn't spotted them, but now—on this second, closer look—he saw the wet footprints, running down the hall but close to the wall at right. Were those Hankins' footprints?

No—his partner was still up on sixth; and anyway, these were smaller than Hankins' big feet would make, not as wide, and longer. And leading to the third door on the left. . . .

Acid churned in Thompson's stomach as he considered what it might be like to go one-on-one with a transgenic. They could vary in strength, in abilities, and defects, depending on what animal DNA had been mixed into their personal genetic soup. Some of them were human, even beautiful.

Others were grotesque combinations of man and beast.

"Hankins," he whispered into the headset.

"Yeah?" The older man's voice sounded resigned and maybe a little pissed off.

"I've got footprints on the second floor. They're wet and they're fresh."

Any skepticism or irritation disappeared from Hankins' voice: "What's the imager say?"

Thompson returned his automatic to its holster and pulled out the imager. Watching the imager drawing blanks as its invisible beam moved up the hallway, he suddenly felt naked without the pistol in his hand, and when a red flare blipped up on the imager's tiny monitor screen, he damn near threw the thing down the hall in his anxiety to reach for his weapon.

"You still with me, kid?" Hankins asked.

In spite of himself, Thompson jumped a little when Hankins' voice made its appearance in his ear.

"Got a hot body," Thompson said, "but its temp is below a hundred."

"Probably not a transgenic."

"Probably not."

"Shit, though—I'm on my way. Hang loose till I get there."

Thompson felt his nerve returning a little as he realized that whatever was in the room ahead probably wasn't a transgenic.

"It's all right, man," he said into the headset. "I'm all over it."

"You sure, kiddo?"

Slipping the imager back into his pocket, Thompson pulled out his Glock; his stomach was still fluttery, but—goddamnit—this was his job, and he would do it. "Yeah, I'm sure."

Hankins' voice came back clearly, all business now. "You let me know what you find. You need me, I'm there in a heartbeat."

"Right," he said, almost feeling affection for the older man—and wasn't *that* a rarity. . . .

Thompson remained cautious, shining his light into each room as he moved down the hall. He wasn't checking them carefully—somebody or something was on this floor, and he was moving it right along, accordingly—but the imager had shown nothing, and the quick playing of the beam around the rooms assured him the new gizmo wasn't on the fritz.

Outside the third door on the left, he stopped, calmed his breathing, and once he was steady, he swung through the open door, his arms extended in front of him, the flashlight moving from right to left.

His flashlight sweep was halfway around the room when he heard the whoosh in the blackness to his left. In the grim darkness, he saw a length of two-by-four arcing through the air!

Before he could react, though, the board crashed down across his arms and the flashlight and pistol went flying in opposite directions, clattering, clanking. The flashlight went out when it hit the floor, the room going completely black. His Glock flew to the floor somewhere as well—didn't go off, thankfully—winding up vaguely to the left, where it skittered along until it smacked into a wall.

Thompson's vision went white, then black, as pain exploded through his being. He heard the whoosh of the board making a second swing, and tried to move out of the way, but then he heard the snap of his left arm breaking, and grunted once before collapsing to the floor. He felt more than saw his attacker, raising the board for a third strike, this one sure to split his head like a melon and leave Melanie a widow and his child fatherless. . . .

Instinctively rolling toward his attacker, Thompson managed to narrow the distance between them enough so that this time when his opponent swung the board, it whizzed over Thompson's head as he crashed into the attacker's legs and sent the man tumbling across the room. Scrabbling to his left, Thompson used his good hand to feel along the floor for his pistol.

Behind him he could hear his attacker cursing under his breath as he struggled to regain his feet in the near darkness. Thompson fumbled along, seeking his gun, dust rising, and he repressed a sneeze as he crawled forward.

Hankins' voice erupted in his headset. "Find anything yet, kid?"

Fine, Thompson thought, *just swell*, but he said nothing, not wanting to give his position away to his unwelcoming host. He continued forward, his good hand searching for the Glock, his bad arm throbbing so badly he wanted to pass out.

"Son of a bitch barge in my house," the attacker muttered thickly behind him in the darkness.

There!

Something cool, something metallic—the Glock. His fingers wrapped around it and in one motion, still on his knees, Thompson pivoted, brought up the pistol and fired blindly three times, left, center, right, covering his options.

Thompson heard the soft thwack of at least one round entering the man's body, heard too the man's involuntary grunt, and finally he heard one more sound: the board dropping from his attacker's hand with a thunk, raising dust. The attacker sagged to the floor, gurgled a couple of times, then was silent.

"Jesus, kid, I'm comin'!" Hankins' voice shouted in the headset.

The pistol still in front of him, in his good hand, Thompson got to his feet, shuffled over, found the body in the dark and kicked it a couple of times.

It didn't move.

Into the headset, Thompson calmly said, "It's okay. Got a guy down—need a medic. My arm's broken, but the attacker's down."

Hankins' voice sounded like he was underwater. "I'm comin', kid! I'll be right there, I'm on the fifth floor and headed down." The poor overweight bastard was probably running, which meant he might be about to have a heart attack.

"It's all right, I said," Thompson insisted. "I've got it covered."

Using his foot, giving the darkness gentle kicks, he finally found the flashlight. He picked the thing up, shook it a couple of times, and was surprised when the beam came back on.

Struggling to juggle both the light and pistol in one hand—not put any more pressure on his aching arm than he had to—he made his way over and pointed the light down at his attacker's face.

An old white man with wispy white hair, an open, mostly toothless mouth, and unblinking milky blue eyes stared up at him—no transgenic . . . just some poor homeless wretch. The old man had been doing nothing more than protecting his squatter's rights in the tiny office . . . and for this, Thompson had killed him.

The young man's stomach turned acidic again, but this time it wasn't from fear. This time it was something far worse—shame . . . guilt.

He didn't know how he'd ever get past this. Since joining White's unit, he'd done some things that he knew he'd eventually regret; but, goddamnit, he'd never killed an innocent man—not until tonight.

Shaking his head, hot tears running down his face, mingling with sweat and rain, Thompson knew that tonight would be his last in this stinking job. Fuck Ames White. He and Hankins would finish here, drive back to the office, where they would make out their report, then he'd be done.

He would go home to his wife, take her and the baby in his arms, and tomorrow they would decide how far away they would move to try to put this night behind them. Somewhere, in the post-Pulse world, there had to be a life better than this one.

Then, in Thompson's ear, Hankins screamed.

"Hankins!" Thompson shouted into his headset.

Nothing.

"Hankins, talk to me!"

Still no response.

Changing frequencies, Thompson sent out an emergency call to headquarters for reinforcements, and a general 911 call that would bring both the local cops and an ambulance. Then he switched back and called Hankins' name again.

More silence.

Stripping off his tie, he made a makeshift splint with the flashlight, so the beam seemed to shoot out the end of his fingers; he tied it off, popped a new clip into the Glock, then took off up the stairs, fast as hell.

But not fast enough.

He found Hankins' body on the fourth floor, where it had been dragged from the stairwell—he knew it was Hankins, though there was no way to recognize the naked, bright gleaming redness of blood and exposed muscle and bone as any particular human.

Merely a skinned one.

Very fresh, this time.

. And the scream he heard in his ears, now, was his own.

Leanly muscular, with spiky brown hair, icy blue eyes, and the empathy of a shark, Ames White pressed the palm of his left hand against his forehead.

He didn't know whether to laugh or scream, so he did what he always did: he smirked, even in the face of death . . . he smirked.

White knew Hankins and Thompson were not the sharpest men on his unit; he had even suspected they were inept—but he'd had no idea that they were this lame.

Yet somehow this seemed typical. He was a man with a mission of almost cosmic importance, in a city, a country, that was a shambles, barely worth ruling . . . though one took one's best option, right? And here he was, with this huge responsibility, surrounded by fools and incompetents. It seemed to White, these days, that he was constantly on the verge of a great victory or a humiliating defeat.

He wondered which column this one would end up in.

The upside of this, if there was one, was that at least he'd be rid of the bungling duo now. Hankins, of course, was dead. White glanced at the skinned body, then looked away again—what a disgusting mess. Thompson, huddled in a corner, a blanket wrapped around his shoulders, cradling his broken arm, seemed unable to tear his eyes from his partner's grotesque corpse.

White already knew the kid was washed up, he could see it in his face. And the fact that Thompson had nearly been taken out by a geriatric homeless person only compounded the failure.

The downside of this was the pair's ineffectiveness would reflect on him, and White despised failure, even if his was only one by association. Shaking his head, he turned to his associate, Otto Gottlieb.

Hispanic-looking with his black hair, dark eyes, and olive skin, Gottlieb was not in the know about government agent White's several secret agendas. In fact, Gottlieb's best trait—as far as White was concerned—was that the man did what he was told.

So far, Gottlieb had resisted the urge to grow a brain and start thinking on his own; but White was afraid that couldn't last forever. And when the moment came, he knew he'd miss Gottlieb. He didn't really like the guy—White didn't really like anyone, and prided himself on a superiority devoid of such weakness as compassion and sentimentality—but he had gotten used to having Gottlieb around, and his associate's presence somehow brought him peace.

Even if the man was a moron.

Motioning toward the two partners—one dead, one alive—White said, "Get him out of here, Otto. He disgusts me. Get him out."

"The body? Shouldn't we wait for—"

"No. That's evidence. Thompson, I mean. Lose him."

Gottlieb, finally getting it, nodded and moved to the other agent. Helping Thompson to his feet, Gottlieb drew the blanket around the man's shoulders and led him toward the door.

When they neared White, Thompson looked at his boss with golf-ball eyes and said, "That transgenic skinned him so fast—so fucking fast. He *skinned* him."

"You screwed up. This was an unacceptable loss."

Now Thompson's eyes tightened and tears began to trickle. "I tried to get to him in time . . . I tried to help . . . I . . ."

White smirked again, and shook his head slowly. "You just don't get it, do you?"

A wide-eyed blank look settled on Thompson's face.

"I'm not talking about Hankins. This transgenic saved me the trouble of firing his fat ass."

"You said . . . it was an unacceptable . . . loss. . . ."

"And it is. The transgenic got the thermal imager." White grabbed the front of Thompson's wet raincoat. "And how long do you suppose it'll be before they figure out what it is, and what it's for?"

White released the young agent's coat. Thompson said nothing, his head turning back to Hankins on the floor. His lower lip trembled as he said, "You . . . you're a monster."

"No. They're the monsters—and you're fired. Get him out of here, Otto."

Gottlieb hauled him away.

Alone but for the body, White slammed his fist into a concrete wall, leaving a fist-sized dent.

To the glistening scarlet corpse, White said, "I can't believe you let a goddamn transgenic get hold of a thermal imager."

But Hankins said nothing—he just grinned stupidly back at his boss, his teeth huge in the raw red pop-eyed mask of his face.

Chapter Two
FREAK NATION

Her heart jackhammering, the transgenic the public knew only as 452 prepared to step out of Jam Pony into a cool night smeared red and blue by the lights of police cars. She and a group of her closest friends—her brothers and sisters in the fight to be free—appeared to be in custody, about to be escorted by what seemed to be a cadre of SWAT officers.

Her long black hair hung loose and her black shirt and snug slacks were smudged with dirt—the aftermath of a vicious round of hand-to-hand combat with a hit squad attached to Ames White. But 452—Max to her friends—was still unbowed, and not even bloodied.

Nonetheless, blood could still flow—and some already had.

The hostage situation at Jam Pony had started by accident—literally. Earlier, before sundown, the lizardish transgenic Mole—brave but impulsive—and her towering friend Joshua—who the tabloids had termed a "dog boy"—had just picked up two transgenics headed for Terminal City, the ten square blocks of biochemical wasteland where the societal outcasts spawned by the gene-manipulating Manticore project had taken up residence. The transgenic squatters could survive behind the fences, despite chemical and biotech spills, where everyday humans would get sick and die; the transgenics—whether beautiful physical specimens like Max or Alec, or genetic "freaks" like the lizard man and dog boy—had been immunized against such poisons . . . one nice thing Manticore had done for them, anyway.

Accompanied by a teenage boy named Dalton, the young woman, Gem—an X5—was pregnant and about to pop, so Mole was in a hurry to get her to the shabby sanctuary that was Terminal City. They had made it less than two blocks when a junk-piled truck backed into their path and what should have been a minor, bumper-bumping accident turned into a disaster.

Forced to make a run for it when a mutant-hating mob gathered, Mole, Joshua, and the two new arrivals had sought refuge at the bike messenger service where Max and two other transgenics, Alec and CeCe, worked. But the cops were already on their heels, and a full-scale hostage crisis quickly developed. Alec and CeCe had posed as hostages along with the ordinaries who became prisoners, though the handsome, usually self-centered Alec eventually outed himself as a transgenic, by coming to Max's aid.

At first Max had not been on the scene, and lizard-man Mole had terrified her friends; when she arrived, Max took over and before long the hostages realized that they and their "captors" were faced with the same challenge—staying alive.

Not so long ago, Max and the police department negotiator, Detective Ramon Clemente, had reached an accord that provided for trading half the hostages for a getaway van. Clemente's rooftop SWAT team had backed off, as promised, but Ames White—that CIA agent with an antitransgenic agenda—had unleashed his own hidden snipers.

Max and company did not make it to the van. If Logan Cale hadn't jumped in on their side, blasting away with his own weapon, driving the snipers back, Max and her group

might never have made it into the building again. But they
did, hustling back into Jam Pony, after taking a casualty in
the cross fire—CeCe—who within moments had become a
fatality.

Even with such a terrible loss, they had survived much in
this single day . . . but they still had a long way to go before
they would be anything like safe. If just one cop out there
noticed that the escorts in SWAT gear were not who they
were supposed to be, the bloodbath would begin again.

If so, if she and Logan Cale died, at least they'd die
together.

She loved this man, who once again was laying his life on
the line for her and her cause—to protect him, she had told
him she no longer loved him, and even tried to convince herself she could live without Logan Cale. But in the glare of
the bright lights—courtesy of the cops and the media—she
knew that wasn't true.

Logan Cale—tall, blue-eyed, with that spiky blond-brown
hair and shy smile . . . how she had longed to kiss him and
tell him how she truly felt. But that was impossible now—
that bitch Renfro, at Manticore, had made certain of that.

*Even with Manticore burned to the ground, the mad sci-
entists who had created her and Alec and Joshua and so
many other troubled souls were still fucking with her life—
that oh so specific virus that the late unlamented Renfro had
infected Max with still had no known cure, and if she
touched Logan, if their flesh met in any way, well, she knew
she would be the death of him.*

Yet despite all the trouble she had caused him, the
heartache she'd brought him, Logan had come to her aid
again, hadn't he? Firing up at the snipers, helping Mole to
keep the killers at bay while the others hightailed it back into
the building. He even stayed by her side, providing cover fire
as she dragged CeCe back inside as well.

The standoff had gone on from there, lasting until well

into the evening, when White had finally brought in his SWAT-geared hit team. Max smiled at the thought. The hit team had been tough, really tough; but she and her brothers and sisters—and even some of the hostages, who were on the transgenics side by now—had taken the suckers down.

Max had worked hard not to take any lives. Joshua, face-to-face with Ames White—a man who had murdered some-one dear to the normally gentle giant—had nearly broken the bastard in two. But Max knew how important it was *not* to kill—not to feed the media frenzy, fueled by White and others, that had convinced so much of the public that the transgenics were monsters, inhuman beasts worthy only of slaughter.

Now they had the opportunity to escape into the night and maybe, for a while anyway, be safe. Just this one last gaunt-let to pass through. . . .

Hiding within the bulky uniform of one of White's SWAT team members, his head covered by a Kevlar helmet, his face behind tinted goggles, Logan shoved the front door open and shouted, "Weapons down! Hold your fire. Team coming out."

Then Logan led the way out into the cool night air. The crowd behind the barricades pushed forward for a better look, their hatred a hot, oppressive slap riding the wind of their angry shouts: *"Death to the freaks!" "Kill 'em all!"*

Max wondered if they would ever be able to make people, those people, understand that all the transgenics desired was a peaceful, quiet life. The "freaks" just wanted to fit in like everybody else, and not be feared for—or judged by—their appearance.

Wasn't that what America was supposed to be about? She and her transgenic clan had been born in the USA, even if it was in a test tube, where they'd been genetically designed to defend this country—the very one that now seemed to want only their extinction—from the rabble on the street to the suits in high places.

With Logan and the others moving into the street, the cops suddenly seemed more interested in containing the crowd than dealing with the federal SWAT team. They backed out of the way as Logan led the parade toward the rear of a waiting police van.

Also dressed for SWAT team duty, complete with the helmet and goggles, Alec held a handcuffed Max by the arm while that lanky goofball, Sketchy—a really unlikely SWAT team member—escorted the cuffed Mole and Joshua. The lizardish Mole still puffed defiantly on his ever-present cigar, while Joshua, with his long brown hair and soulful canine-tinged features, looked more like a beaten puppy as Sketchy led him to the van.

"Federal agents," Logan announced, his voice cool and authoritative. "I need you to move back. Step away. We may have a biohazard here, people. . . . Make a hole!"

All of the cops—except Clemente, the intelligent, no-nonsense detective who'd served as negotiator during most of the siege, only to be usurped by Ames White—stepped back.

Clemente, a slender, well-chiseled African-American in his forties, looked like he probably felt much older now; but his brown eyes were still alert, and he obviously wanted to know what was happening. He wore a rumpled gray sport coat over a Kevlar vest, blue tie, and white shirt, his gold shield dangling from a necklace. As they passed, he said nothing, his pistol still in his hands, the barrel pointed toward the ground.

Logan turned to him. "Agent White wants your people in there to secure the crime scene, ASAP."

Clemente made no move, standing with wide eyes and perhaps just a hint of skepticism as Logan yanked open the van's rear doors. Alec loaded Max in, then Sketchy shoved

Mole and Joshua up and in. Alec climbed into the van with the prisoners while Logan, businesslike, said, "We're going to have to commandeer this ambulance."

Sketchy peeled off to help ease Gem—the X5 who'd given birth during the siege—and her new baby into the ambulance parked next to the van. Dalton, the short blond male X5 who'd been traveling with Gem, climbed aboard as well. Original Cindy—the beautiful African-American bike messenger who was Max's best friend in Seattle—followed suit.

Logan turned back to Clemente and said, with the faintest hint of sarcasm in his voice, "Agent White is not a man who likes to be kept waiting."

The driver of the ambulance slowly climbed down from his seat, and Sketchy stepped into the man's space. "We'll take over from here," Sketch said, playing his macho SWAT role to the hilt. "Unless you wanna buy yourself a six-hour decontamination hose-down."

The driver wanted none of that, and backed off, while Sketchy climbed behind the wheel of the ambulance. Not waiting for Clemente to move, Logan slammed the door of the police van and jumped into the driver's seat.

Inside, Max and the others slipped the unfastened cuffs off as Logan started the vehicle.

"Move the barricades," he shouted through the windshield, waving for the officers in front of the van to clear the long sawhorses that kept the crowd back. The headlights of the van and the ambulance painted the mob a ghostly white.

With the crowd still screaming, *"Kill the freaks,"* Logan shifted into gear and let the vehicle roll gently forward.

Behind him, Max encouraged this approach, saying, "Nice and easy."

The van moved through the crowd to screams of *"Monsters!"* and *"Kill 'em now!"*

Looking out the back window, Max watched Clemente melt into the crowd, then the crowd melt into the night, as the two vehicles rolled off into the darkness. Tension seemed to palpably dissipate—the crisis was over.

Finally, when Max saw no one following them except the ambulance with the others, she let out a long sigh of relief. "We're clear."

The van filled with whoops and cheers as Joshua and Mole knocked fists.

"Now *that's* what I'm talkin' about!" Mole yelled.

"It's all good," said Alec, a wide smile breaking his normally laid-back demeanor.

Grinning into the rearview mirror, Logan said, "Just for the record, that girl was kickin' your ass."

Logan was referring to a particularly bulked-up female fighter on Ames White's hit squad, back at Jam Pony.

Alec's smile tightened a fraction. "I had her. I was just settin' her up."

Everyone laughed.

Keeping her voice low and even, knowing they weren't really in the clear yet, Max said, "All right, head for Terminal City."

Something nagged at Clemente—this just didn't *feel* right—and when he entered Jam Pony it was with gun drawn and both arms extended, his flashlight in his left hand, his pistol in his right.

Behind him, four members of the SWAT team—the PD's men, not White's—fell into a loose line and then spread out once they were inside the door. The power was still out and the place was bathed in eerie shadows, strangely quiet after the tension of the day. It was almost as if the building needed a rest too. . . .

Coming around a corner, Clemente saw three people sitting on a bench, apparently just waiting for the police to enter. Nearest him sat a young woman of perhaps twenty, her

short brown hair tied into two tiny pigtails. She wore a tan
hooded pullover and khakis.

Next to her sat a taller, muscular, nerdy guy with black-
rimmed glasses, a blond flattop, wearing a blue pullover
short-sleeve shirt and jeans. Beyond him, a tiny bald guy,
also in his early twenties, wore a plaid flannel shirt and
jeans. They all seemed calm.

Very damn calm, for just-released hostages.

"Anyone hurt?" Clemente asked, shining his flashlight toward them, but not into their eyes.

"No," the young woman said. "We're okay . . . but you
better go look upstairs."

Was there something . . . *mocking* in her voice?

Slowly, all his attention focused on the doorway ahead,
Clemente led the way up the stairs. On the landing, he hesitated for only a second before swinging through the door
with his pistol outstretched. Behind him, the SWAT team
fanned out into the room.

It was immediately obvious that a ferocious battle had
taken place up here. Nearly every pane of glass in the windows and in the top half of the wall that separated the warehouse space from the office space lay in shards on the dusty
floor. Shelves had been tipped over, furniture broken—the
place was a shambles.

Playing his light around the room, Clemente settled his
beam first on a muscular redheaded woman lashed to a cement support. She had been gagged and taped to the pillar
with packaging tape, as if waiting delivery, perhaps by one
of the bike messengers.

Swinging farther around, Clemente's light fell on a trio in
their underwear—they'd been stripped of their uniforms and
lashed to another pillar. They too had been trussed up and
gagged with packing tape.

Clemente realized at once that this meant the SWAT team
members who'd seemingly hauled off 452 and the rest were

impostors, wearing the uniforms of the SWAT team they'd defeated. And he knew he should spring into action, but . . .

He couldn't keep a wide smile from spreading across his face.

"Special Agent in Charge White," Clemente said, in mock good humor.

The normally smug and very trussed-up government man, Ames White, growled something that came out garbled because of the packing-tape gag. He had not been stripped of his clothes—just his dignity.

"What was that?" Clemente asked, as if actually understanding the agent's muffled outraged words from beneath the packing tape. "The transgenics tied you up and took your uniforms?"

Another growl erupted from the agent as he fought against the tape that bound him.

The detective chuckled and his grin grew even wider. "No way!"

White's eyes went wide with anger and he yelled something—probably obscene—that was again swallowed by the tape.

As if making sure he was understanding White correctly, Clemente asked, "And you want me to go after them?"

The NSA agent's cold stare carried every ounce of anger and hatred that the tape wouldn't allow him to utter.

"Now that's a good idea," Clemente said as he rose. He went to the door with his men on his tail, none of them making any move to untie White or his cronies.

As he stepped into the hall, the detective heard another muffled scream from White. It sounded quite a bit like, "Son of a bitch," even with the tape over the man's mouth. Clemente allowed himself to enjoy the moment, then took off at a run for his car.

White wasn't the only one who'd been fooled by the transgenics, and Clemente—the pleasure of seeing the arrogant

White hung out to dry receding in his mind as his duty kicked in—wasn't going to let this slide. Now he would catch the transgenics, and succeed where White had screwed up.

And let Ames White stare into Clemente's smug smile, for a change.

The crew had lapsed into silence; the tension of the long day finally seemed to be leaking out of them, and they all looked beat. Max was proud of her family, her friends. This day could have ended as the bloodbath Ames White had sought, and the transgenics' cause irrevocably hurt, had anyone besides CeCe—one of their own—been killed or injured.

Not that Max and the others didn't hurt because of the loss of their sister; but had any of the "ordinaries" died, well, that would have been the end of her hope of getting the humans to accept them as equals. She was just settling down to rest herself, in the back of the van, when she heard the first siren.

She looked out the rear window at the same moment Logan spotted the flashing lights in his mirror.

"We've got company," he announced.

Clemente's voice came to them over a loudspeaker from the lead car. *"Stop your vehicles now or you will be fired upon!"*

Logan ignored him and kept driving.

Again Clemente's voice came over the loudspeaker: *"Pull over now or we will use deadly force to stop you."*

Looking out the windshield, Max said, "Don't stop—keep moving."

Not slowing, Logan kept the van going straight down the middle of the street, Sketchy at the wheel of the ambulance behind him, following Logan's lead, the police cars close behind, but none of them moving forward to try and block their path.

To Max, the trip to Terminal City seemed as though it took

hours, not minutes. But finally they approached the locked gate of the no-man's-land the transgenics had claimed for themselves, signs proclaiming, NO TRESPASSING. IT IS A FELONY TO PASS THIS POINT, and BIOHAZARD. UNSAFE FOR HUMAN OCCUPANCY.

"Go straight through," Max said, almost casually.

Logan didn't hesitate in following her instructions—he pressed down steadily on the accelerator and slowly the van gained momentum as it neared the gate.

"Hold on," he advised, and everyone in the van tried to burrow in for the impact.

They slammed crunchingly through, the ambulance roaring in after them, right on their back bumper, police cars in a long line behind them. Inside the van, they rocked with the impact, then settled as they sped into the makeshift compound.

"Right, left, then straight up the ramp," Max said.

Driving like a lifelong racer, Logan followed her orders.

As they accelerated up the incline, Max said, "Straight through the building."

Again Logan complied, steering through the maze of concrete pillars as fast as was possible in the unwieldy van. Finally, they reached a barricade of junk that not only prevented them from moving forward, but cut them off to the left and right as well.

"End of the line," Logan declared as he braked the van to a stop.

Sketchy stopped the ambulance next to the van, and the police cars quickly formed a semicircle behind them to keep Max and crew from turning around and making a break for it. The light bars atop the police cars painted the scene red, blue, and shades of purple where the two colors met. Pouring out of their cars, twenty or so officers drew their guns, and Clemente's voice once again came over a loudspeaker: *"Throw down your weapons and let me see your hands. Now!"*

Mole spun angrily toward Max. "What's your plan *now*?"

"Show me your hands," Clemente said over the speaker.

Looking a little panicked, and sounding like a small boy and not a massive dog of a man, Joshua asked plaintively, "Max . . . ?"

"Throw your weapons out now!"

Max looked from face to face, seeing defeat, even despair, but she was unwilling to accept either.

She made her decision. "You heard the man."

"Well," Mole said, "this sucks."

Logan dropped his pistol through the open driver's side window and it hit the concrete floor with a dull smack.

"I fought the law and the law won," Alec said, wry resignation in his voice.

Moving to the back door and opening it a crack, Max dropped out Alec's weapon and it clattered to the concrete.

"Step out of the van with your hands up."

Grumbling the whole time, Mole followed suit, handing his gun to Max, who tossed it outside.

Clemente's voice came over the speaker again. *"Do it—step away from the van, and keep your hands up!"*

Original Cindy, in her SWAT team drag, dropped her gun and Sketchy's gun out the back of the ambulance as well.

Max came out first, followed by Mole; then came Cindy, without her helmet and goggles; Gem and her new baby; Sketchy—also without his SWAT headgear—and finally young Dalton exited the ambulance.

As Clemente and his men kept their guns trained on the transgenics, Max kicked a couple of the rifles even farther away so the cops wouldn't think they were up to something. Joshua helped Alec down, Alec's shoulder still giving him trouble from a bullet he'd taken early in the siege. Logan came out the driver's side and marched to the back of the van to join the others.

"Step away from the vehicles!" Clemente commanded. *"On your knees—hands on top of your heads!"*

Sketchy dropped first, as if suddenly taken by the urge to pray, his hands shooting to the top of his head. Slowly, the others fell in line as well—Mole, then Alec, Logan, Original Cindy, Dalton, and Gem—all on their knees in defeat, all of them putting their hands on their heads, except Gem, who held her baby.

All but Max.

Max remained standing, her hands dangling at her sides. She kept her face calm, passive, showing neither anger nor deception. And yet her very failure to follow orders made her a pillar of defiance.

"On your knees," Clemente yelled, no longer on the loud-speaker.

Instead, Max took two tentative steps forward.

"Do it, now!"

Ignoring the instruction, Max walked forward a few more steps, then stopped just a few feet from the police, their headlights bathing her and her friends in bright white light.

"452?" Clemente asked, frowning. That was what she had told the cop to call her when they'd been negotiating the hostage crisis.

But why hide any longer?

She said, "You can call me Max."

He drew a breath. Then he said, "I think you should get on the ground."

Max's face remained placid. "I think you should probably go."

Now Clemente's expression hardened. "I'm not going to tell *you* again."

She gave him the tiniest of shrugs. "I'm not going to tell *you* again."

Luke and Dix—two of the transgenics that had started the settlement within the fences of the dead industrial park that was now Terminal City—stepped out of the shadows, pumping shotguns.

In front of Max, the officers cocked their own guns and drew beads on the transgenics.

Then, from the darkness, other armed transgenics emerged on nearby rooftops and on either flank of the policemen. The eerie, half-lit forms of these feared freaks could only give the police pause . . . and there were more and more of the figures. . . .

The only escape route for the cops was to their rear. And by the time all the transgenics made their appearance known, over one hundred of them had the officers in their crosshairs.

Max could see on Clemente's face the realization that his forces were hopelessly outgunned.

"You can try to arrest us all," she suggested affably, her arms widening to include the whole group, "but you guys might want to call it a night . . . and go have a beer."

Clemente needed only a second to make up his mind. "Back it up! Outside the fence, people. Let's go, move it back!"

The officers looked from the transgenics to their leader, then started looking at one another.

"Now!" Clemente yelled.

Cops began holstering their weapons, jumping into cars, and soon police cruisers were moving in every direction as they tried to find the fastest way out of Terminal City. As the long line of cars broke and headed for the gate, Clemente watched them for a moment, then gingerly holstered his pistol and turned toward Max. Walking slowly, he crossed the short distance to her.

Barely a foot from her, he said, "You kept today from turning into a bloodbath . . . and I respect that . . ."

She gave him a slight nod. "You held up your end too."

The detective's face remained a solemn mask. ". . . but you haven't won anything. This is going to get ugly . . . and it's way over my head now. These people's lives depend on the decisions you make next."

Their eyes locked.

He went on: "And I pray you make the right ones . . ."

She stared at him, waiting.

". . . Max."

She was unprepared for the swell of pride she got when he said her name. Why couldn't more of the "ordinaries" be like this one? Yes, they were adversaries—those lines had been drawn long ago. But in the tone of that one syllable, "Max," she could tell they were not enemies.

Turning on his heel, Clemente got into his car, dropped it into reverse, and backed out of the building toward the gate of Terminal City.

The lights of the car weren't even out of sight before Mole—ever the hotheaded activist—went to work. "Escape and evade. We divide into teams, pick a compass point, and go to ground."

Max surprised even herself when the words jumped out of her mouth: "*No!* . . . We stay here."

Mole spun to face her, his harsh-sounding voice even harsher than usual. "In a couple of hours that perimeter'll be totally locked down . . . tanks, National Guard, and every cop within a hundred miles."

Stepping forward, Dix—a transgenic with a face like a pile of lumpy mashed potatoes and a half-assed goggle-cummonocle strapped to his one good eye—said, "We'll be digging our own grave."

"Mole's right," said Luke, a transgenic with a cue ball for a head, red bags under his black eyes, and huge flaps over his tiny ears. "We move now, they won't be able to catch us all."

"Where are you going to go?" Max asked, then turning her

attention to the misfit throng, she added, "Look—I can't stop anyone from leaving. But I'm through running and hiding and being afraid." Making her point with a forceful pirouette, she said, "I'm not gonna live like that anymore. Aren't you tired of living in darkness?"

She saw a few nods and heard a few scattered mumbles of agreement.

"Don't you want to feel the sun on your face? Don't you want to have a place of your own? A place where you can walk down the street without being afraid?"

The noises of agreement grew louder.

"They made us and they trained us to be soldiers . . . to defend this country. It's time they face us and take responsibility for us instead of trying to sweep us away like garbage. We were made in America. And we aren't going anywhere."

Original Cindy, nodding, said, "Speak your word."

Max looked at her for a split second, loving her sister, who had been with her since the very beginning; then she went on: "They call us freaks? Well, okay. Today . . . I'm proud to be a freak. And today, we're gonna make our stand, right here."

Looking around her, she studied the faces, so many faces, of those she knew and those she didn't know, but in her heart they were all her family. *"Who's with me?"* Calmly, Max raised a fist in the air.

Joshua's fist shot up instantly and Original Cindy's and Logan's and Alec's and one by one the others, even Dix and Luke. This was a solidarity none of them had ever known, not even back at Manticore. They were together, proud and defiant. Finally, only Mole stood alone, arms at his sides.

Max studied the lizard-faced commando. As she watched him gazing from face to face, she could see he felt it too— brotherhood was in the air. Sisterhood too.

Slowly, his fist rose in the air and something like a grin appeared on that lizard puss. "Aw, what the hell. . . ."

A smile broke across Original Cindy's face; few smiles on the planet were brighter. "Right on!"

Feeling hope flood through her system like adrenaline, Max thought of the ancient Chinese philosopher, Lao Tze, who said, "A journey of a thousand miles begins with a single step."

She hoped they were getting off on the right foot.

For the next forty-eight hours the transgenics fortified their position inside and kept a careful eye on the police and National Guard outside, who—true to Mole's prediction—had locked down the perimeter of Terminal City. Already a chain of command seemed to be establishing itself. Alec and Mole oversaw the upgrade in security, and Dix and Luke monitored the media—whose cameras gave them a nice look at the National Guard and police forces outside the fence. Joshua appointed himself Max's personal bodyguard, while Logan and Max pored over strategies for their next step.

It was late the second night when Dix called them into the transgenics' makeshift media center. A dozen monitors were built into a pyramid, with four of their brethren watching them, sifting through the information from the various sources both local and national. Off to the left another baker's dozen of monitors kept track of the security system the transgenics had installed and been upgrading since they first settled in the restricted area.

"What's going on?" Max asked.

Dix pointed to a monitor in the third row; and an X5, a redheaded young woman about Max's age, pointed a remote that raised the volume.

On the screen, a reporter stood in front of Jam Pony, Normal standing next to the man. "But about your captors . . . what are these creatures like? Is it true you delivered a transgenic baby?"

Normal beamed. He couldn't have been any happier if he'd been the father himself. "I did, and a beautiful, bouncing baby girl she is."

The reporter asked, "So—you're saying they're not all monsters, then?"

"Monsters?" Normal asked with a shake of his head, as if such a thought were foreign to him. "No more than you or me."

And with that he turned away and swept the sidewalk in front of Jam Pony. When he saw two of his riders not moving fast enough, he said, "Hey, Sparky—not a country club, get moving. Bip bip bip!"

The two slackers headed off in opposite directions, each trying to get as far away from Normal as fast as they could.

Max turned to Logan. "What do you make of that?"

Grinning, Logan said, "Looks like you've got another convert."

With a perplexed look, Max asked, "Normal?"

Logan shrugged. "Could be helpful to have another friend on the outside."

She nodded. "Can't ever hurt to have another friend." Turning to Dix, she said, "Anything else?"

He shook his mashed-potato head. "You should get some rest, Max."

A yawn escaped from her. "Maybe you're right." She and Logan, as well as most of the rest of them, hadn't slept for at least the last two days. A nap wouldn't hurt her, and she knew Logan needed the rest even more than she. "Can you get somebody to wake us at dawn?"

Dix nodded. "Take my room," he said, pointing to a door off to the right.

She took a few steps then turned back to Logan. "You comin'?"

A small smile appeared and he said, "Yeah."

Dix's room was a far cry from the penthouse apartment

where not so long ago Logan had lived, or even Max's condemned-building crib, for that matter; but it would do, for tonight anyway. About as big as a good-sized bathroom and illuminated by a single lightbulb dangling from a cord, it had an old double mattress on the floor in one corner, some bookshelves with a few volumes on the opposite wall to the left, a small round table near them with two chairs, and in the front left corner—below some steam pipes that Logan had to duck beneath—an old leather recliner that had been salvaged from God knew where.

"You take the bed," Max said. "I'll take this." She patted the recliner.

"No," Logan said. "You take the bed. . . ."

She gave him a sharp look. "When was the last time you slept?"

He shrugged, but said, "Can't you let me be a gentleman about it?"

She waggled a finger at him. "Who's a genetically enhanced killing machine that can go days without sleep?"

"You are," he said hopelessly.

She knew she had him now.

Without any more argument, he spilled into the bed, took off his glasses, and instantly fell asleep. He hadn't even bothered to take off the exoskeleton—the device affixed to the lower half of him that allowed him to walk. His wheelchair, the contraption he'd spent so much time in the last two years, lay in the pile of rubble that had been his apartment before White's people trashed it.

Logan Cale was, after all, Eyes Only—the cyber freedom fighter, a terrorist to the authorities, an identity secret to most (but not Max). Scion of a wealthy family, Logan used his inherited money to help those less fortunate than himself—like the transgenics; these efforts had led to the bullets that had put him into a wheelchair.

Plopping onto the recliner, Max kicked back and listened

as Logan started to snore softly. She couldn't think of a prettier sound. Pulling the string on the light and grinning, she looked over at this man who she loved and adored, asleep in the darkness. "I love you," she said quietly.

He snorted a snore in response, and Max suddenly realized this was what they all wanted, what they were all fighting for—just a little peace and quiet in this big, noisy world.

Logan's snoring grew louder, and Max decided that even peace without quiet was good enough for her. Closing her eyes, she drifted off in a cloud of hope that carried over into sweet dreams.

Which, when so many of her days were waking nightmares, was one small blessing, anyway.

Chapter Three
SIEGING IS BELIEVING

The next morning, rested and refreshed, Max and Logan joined a number of their fellow outcasts in the Terminal City media center and watched the early morning news on KIPR. The picture showed a dozen police cars layered in front of the main gate in multiple barricades, their light bars flashing red and blue, heavily armed and armored officers running around behind the barricade.

"Tell me something I don't know," Max said dryly.

"Maybe *she* will," Logan said, with a nod to the screen.

The camera had settled on a female newscaster wearing too much lipstick. "As dawn breaks on the siege at Terminal City, the situation is tense but unchanged. While several hundred transgenics remain barricaded inside the restricted area, police and National Guard stand an uneasy watch at the perimeter, each side seemingly waiting to see what the other will do next."

"No kidding," Max said to the TV.

"You think they're coming in?" Logan asked.

She shook her head. "I don't think they're that stupid."

Logan shot her a quick grin. "What about White?"

They exchanged glances—neither really considered Ames White stupid, but both knew him to be incredibly ruthless and reckless, with other people's lives at least. White, with his antitransgenic agenda, had the most to gain if this siege turned into a slaughter. It didn't even matter who on which side *got* slaughtered. . . .

At the thought, Max's face turned sour and an epithet formed on her pretty mouth. Just as she was about to let it explode out, the hulking figure that was Joshua burst through the door.

"Everyone, come up to the roof," he shouted, his canine face turned up in a broad smile, his eyes bright with excitement, alive with enthusiasm.

Max turned to Logan, whose shrug and expression said, *I have no idea—don't ask me!*

Dix asked, "What?"

But it was too late, Joshua had already bounded back through the door again and they could hear him pounding up the stairs just beyond the wall of the media center.

"Better go see," Max said. She had great affection for the keenly intelligent but childlike Joshua, and would gladly take time to humor him, even under these circumstances.

Dutifully, they all fell in line behind Max and followed her out the door, then up the stairs, quickly taking the three flights to the roof. When she opened the door, golden sunlight flooded the stairwell. The little ragtag group—Max, Logan, Dix, Luke, and Mole—walked out onto the flat concrete roof, where they found a couple of dozen transgenics already there, including Joshua, Alec, Gem, and her new baby.

With no preamble, Joshua, a couple of X5s, and an X3 raised a makeshift steel flagpole into a base they had built. As Max and the others watched, the quartet hoisted the pole, with the transgenics' flag—recently painted by Joshua, whose considerable artistic abilities were known to all of them—attached to the top.

Once the pole was in place, they all stepped back and

looked up at the banner waving gently in the morning breeze, the sun seeming to make it glow.

Not fighting the swell of emotion, Max stared at the flapping flag, remembering Joshua's description of the banner's design.

"This is where we come from," Joshua had said, "where they tried to keep us." And he'd pointed to the banner's bottom third, a broad black band bisected by a red bar code.

"In the dark," Max had said.

Joshua nodded. "A secret."

Pointing to the middle band—a wide crimson stretch with a white dove rising from the bar code beneath—Joshua said, "Where we are now . . . because our blood is being spilled."

She nodded her acceptance of the appropriateness of that.

Finally, the dogfaced man pointed to the topmost third, a white band. "And this . . . is where we want to go."

Max had gotten it immediately. "Into the light," she said, her voice betraying a gentleness few saw in her.

Now, looking up at Joshua's design riding the breeze, Max seemed about to burst—partly from pride for what they had accomplished, partly from apprehension for what was to come. Still, for the most part, it was a good feeling.

More important, she thought, how right it felt to be standing here with their own flag.

Max glanced over at Gem and the baby, and another feeling settled on her—as if a great weight were now resting on her shoulders. After all, she was the one who had destroyed Manticore, who had unleashed the transgenics—from beauties like Alec and the late CeCe to beasts like Joshua and Mole; and, free or not, none of them would be under siege in Terminal City if not for her.

But she had carried weight before and survived. Hell, she'd even flourished. She vowed to herself that she would carry this weight too. Logan had said it best, hadn't he? Freedom wasn't free.

Alec seemed moved by the moment, and Mole lit up a big cigar and puffed it with pride. They all appeared in better spirits this morning, with the sun shining and their flag flying. They actually had something of their own, and not just a flag: forsaken by God and man, Terminal City was, for good or ill, their own little chunk of the Seattle landscape.

Logan's hand encased in a white surgical glove, hers in a black leather one, she felt the man she loved take her hand and give it a gentle squeeze. Without looking away from the flag, he said, gently mocking, "Now look what you've done."

It felt so good to be at his side, hand in hand; but she could never let her guard down: if their flesh touched, even if all she did was absently wipe a stray hair from his eyes, even if she accidentally brushed her hand against an exposed section above the surgical gloves, Logan Cale would be seized by that Manticore-implanted virus—specific to his DNA— and he would in all likelihood die.

A tiny smirk dug into her cheek. Most men were allergic to commitment; her man was allergic to her.

They all stayed there for a long time after that, just watching the flag flutter. After a while, Logan finally said, "We need to talk."

Max looked at him, and he glanced meaningfully toward the door.

She nodded.

Joshua ambled over to them, a shy smile on his snout-mouth. He was proud of himself, but obviously embarrassed by the feeling.

"Nice job," Logan said. "It looks good, Joshua. You have a real touch."

The one who had been the first of the transgenics—an unfortunate failed experiment who was in some ways the best of them all—shook his wooly mane. "Thanks, Logan." He turned to Max, who enveloped him in a hug.

"You did good, Big Fella," she said.

"Thanks, Little Fella," he said, returning the hug hugely.

The silly nicknames were a small indication of the big brother and sisterly affection these two shared.

The rest of the transgenics broke up and headed back downstairs, their conversation light and hopeful. Taking one last look at the flag, Max allowed herself a little smile, then followed.

Logan and Joshua stood at the bottom of the stairwell, waiting for her to join them, which she did.

"I just want to check the monitors one more time," Max said. "Before we talk?"

Logan shrugged; he always deferred to her—almost always. "Sure."

The two men followed her into the media center, where Dix, Luke, and their merry misfit band were back to watching all twenty-five monitors at once.

"Any movement?" Max asked.

Luke shook his head, which more or less resembled a soft-white lightbulb. "The cops seem happy just to keep us in here for now."

Reverting to his cynical activist mode, Mole asked, "And how long do you think that'll last?"

No one said anything.

On one of the media monitors a superimposed announcement of a special bulletin flashed across the screen.

"What's this now?" Dix asked.

The picture abandoned the police barricades beyond the Terminal City fence in favor of an area just outside a checkpoint in another sector, where three police cars and an ambulance sat parked, their lights flashing.

A female voice-over intoned somberly, "A sector officer was found murdered this morning, when his replacement reported for duty."

The video cut to a pair of EMTs pushing a gurney up to the back doors of the ambulance. Whatever was underneath the sheet on the stretcher, it seemed to be bleeding through everywhere, damp crimson splotches making terrible polka dots.

The female newscaster continued: "Police refuse to comment on the rumor that the officer had been skinned."

"Skinned?" Luke asked with a touch of disgust, wincing at the thought.

As the ambulance doors closed, the voice-over continued, "If this officer was skinned, it would mark the second such murder in the Seattle metroplex in the last four months."

Mole harrumphed. "And they're worried about us?"

"The previous victim, Henry Calvin, a shoe salesman, turned up last March in a part of Sector Three known to be heavily frequented by transgenics."

"Didn't take 'em long to try to pin this shit on us," Dix said.

"One of White's men?" Logan wondered aloud.

Mole said, "They're reachin'—any way to blame this damn thing on us, they'll find."

But that was the end of the coverage of the sector cop's murder, and the news broadcast returned to the studio for other local news. There was a perverse sense of disappointment among the transgenics monitoring the coverage now that the focus was no longer on them.

Turning to Dix and Luke, Max said, "Logan and I have some things to talk over. We'll be back in twenty." She glanced at Logan for confirmation and he nodded.

Walking out next to each other, they barely noticed Joshua hanging back far enough to give them privacy, but close enough that—should anything bad happen—he could get to them to protect Max. Girl's best friend. . . .

Even though she could more than take care of herself, Max didn't mind the idea of Joshua staying close. Now that Ames White knew where she was, it would only be a matter of time before he and his next squad of muscle bitches came calling again.

They left the building that housed the media center and walked down the rubble-strewn middle of the twenty square blocks that made up Terminal City. Mostly biotech companies back in their day, several had lost containment when the Pulse hit, and the area had long ago been declared off limits to the citizens.

Though the transgenics had been treated against biowarfare agents, the ordinaries couldn't last for extended periods within the restricted area. No one had any sense of the specifics of that, just the inevitable danger of prolonged toxic exposure. Sooner or later some biological agent or other would take nontransgenics down—which meant Logan, Sketchy, and Original Cindy would have to move on, before long.

Most of the buildings within the walls not only were crumbling, but had long since been ransacked for any valuables. Occasionally the transgenics would find a piece of equipment they could use or cannibalize, but mostly what Terminal City was—before the transgenic squatters moved in, anyway—was a ghost town.

The couple let the first few blocks pass in silence, Max waiting for Logan to get around to telling her whatever it was he had to say. Behind them Joshua—the world's biggest puppy tagging along—seemed fine about keeping his own company while watching them.

At last Max's patience reached its limit. "You gonna tell me where we're goin'?"

Logan, with a tiny smirk, checked his watch. "I wondered how long you could go." Reaching into his pocket, he pulled out a five-dollar bill and held it up. "You were right, Joshua. Eight-fourteen. She couldn't go ten minutes without asking."

The big fella came forward, accepted the bill, turned to Max and said, "Thanks, Little Fella."

She stopped, looked from one to the other, then shook her head, not nearly as amused as they were. As she and Logan started forward again, Joshua again hung back, letting the distance widen.

"Okay," she said, a tiny edge in her voice. "We've demonstrated I'm not the most patient person in the world. Granted. I do like to know what's going on, and where I'm headed."

"You're a control freak. Admit it."

She whispered, "Is Eyes Only calling somebody else a control freak?"

He gave her that sideways, amused, look of his. "We're all freaks here, right?"

Now she smiled. "Yes we are. . . . Now, are you gonna tell me why we've marched all the way back to the ass end of Terminal City?"

Logan pointed at a low-slung concrete building in front of them.

"Medtronics," Max said, reading the faded sign with the bold blue letters. "Yeah. So?"

"You know what's behind this building?" Logan asked, something impish in his tone.

What was up with him? She shrugged elaborately. "Let me guess, since you seem to want me to—a parking lot?"

"And beyond that?"

Another shrug. "The back fence and, oh, maybe a bunch of pissed-off cops and National Guardsmen."

He smiled enigmatically and started walking again, this time toward the front entryway of Medtronics. When they got to the metal door, Logan produced a key that he slipped into the lock, then turned and opened the door. He waved for her to enter.

"Neat trick," she admitted. "And where did you get the key?"

Yet another shrug—a matter-of-fact one this time. "I own the building."

Stepping inside, she took a quick glance at the dust-covered receptionist's desk and pitiful little waiting room. "You owned Medtronics?"

"Not exactly. My uncle Jonas did. After the Pulse, naturally, he couldn't give it away. When I offered him a pittance for it, a while back, he sold it to me without even a question. Glad to be rid of any real estate attached to Terminal City."

"I hear that."

Moving to a door to the right, Logan said, "Come on, Max—you too, Joshua."

Logan produced a small flashlight, as the building was windowless and dark. His penlight's small beam was the only illumination as they walked down a long, narrow flight of stairs.

In the basement, he gave the flash to Max. "Hold this a minute, will you?"

She pointed the light at a stack of heavy boxes against the wall where Logan had moved.

"Give me a hand, Joshua?"

The two of them moved the stack out of the way and, to Max's surprise, their efforts revealed a door with a lock, but no knob.

Inserting another key, Logan pushed the door open, flipped a light switch, and Max found herself at one end of a long tunnel with fluorescent lights strung from the ceiling every thirty feet or so. Still, it seemed dim. The concrete walls had been painted a very pale green, and the tile floor was about the same color. Unlike Medtronics, this area was free of dust, even clean. With the lighting, the effect was of a hospital, or worse, Max thought, a morgue.

"Where does this lead?" she asked. "If I'm right about my directions, we're at the back of the building."

Logan nodded. "Tunnel goes under the parking lot."

"We're beyond the fence?"

"Yes. This passage leads under the street—and the police

barricade and National Guard—and comes up in a building in the next block."

She struggled to see Logan's face in the dim light. "A building *outside* Terminal City?"

"That's right," he said with a small self-satisfied smile. "Outside Terminal City."

"How did Logan know about the tunnel?" Joshua asked him, eyes tight with the desire for knowledge.

Another matter-of-fact shrug. "My uncle built it. There are things like this in a lot of buildings he's owned. He'd always been a little paranoid, and after the Pulse, he felt vindicated. I knew the tunnel was here when I bought the building, even though my uncle left it off the blueprints and any other documents filed with the city."

"You knew this tunnel was here," Max said, the significance slowly dawning on her, "when you bought Medtronics."

"It's *why* I bought Medtronics—the building this leads to is part of Medtronics too, actually. The borders of Terminal City weren't established until the containment fences went up."

"Are you telling me you anticipated this siege and—"

"Of course not. But with the influx of transgenics into Terminal City, I thought it might be an advantage to have some real estate nearby. Plus, it was only a matter of time until Eyes Only was going to need a new home anyway."

"A point Ames White drove home," Max said, referring to the discovery and destruction of Logan's penthouse Eyes Only headquarters. Logan had been squatting himself, lately, in Joshua's old digs, an abandoned house.

"I started looking for new quarters a while ago," Logan said.

"So you own both these buildings."

"Yeah. The remains of Medtronics."

She frowned. "In your name?"

He shook his head. "Dummy corporation. Called Sowley Opticals."

Now it was her turn to smirk. "That's a little cute, isn't it? Nobody'll ever figure that one out!"

Joshua was frowning. "Figure what, Max?"

"Nothing," she said.

Logan said, "Eyes Only has a friend in the Records department at City Hall. The records show that Sowley Opticals owned this building from the day before the Pulse. Maybe it is too cute, but in an area of medtech companies, it will actually look legit." He stepped into the tunnel. "Come on, take a walk with me, Max—and take this, you'll need it. I've got my own." He handed her the key to unlock the knobless door.

"Thanks," she said, but she was having trouble processing this. She knew she should be grateful that Logan had done such shrewd planning, but she felt somehow . . . betrayed. No, that was too strong. He hadn't taken her into his confidence—he was up to his old, Eyes Only, secret ways again.

As before, Joshua let the distance grow so the two of them could have some privacy. Their feet barely made a sound as they strode down the tile floor.

"Something wrong, Max?" Logan said, the smirk gone.

"No."

"Max, I can read you better than that."

". . . You did all this without telling me?"

"Some things are on a need-to-know basis, Max . . . and you didn't need to know this yet. I'm sure you have secrets you're keeping, to protect me better."

That was true.

Logan kept his voice low. "You're going to have to talk to them, you know."

"Who?"

"The cops, the National Guard . . . probably even some-one from the feds."

Max shook her head slowly. "All I want is for us to be left alone."

"Terminal City is a toxic island, Max. The time for speeches is over. Brass tacks now."

"Okay. Say it."

"If you initiate negotiations, Eyes Only can get that word out to the world. If you do nothing, sooner or later, they're going to come in . . . and you know what that means."

Genocide.

"Like it or not," Logan was saying, "we're about to enter a media war . . . and we need all the good press we can get."

She winced in confusion as they walked along. "A media war? How is this—"

"Why do you think White tried to turn Jam Pony into a bloodbath?"

"To kill me."

"That's one reason . . . but he was going to kill everyone in the place. Ordinaries like me and Cindy and Sketchy too."

"Yeah, I know—that's why I stopped Joshua from snap-ping White's spine. Carnage makes us look like the monsters everybody thinks we are."

"Bingo. Now you're gettin' media savvy."

She grunted something like a laugh and it echoed in the tunnel. "Don't you ever get tired of being right?"

"I'm always tired of being right, Max. . . . Ames White is going to fight you—not just you, Max, *all* of you—and not inside the gates of Terminal City, not right away. But in the media."

"It won't be hard," she said. "You saw those crazy assholes outside Jam Pony, and on TV. Everybody in Seattle already thinks we're monsters."

Logan stopped for a moment; he seemed about to touch her, but he didn't. Instead, his eyes held her.

"Not everybody," he said. "Not me, not Original Cindy, not Sketchy . . . and now not even Normal."

"And you think we can convince everyone?"

"If a right-wing nutcase like Normal can be brought around, anything is possible."

Now that they'd stopped, Joshua was catching up to them.

"Have to convince people, Little Fella," he said, those soulful puppy-dog eyes cutting to her core. "People are afraid of what they don't understand. Have to change their minds. Make them understand."

She stared into Joshua's unabashed sincerity, knowing he was right, but also knowing—even after all they'd suffered, all Joshua had suffered—that he was naive.

"There's an old pre-Pulse saying among the Normals of the world," Max said. "Shoot first and ask questions later."

Logan said, "That's another reason for you to start negotiations as soon as possible, Max . . . *before* they start shooting. Besides, how much food and water is there in Terminal City? Realistically, how long can you hold out here?"

"Longer than they think we can," she said automatically.

"But is living the rest of your life in Terminal City—just waiting for the day they storm the place—is that what you're looking for?"

Max shook her head. "Of course not."

"Well, you've had your moment of triumph—we have a flag flying. But it's time for a reality check, Max. You better get started talking to the other side."

They had made it to the end of the tunnel now, and Logan unlocked another door. They all passed through and found themselves in the basement of a darkened building, where feline DNA allowed her to see the piles of desks, filling cabinets, and office chairs around them.

Logan clicked his flashlight back on and led the way up the stairs to the first floor. Though the windows were all boarded, this floor was much cleaner than the basement, and a revelation compared to the other Medtronics building back in Terminal City.

High-ceilinged, with a tile floor, the large room was separated by partitions into an office on the right, a living room in the center, and a kitchen and dining area to the left. Numerous monitors and a pile of computer equipment cluttered two desks in the office area, and miles of wire seemed to snake everywhere. There was also a video camera that would serve as the new Eyes Only link to the world. The living room was home to a large leather sofa, three chairs, and a coffee table. A giant area rug only slightly smaller than a city bus covered the floor. The kitchen had a big fridge, a huge oven, a microwave, and even a butcher block island in the middle, and a cozy dining area with room for six. Two doors at the far end of the room led to a bathroom and bedroom respectively.

"Pretty cool," Max said, eyes wide, impressed.

It reminded her of Logan's old apartment. The penthouse had been beautiful, always spotlessly clean, and decorated in a spare modern manner that truly reflected Logan. That had been before Ames White traced an Eyes Only transmission, and his minions had trashed the place, shot it to hell, wrecking everything and sending Logan into hiding.

Fortunately, the penthouse had been off-the-books, and in the many weeks of Logan keeping a low profile, White had apparently not been able to trace it to its true occupant. So both Logan—and his Eyes Only identity—seemed secure.

"It's time," Logan said to her, "to get Eyes Only up and running again anyway—we've been off the air too long."

As she looked around Logan's new quarters, she said, "This didn't happen overnight."

"I've been working on this pad for a while," Logan admitted, "sort of having it as a backup."

"Then you'll move here, from Joshua's?"

"The plan is, kind of hop back and forth. I think it's probably wise to maintain two bases of operations, for Eyes Only—Joshua's place gives us a sort of safe house, away from Terminal City."

Smiling, nodding, she said, "You did really good."

He liked hearing that. "Did I?"

"You couldn't stay in Terminal City without risking a toxic backlash."

"So I've left—but I'm still in your backyard."

"Right. And we have a way in and out of here . . . starting with getting Sketchy and Original Cindy back to Jam Pony. We can *use* contacts in the outside world."

From the far end of the room, by the boarded windows, Joshua said, "Cops."

"Say what?" Max asked, coming over.

Turning to her, Joshua said, "Hole in one of the boards. I can see police." He returned to his post, peeking through the tiny hole.

Logan joined Max and the dog man. They took turns looking through the spy hole, Logan first, then Max. She saw pretty much the same thing she'd seen on the monitor, only now from the opposite angle, from behind the barricade.

Stepping away, she said, "Looks like they're digging in."

"You knew they would," Logan said.

She gestured to the window. "You better cover that hole at night—even a pinhole of light could give away your position."

"I'll take care of it."

"Just remember, that tunnel of yours runs in two directions. . . . Are you sure it's safe here for you?"

He looked at her thoughtfully, and his answer was no glib comeback. "I wish I could say I'm certain, but that's just not how this works. I can tell you, there's no record of the building being anything but abandoned since my uncle ceased its use. And, thanks to his paranoia, there's another tunnel down there that leads to another Cale-owned building on the other side of this block . . . well away from these barricades."

"Good," she said.

"I can use that to get in and out. The police are all concentrating on what's in front of them. They don't seem worried about what's behind them. When we need to, we can even use the tunnels as a supply line."

"You make a habit of it, don't you?"

"Of what?"

"Coming through for me."

He looked at her and she at him, and that would just have to do—no touching. Love didn't just hurt, it killed.

"We better get back," she said.

"Better," he said.

On the walk back, down in the fluorescent-lit tunnel, Joshua seemed lost in thought and hung back even farther than before. When he finally exited the tunnel, Max asked, "What's up, Big Fella?"

He shook his head, the mane bouncing. "Thinking."

"What about?"

"The ones still outside."

Logan frowned. "What 'ones,' Joshua. . . . You mean the transgenics outside of Terminal City?"

"Yes," Joshua said.

"What about them?" Max asked.

"Not sure yet. Still thinking."

Without another word, the big man brushed by them and up the stairs to the first floor of the Terminal City branch of Medtronics.

Though Max wanted to, she didn't press him. Joshua, like most men, only talked when he wanted to, and pushing him wouldn't help.

"Maybe he's wondering," Logan said, "if we can safely bring any straggling transgenics inside Terminal City?"

"Through your tunnel, maybe? A sort of underground rail-road?"

Logan lifted both eyebrows. "Frankly, they're probably safer in the outside world."

"Probably. But at least in Terminal City they have an iden-tity . . . a 'country.' And they don't have to 'pass' as ordinar-ies."

When she and Logan got back to the media center, Dix greeted them with, "Nothing's changed. They seem to be set-tling in now. They must think they're going to wait us out."

"All right," Max said. "You know where Original Cindy and Sketchy are?"

Dix checked the monitors of their security system. "I think Sketch is asleep in the back of the ambulance . . . and Original Cindy is up on the roof."

"Get someone to wake Sketchy, would you? And send him up to join us on the roof. I need to talk to both of them."

She and Logan went upstairs. Since the police hadn't sent up so much as a hoverdrone, the roof seemed safe enough. Original Cindy stood just this side of the flagpole, watching the barricade at the main gate. The roof gave them a pretty good vantage point to watch what the police were up to, at least at the main gate.

When she heard them, Original Cindy turned. "Whassup?"

Max took a step forward. "We were just talking about you."

"Original Cindy's always a popular topic of conversation."

"Cin, we're talking about you getting out of Terminal City."

Original Cindy frowned and waved that off. "Girl, you ain't gettin' rid of me that easy. You just afraid with my natural leadership, these fools are all gonna gravitate to-ward me."

With a light laugh, Max put a hand on Original Cindy's shoulder. "You gotta go, girl—it's for your own good."

"*My* own good?" She shook her curly Afro. "This about *your* own good. See, you my Boo, and I ain't walkin' out on your puny ass while you're in the middle of some heavy shit."

Max felt a wave of affection for her attitude-filled friend. "You know you can't stay here. Sooner or later, this bad bioshit's gonna take a toll on you."

"So if I feel sick, I'll come up here on the roof and breathe the sweet Seattle air, smog and all. Right now I feel as fine as I look, and you know how fine *that* is. Anyway, this is about something bigger than feeling sick and shit."

Logan stepped between them, a friendly referee. "The truth is, Cindy, you can do Max more good on the outside."

She smirked and put her hands on her hips. "Why don't *you* do her some good on the outside?"

"I plan to," Logan said, his voice quiet but firm. "I'm leaving Terminal City tonight."

"You bailin'?"

"Hardly. Cindy, we can do Max and her people more good—and be safer, ourselves—out there." He gestured toward the city on the horizon.

"I ain't worried about bein' safe. Do I look like I'm worried about—"

Max stepped forward and touched Cindy's shoulder. "I need live allies, not dead martyrs. You dig?"

As Original Cindy chewed on that, Logan pressed closer to her. "Look at her! Max is worried about both of us, and Sketchy too. And if she's got us on her mind, she's not keeping her eye on the prize."

Her face creasing into a severe frown, Original Cindy said, "Well, hell—when you put it like that . . ."

"We do need you outside," Max said. "You *and* Sketchy. . . ."

"You rang?" Sketchy said as he ambled across the roof. Still wearing the SWAT suit, he looked like a lanky cross between a surf bum and a storm trooper.

"We were talking," Max said, "about you, Original Cindy, and Logan leaving Terminal City."

Sketchy's long, narrow face contorted into a frown, and Max thought, *Great, here we go again. . . .*

But Logan pulled the blond-haired bike messenger turned reporter off to one side. "You've already helped a hell of a lot, Sketch. You know the transgenics all appreciate that—Max especially."

Sketchy glanced at Max and Original Cindy, then looked back at Logan and said, "Yeah. I caught that drift. Me and the dudes downstairs, we been . . . bondin'."

Logan managed to hide his amusement at this stoneresque response. "Well, good," he said. " 'Cause now we need your help on the outside."

"Outside?" Sketch asked. "As in . . . *on* the outside?"

"Yeah."

"*Is* there a way out?"

Logan said, "If there was a way to get you out, safely out . . . would you be willing to help?"

Sketchy shrugged. "I came this far. How?"

"For one thing, as a reporter."

Brightening, Sketch said, "You're kidding! That's what I do, man."

And that was true—sort of. For most of the last year—in addition to working at Jam Pony—Sketch had taken a job as a stringer and part-time photographer for one of the local tabloid papers. It wasn't exactly the *Washington Post*, but Max and Logan—in the coming media war—were in no position to be choosy—they needed all the help they could get.

And they all knew that the rag Sketchy worked for loved nothing more than stories about transgenics.

"I know Eyes Only is trying to help," Logan said. Only

Max and a small handful knew that Logan was Eyes Only; the others, like Sketchy, thought Logan was merely an Eyes Only source. "But Eyes Only is just one man . . . and he's not in the print media. You could be a big help."

Standing just close enough to hear, Max watched as Sketchy's head seemed about to explode with pride and possibilities.

"I could do that," Sketch said. "I was born to do that!"

"You think your editor will go along?" Logan asked.

"Why wouldn't he? Transgenics make great copy!"

"That paper's been feeding the fear, Sketch. The paranoia. We need to get the real story out."

Sketchy considered that, then said, "You want positive stories about transgenics, right?"

"Yes. Otherwise, you're part of the problem."

"I'm not part of the problem! . . . Can I get pictures?"

Logan shot a glance at Max, who nodded. "We'll get whatever we can," Logan said.

"With exclusive pics," Sketch said, "I think my editor'll go along, and be happy to! I mean, if we're the only protransgenic newspaper in the city, that's got to sell some copies, right?"

Logan nodded, put a hand on the skinny guy's shoulder. "Now you're thinking like a newspaperman."

Sketchy beamed. "I could get a byline and everything. . . ."

"If this fool can be a help out there," Original Cindy said, "Original Cindy can do some real shit. What you got in mind?"

Max turned her attention back to her best friend. "You can help get us supplies in, for one thing. And you can get us information, and we may even need you to deal with some hot-property fences and stuff, should we be forced to make our living by . . . well, less honorable methods than bike messengering."

"If you mean takin' down some more dope dealers,"

Original Cindy said, "they ain't nothin' more honorable than
that. . . . Hell yes, I could do all that, girl."

Max knocked fists with her friend, and felt like one of the
weights had at least shifted, if not totally lifted off her shoulders.

That night, she, Logan, and Joshua led Original Cindy and
Sketchy to the Medtronics building, down the stairs and into
the tunnel. They spoke as they walked, voices echoing a
little.

"How we gonna stay hooked up, girl?" Original Cindy
asked Max. "You got your cell?"

Max shook her head. "Cell phones are no good. The police will be monitoring all signals coming in or going out of
Terminal City."

"For some messages," Logan said, "we can use Eyes Only
bulletins."

"Busting in on TV transmissions," Sketchy said. "Sweet—
but you think he'll help?"

Logan nodded. "I know Eyes Only, and he's always been
on the transgenics' side."

"Cool dude," Sketchy said.

"Yeah, I'd say Eyes Only is a pretty cool dude," Max said,
glancing at Logan and giving him a secret smile.

"So what else we going to do to stay connected?" Original
Cindy asked.

Logan asked Max, "You think Cindy and Sketch'll be
watched by the police or White's people?"

Max shook her head. "I don't think either White or the
cops know that these guys helped us—" She turned toward
Cindy and Sketchy. "—so there's no reason for them to sur-
veil you. But watch your backs."

"Always," Original Cindy said.

"Then," Logan went on, "how about using Joshua's house
as a drop site?"

The house was a condemned, abandoned one, where the mysterious Sandeman—a key figure at Manticore, and by some accounts the "father" of all the transgenics—had once lived. Joshua had squatted there, and then Logan, and its appearance as a run-down derelict structure kept it useful.

"I like that," Max said with a short nod.

Not missing a beat, Logan kept going. "If the blinds are up, there will be a message inside; if the blinds are down, nothing."

"Rad," Original Cindy said.

Sketchy said, "*Not* rad—what are you talking about? Joshua's house . . . ?"

"Original Cindy will show you where it is," Max said.

"Where exactly will the message be?" Sketch asked.

Logan and Max traded looks.

Then Max said, "There's a desk in the living room. We'll put any messages in the top center drawer."

Sketchy looked perplexed. "Life and death riding on this, and the secret hiding place is a desk drawer?"

Max explained: "There's no reason to hide anything any more than that. The house looks abandoned, and anyone who's coming poking around has run into Joshua . . . and those people usually don't come back."

"So," Sketch said, nodding, concentrating, "best not to overthink it."

"Truer words," Max said.

Original Cindy said, "Yeah, Sketch—don't pop a vein over it, 'kay?"

"As Max would put it," Logan said, "we better jet—it's dark, but those cops are going to start getting restless . . . and we don't want to get caught on the street."

Max and Logan had worked out the escape plan during the day. Logan had sent an e-mail message to Bling, his physical therapist and occasional Eyes Only associate, to bring Logan's car to the end of the second tunnel at precisely nine o'clock. By then Logan would be there with Sketchy and Original Cindy and the three of them would pile into the car and disappear into the night.

Just in case, Max would pick that moment to call the cops and suggest the beginning of negotiations. They figured the police would get so wrapped up in that, they wouldn't give a civilian car driving out of the neighborhood beyond Terminal City a second glance.

Sketchy gave Max a quick hug. "I'm sorry for all the times I let you down . . . I didn't mean to—"

"Forget it," Max interrupted. "When it mattered, you came through."

Nodding feebly, Sketchy said, "Thanks. I'll make it up to you—I'll do the best I can to help."

She grinned. "Always knew you would. You may be a lard-ass bike messenger, but you got a good heart, Sketch. You should remember that more often."

The goofus was starting to tear up.

"Don't *even*," she said, raising a single digit. "Get the hell out of here and get back to work. You'll be lucky if Normal doesn't fire your lazy ass."

Grinning again, Sketchy slipped through the door.

Original Cindy put her arms around Max. "You watch behind you, Boo, 'cause I ain't got your back."

"You too."

Original Cindy's smirk dug a dimple. "You think Normal's holding a job for a bitchin' Nubian princess who just happens to be playin' for the home team?"

Max grinned. "In a lot of ways I think you scare him more than I do. . . . Oh yeah, he'll have a job for you."

The hug went on a few seconds longer, neither of them wanting to let go. Then Sketchy ducked back in and said, "Group hug! Can I join in?"

"In your skinny-ass dreams, maybe!" Original Cindy said. He disappeared back through the door, Original Cindy sprinting behind him, yelling something about kicking his ass until his ears bled.

With her friends this close to safety, Max couldn't help but smile.

Logan hung back and said, "So . . . I'll see you soon."

"Yeah. Take care out there."

"I will," he said, his eyes boring into hers, their feelings burning back and forth, riding the connection. "And you too."

She gave him a little nod. "I will. You better get going before Cindy kills Sketchy's skinny ass. Of course, if she does, we won't need my diversion."

Still refusing to take his eyes from hers, he said, "Seeya."

"Yeah, seeya."

This is where they would have kissed—if hers wasn't a literal kiss of death.

Then Logan Cale edged through the door, paused for one last look at her, and shut the door. Joshua stepped forward, gave her a quick hug.

"Gonna be okay, Little Fella," he said.

"Yeah, I know."

He said, "We better go."

She took a last glance at the door and said, "Yeah, we better."

As they walked back down the tunnel, Joshua's face turned somber again, just as it had that morning.

"You still worried about our brothers and sisters outside?" Max asked.

"They don't have family out there. Even Freak Nation has freak family. But out there," he said, and pointed vaguely toward the ceiling, "out there, they're alone. Might get scared by things they don't understand."

"What?" Max asked.

"Like Isaac. Afraid."

Isaac had been Joshua's test-tube twin brother, a gentle soul. But abuse from the guards at Manticore had snapped the young transgenic's mind, and when Max had set them all free, she'd turned loose a serial killer who preyed on men in uniform.

But she couldn't figure how Isaac tied in with whatever was bothering Joshua.

"What are you talking about?" she asked him.

"What Mole said this morning."

That only served to confuse Max more. "What did Mole say this morning?"

"When we saw the news story about the murdered policeman."

"Yeah?"

"Mole said, 'And they're worried about us?' "

"Go on."

"What if the one who killed the cop is one of us?"

"Joshua, don't pay any attention to what they said on TV—they're going to blame us for every bad thing that happens in the city, for a while."

He turned those soulful, sorrowful eyes on her. "What if—we deserve the blame?"

"Why would you even think that?"

The dog man gazed toward the city. "Our brothers, our sisters . . . they could be out there now, alone. Scared, like Isaac."

All of a sudden, Max saw where he was going. "You think a transgenic really may have killed that cop?"

Joshua shrugged. "People are afraid of what they don't understand. We are people too. . . . Could be."

"But it could just as easily be one of them too."

He shrugged again. "Could be."

"You . . . you think it's one of the basement people?"

She was referring to the animal DNA experiments—like Joshua himself—who'd literally been caged up in Manticore's basement.

"A lot down there had it bad, Max . . . real bad. Isaac, Dill,

Oshi, Kelpy, Gabriel. Many bad things done to our brothers. Guards were afraid of what they didn't understand and they did bad things."

Joshua didn't have a theory—he had nothing to go on but his experience, and in his life, if someone was killing men in uniform, it was a transgenic. Like Issac. Max tried to rid herself of the thought . . .

. . . but it didn't go away easily.

Hustling back to the media center, Max laid out her orders, then, with Joshua and Alec accompanying her, she walked up to the blockade at the main gate at exactly nine P.M.

Half a dozen officers pointed guns at them from behind cars. Illuminated only by the light bars, Max could nonetheless see the hatred in their eyes. She knew that each now fought the impulse to pull the trigger and kill the three transgenics without hearing a single word.

In her earphone came Dix's voice: *"Jesus, Max, you really set them off. Security cameras show them hunkering down at every post. They're getting ready for a fight."*

Not changing her passive expression, she yelled, "Where's Detective Clemente?"

A very white man in a camouflage uniform and Kevlar helmet inched up so his head and neck were visible above the roof of a police car. "I'm Colonel Nickerson, National Guard! . . . I'm in charge here."

"You may be in charge of them, Colonel, but you're not in charge of me . . . and I only talk to Clemente."

"He's not part of this anymore," Nickerson said. He was practically yelling, and Max didn't know if it was because he wanted to be heard . . . or just because he was scared.

"They're on the street," Dix said in her ear, meaning Logan, Cindy, and Sketch. *"Everything's go so far."*

"Colonel Nickerson," she said, her voice emotionless and almost bland, "do you want to see a peaceful end to this little situation?"

"Yes, I do. The question is . . . do you?"

Max nodded and took a couple of steps toward the fence. She heard guns being cocked as she moved—deadly little echoey clicks in the night.

Nickerson came out from behind his car and faced her.

"I've never wanted anything but to live peacefully," Max said.

In her ear Dix said, *"They're in the car—it's started and they're moving off. No one seems to have even noticed their asses!"*

"Then why the hostage situation at Jam Pony?" Nickerson asked, with some edge in his voice. "And why all this?"

"Do you know an NSA agent named Ames White?"

The question seemed to catch Nickerson off guard. "No—never heard of him."

Max could buy that—just as White had excluded the local PD from carrying out his dark agenda at Jam Pony, the National Guard colonel might well be out of the Ames White loop here at Terminal City. "That's why I need to talk to Detective Clemente."

Nickerson looked confused.

"By the time I get you up to speed, this mess may have blown up in all our faces. . . . The clock's ticking, Colonel, and there's nothing you or I can do to slow it down. The only thing we can do is work with it, and if you really want a peaceful ending to this, then you'll do what expedites that. And that would start with finding Detective Clemente and getting his ass down here . . . now."

"I don't know . . ."

"Otherwise, you're lying about not knowing Ames White . . . and I'll know where I stand with you." Max looked at him hard. "Bip bip bip, Colonel."

Then she, Alec, and Joshua turned and walked into the welcoming gloom that was their Terminal City home.

Chapter Four
OTTO BODY EXPERIENCE

SECTOR ELEVEN, 9:28 P.M.
SUNDAY, MAY 9, 2021

Bobby Kawasaki could feel the inner him—the *real* him—coming out. He had more energy now, though he still had not been off the sofa all day. The drug was finally winding down, and he could feel his true strength returning.

On a normal weekend Bobby would have already been out; but even before it started, this weekend had been screwed up. He felt lucky that he'd gone out Thursday and gotten a jump on the weekend's shopping. If he hadn't done that, he'd be further behind—further from his goal—and he would have felt even more lethargic than he did now.

The hostage situation at Jam Pony had almost screwed up everything. Bobby was a transgenic passing as an ordinary, and not even Max or Alec had known; not CeCe, either. Max and Alec he admired for helping other transgenics; but he'd been unable to find the courage to join in.

Maybe he would find that courage, one day soon—after he reached his goal.

In his run-down rattrap of an apartment on the eighth floor of a condemned building, Bobby was glued to his tiny used television—which he'd liberated from a sector checkpoint—carrying coverage of the hostage situation at Terminal City. This shabby studio apartment with its tiny stove, dwarf refrigerator, a coffee table that Bobby also ate on, and worn-out sofa was not going to be his home for much longer. Once he reached his goal, and finished his project, and could truly pass as human, things would change for the better.

And Bobby Kawasaki would finally have everything he wanted.

Rising, Bobby wandered into the bathroom and looked in the mirror. He stared at himself—the white face, the features sort of pinched, the bone structure vaguely reptilian—in a manner reserved only for the vain and the self-loathing.

He knew very well he'd been an experiment—something involving splicing chameleon DNA into his human genetics—though the Manticore scientists (his abusive "parents") had reminded him over and over that he'd been a disappointment to them. Their goal, their project, had been for him to blend in with his surroundings on command; but as it turned out, this ability only manifested itself when his adrenaline spiked—something over which he had no control.

Fear, anger, anxiousness, any extreme emotion set him off; but any other time—zippo. Oh, he sort of blended in anyway, in a more subtle manner; just not to the extremes his Manticore creators had intended for their projected military uses.

The scientists had tested him extensively. In a crowd of Asians, Bobby appeared somewhat Asian, while in a crowd of Caucasians, he took on the poly-Euro cast thought of as all-American; if he'd been sitting with African-Americans, they'd remember him as a light-skinned brother, albeit a quiet, unremarkable, definitely undistinctive one.

Of course, that had been too distinctive for Manticore—the point had been for him to blend in so well, he would virtually slip away, and if anyone remembered Bobby at all, that was seen as a failure.

Manticore was looking for an invisible man.

And sometimes Bobby was just that—that was the worst part. On occasion the blending effect happened at the most inopportune times, as well. He'd lost a couple of job interviews and more than a few first dates when he'd simply blended out of sight in his nervousness to please.

And once the blending began, once he had faded into the woodwork, he could not speak, did not dare call attention to himself, lest he expose himself as the freak he was.

That had been the case until the drug, anyway.

The drug—Tryptophan, to be exact—worked differently on his X3 metabolism than it did on his later X5 brothers and sisters. He knew that in them it controlled their seizures, made them more human. In Bobby the results were much more extreme. Sure, it kept him from blending in, but it also kept him from living.

The pills made him feel like a hundred pound weight had settled on his chest. He felt drowsy, slow, and unable to connect with the world. They did allow him to hold down a job, though they had made him a different kind of invisible man: no one, not even at the hectic Jam Pony, seemed to notice either Bobby or his lethargy. His boss, Normal, dismissed Bobby's listlessness as typical behavior, commonplace conduct among his regular layabout employees.

"Bip bip bip, Bobby."

The words still echoed proudly in Bobby's head. When Normal yelled at him, he was just like everybody else—human.

The recent hostage crisis had exacerbated his already high anxiety level, however, and he'd had to double his Tryptophan dosage to keep from blending during the crisis. If he'd blended then, there was no telling how much damage it would have done. The ordinaries would have seen him as a transgenic—he would have been exposed, as Alec and Max had been—and any chance to keep up his human life would have been gone.

Even the transgenics might have reacted badly, would finally realize he was one of their own, and perhaps see his blending as a betrayal. Either way, both sides would have hated him.

And hatred was one kind of attention Bobby Kawasaki did not crave.

Now, though, Bobby struggled to fight off the dulling throb of the drug. Tomorrow he'd have to be at work, and Normal wouldn't expect any less from him. That meant by tomorrow he'd need to get back on his damn meds, so he'd have to pursue his project tonight, or else it would need to wait clear till next weekend. Though Thursday's shopping hadn't been discovered until yesterday, the effort of a midweek foray had weakened him considerably, and the double dose of Tryptophan on Friday had practically turned him into a zombie.

He needed to go shopping—he was *so* close! One, maybe two more trips, then the big one . . .

. . . and Kelpy—the name he'd been called by the other transgenics at Manticore—would be gone forever, and so would Bobby Kawasaki . . . gone, history, a ghost . . . as he evolved into the person he'd always wanted to be, the one person that would gain him access to the affections of the only woman who had ever meant anything to him . . .

. . . Max Guevera.

Looking into the mirror again, Bobby—for now he was still Bobby, stuck with Bobby—realized that he was starting to blend into the bathroom wall behind him. The drug was almost gone now. He would soon be at full strength and then he'd go shopping for material.

After all, he had a human suit—a suit of flesh—to complete.

Even though he bore a German name, Otto Gottlieb strongly resembled the Hispanic portion of his lineage.

Otto's Jewish great-grandfather had smuggled his wife
and two boys out of Nazi Germany just before the onset of
the Second World War. The family had ended up in South
America, where the two brothers, Otto and Fritz, had grown
up safe from Hitler's clutches. Though many Nazis came to
Argentina after the war, the Gottliebs were already firmly
entrenched and the family furniture business had flourished.

Otto's grandfather had eventually married an Argentinian
woman and they had a son, Samuel, who went to school in
the United States, where he married an American woman
and put down roots. Samuel and his wife, Eliza, lived the
American dream. Selling furniture to families in Bloomfield
Heights, Michigan, the Gottlieb family included Samuel, his
wife, and two children—a girl, Elizabeth, and Otto, named
after his father's uncle.

Brought up with a deep love of justice and an even more
deeply ingrained sense of patriotism, Otto joined the Army
straight out of high school. Then, following his service stint,
where he had nearly made a career of it, he went to the
University of Michigan for his bachelor's degree, followed
by earning a master's degree in Criminology. Not long after
that, Otto had been recruited into the NSA and—after four
years of dedicated service—found himself partnered with
the enigma known as Ames White.

Not quite six feet tall, Otto liked to play basketball to stay
in shape, but mostly he jogged, or really, ran—like he was
right now. Sweat dripped onto the front of his gray T-shirt
and his feet thudded on the concrete of the street as he ran
alone in the cool evening silence. The shirt and his matching
gray shorts were both emblazoned with the logo of the FBI;
but being with NSA, Otto had many clothes and many IDs
with the names of various agencies on them.

Working on mile seven of a ten-mile run, Otto huffed a little, but otherwise ran easily, arms and legs pumping in a natural rhythm. He loved this time of night. Darkness settled on

the city, a gentle blue softening the edges of what Seattle had become, post-Pulse; no one to bother him, the job wasn't pressing on him, the day's work behind him, and, most important, time to himself, to sort out whatever problems occupied him at the moment.

Tonight's problem had to do with his boss and partner—that lovely specimen of humanity known as Ames White.

Something was going on behind Otto's back—or anyway, White was up to something behind Otto's back—and the NSA agent hated that. He'd suspected White was pursuing a secret agenda, well before the crisis situation at Jam Pony; but, before, Otto had always been able to write off his suspicions about White to the man just being a little . . . odd.

Otto knew plenty of government agents, and they were all—including himself, he realized—wired up wrong, in some way—even twisted in one fashion or another. Scratch a cop, and find a guy who's looking for a little piece of personal power; scratch a government agent, and find the same sickness, writ larger.

For the most part, though, these quirks were harmless, outweighed by the sense of civic responsibility that attracted a man to government service. White, however, was a weird, self-absorbed, negative son of a bitch . . . no question. The man seemed to have two saving graces: competence and patriotism. Only, Otto had started to doubt the latter attribute, wondering if White served some secret master. . . .

Running like this, getting the poison out, usually made Otto dismiss such thoughts as absurd, even silly. But now—after the weird climax of the Jam Pony hostage crisis—whatever suspicions Otto had about White were only magnified, and given weight.

His feet pounding the pavement, Otto let the movie of that night run in his head. . . .

The Seattle detective in charge of the situation, Clemente, seemed to have things in hand until he tried to trade a truck for hostages. Sometime during the exchange, shooting had erupted from somewhere. Otto had seen Clemente order his snipers to pull back, and the snipers did visibly withdraw.

Though he couldn't prove it, Otto had a suspicion that one of the endless phone calls White made that day was to bring in the group of shooters that queered the exchange.

Otto didn't know why he felt that—it was just his gut— but over the years, he'd learned to trust his instincts. Then later, after dark, after White had used the botched exchange to gain control of the hostage crisis, Otto approached White just as his partner was slipping on a Kevlar vest handed to him by the female leader of some kind of tactical insertion team—a team unlike any Otto knew of in the NSA lexicon. The group—bizarrely bulked-up types—kept moving, and Otto fell into step with them.

"Sir, what is this?" Otto had asked. "Who are these people?"

White glared at him with typical impatience. "They're assigned from another agency."

"*What* agency? I don't understand . . ."

Stopping and turning to face Otto, his sneering features only inches away, White growled, "And let's keep it that way. You're not cleared for this op—so pull the men back and secure the perimeter."

Otto froze, his mind bubbling with protests that couldn't seem to find their way out through his mouth.

White's expression tightened further—a handsome man, Ames White became ugly when lines of anger grooved his face . . . which was frequently. His voice rose: "Walk away. Do it now."

Not understanding, but unwilling to question a senior officer, Otto had done as he was told.

And it had been less than a half hour later—after the unknown agency's super-SWAT team emerged from Jam Pony with the perps, loading them into a van and a commandeered ambulance—that one of Clemente's uniformed cops came up to Otto near the perimeter. The man seemed on the verge of laughter, and Otto couldn't imagine what there was to laugh about in a hostage crisis.

"They need you inside," the uniform had said, the words burbling out, mixed in with chuckles.

How weird, how inappropriate, that seemed. . . .

Otto started to call to the other agents, but the uniformed cop put a hand on his shoulder.

"You better go in alone, sir," the officer said, his amusement lessened, but still there.

Confused, Otto made his way inside the building. He walked slowly through the first floor, where some other uniformed cops were leading three of the hostages toward the door.

"Can you direct me to Agent White?" Otto asked.

One of the uniforms pointed toward the ceiling and walked out, laughing.

What the hell was this?

Climbing the stairs to the second floor, Otto thought he heard what sounded like muffled voices—*angry* muffled voices. The building was supposed to be secure, but Otto slipped his pistol out of the holster anyway and pulled a penlight from his jacket pocket. Checking carefully, he went through the door of the second floor—it appeared to have been a dressmaker's loft, long since abandoned, a few naked female mannequins holding court surrealistically among various detritus—and moved closer to the voices.

Coming around a corner, he found the TAC insertion team, in their skivvies, and a fully dressed Agent White—all secured to pillars with Jam Pony packaging tape . . . all screaming what seemed to be obscenities through the tape gags that covered their mouths, in particular Ames White.

Suddenly Otto knew what the cops were all laughing about, though he himself found the situation humorless.

He holstered his pistol, pocketed the flash, and rummaged in his pants pocket for his knife. "Sir, what happened?" he asked.

White's answer was thankfully muffled—and for a split second Otto considered turning around and walking out; but he knew it would mean his career. Biting his tongue, he cut them loose, White first, then the others.

The muscular, half-naked commando team left without so much as a thank you—their displeasure (with themselves?) palpable.

Standing there in his ripped suit, peeling pieces of tape off his jacket, his scowling face bloodied, White said, "Go home, Otto. I'll write up the report and let you see it in the morning."

"But . . . what *happened* here, sir?"

White closed his eyes, obviously fighting for control. One fist balled at his side while the other grabbed a hank of his own hair. He stayed like that for a long moment. Otto realized his boss considered himself a cool customer; but Otto knew that White was in reality a hothead. Anger, frustration, desperation, and finally a kind of unearthly calm all crossed White's face before he opened his eyes again.

"Now is not the time, Otto," he said. "Go home and wait for me to call. . . . It might be tomorrow, it might be the next day. Maybe it'll be Christmas. But just *go home*—relax. And wait."

Otto was about to tell White that he couldn't do that—that standard agency policy demanded otherwise—when the superior agent simply turned and walked out of the cluttered loft. A voice in his head told Otto not to follow, and because the voice—whose message had often been, *Cover your ass*—had been right so many times in the past, he listened to it.

So instead of going after his partner and bringing the craziness to a head, Otto simply went home and waited.

That had been two days ago, and the phone had yet to ring. Tomorrow, whether White called or not, Otto was going to report back to work. There might be hell to pay, if White considered that a breach of orders; but maybe it was time to go over Ames White's head and report what he suspected . . . what he'd observed. . . .

As he entered the eighth mile of his run, Otto prayed that he was doing the right thing . . . because Otto Gottlieb truly wanted to do what was best not just for himself, not just to cover his ass, but for his job. His country.

That settled, Otto tried to empty his head of everything except the run. The sound of his own blood in his ears, the smack of his shoes on the pavement, breath rushing in through his nose, out through his mouth, feeling the sweat run down his face . . . this became his world. Everything else was left behind.

The rest of the eighth mile flew by. He was nearly to the end of the ninth mile, really getting into the run now, when the cell phone clipped to his waistband chirped.

"Damnit," Otto muttered as he slowed to a walk, and tried to control his breathing so he wouldn't sound winded. He answered on the third ring.

"It's me," came Ames White's voice.

Otto cursed silently. He wanted to ask where the hell White had been, but he said, "Yes, sir."

"Sounds like you've been running."

"Yes, sir."

"Good. You could stand to take off some of that gut."

" . . . Yes, sir."

"Have you talked to anyone since we last spoke?"

"No, sir."

"Good. We need to meet."

"Yes, sir." Otto hated himself for falling back into ass-kissing mode so easily, but he didn't really know what else to do at this point.

"I'm bringing you in more fully on this op. You'd like that, wouldn't you, Otto?"

"Yes, sir."

"You know the Three Girls?"

"Yes—bakery at Pike Place Market." White couldn't have picked someplace closer, of course; he had to pick somewhere clear across the city from where Otto lived.

"You being watched, Otto?"

"No." *Why would he be watched?*

"Good. Twenty minutes. Come on foot."

"I'll never make it."

"Half an hour, then. And run faster."

Otto knew that not only was White a sucker for the meat-loaf sandwiches at Three Girls Bakery, the man also liked the fact that the L-shaped counter only had thirteen seats. Most people didn't hang around long, and the chances of them being spotted by someone from the office were minimal, especially at this time of night.

White sat at the far end of the counter, waiting over coffee and a scone, when Otto—in his running togs, breathing hard—entered thirty-five minutes later. Two days had allowed White a change of clothes and the opportunity to clean his wounds. They seemed to be healing nicely, from what Otto could see.

The runner sat down next to his partner and boss, and when the counterman promptly came over, Otto said, "I'll have the same. Decaf, though," and gestured toward White's meal.

A skinny man in his late fifties, and obviously not one of the three girls, the guy grunted and went back to the other end of the counter.

"You're late," White said quietly.

Otto ignored that. "Are you going to tell me what happened at Jam Pony?"

The counterman brought a cup of coffee, a scone on a

small plate, and set them both on the counter in front of Otto. "Anything else?"

"No," Otto said.

The counterman left the check and went away.

Finally, satisfied they were alone, White shrugged. "They got the best of us. They *are* transgenics, after all."

Otto nodded. "That TAC team of yours looked like they coulda been transgenics themselves."

"You think the NSA has transies working for them now, Otto? Please. Those were just top physical specimens—the kind who could've run over here in *less* than half an hour."

"Maybe so—but, like you said, the bad guys got the best of them anyway."

"Let that go. We have something more important than that now."

"Yes?"

White sat forward, kept his voice down. "You recall the thermal imager that was taken off Hankins?"

Otto took a bite of his scone, but wished he hadn't when the picture of the red-glistening skinned Hankins popped into his mind. He washed the bite down with some coffee. "Hard to forget," he managed finally.

"The imager has turned up."

"Good news. Where?"

White took his time now, nibbling at his own scone and taking a swallow of coffee before continuing. "A sector cop found it, not long after the murder at the warehouse. He was one of the perimeter guys. Apparently the monster that skinned Hankins didn't know the device's value—just threw it away. Interestingly, Hankins' skin didn't turn up—the perp took it with him."

Otto put down his scone.

"Anyway, the sector cop who found it knew the thing was valuable. Somehow he got my cell number and got through

to me. Name's Dunphy, Brian Dunphy. He's willing to return
the imager—for a price."

"How much?"

"Ten grand."

"No way!"

White's smile put nasty grooves in his face. "That's what
I told him. He settled for five."

"That's still robbery."

"More like blackmail. But the agency is willing to cover
it—if one of those transgenics got hold of an imager, and
was smart enough to figure out its use, well . . ."

"When's the drop?"

"Tonight."

"Where's the money?"

Glancing down, White drank some more coffee.

Otto followed the man's gaze, saw a briefcase on the floor
next to White, and looked back up at his partner. "You
brought it here?"

"I needed to pass it to you."

"Me?"

"Yeah," White said. "You're going to make the delivery."

The scone and coffee rolled over in Otto's stomach. "Sir,
without proper paperwork, I don't think I can—"

White interrupted. "You have to. I'm going to be in meet-
ings for the next twenty-four hours trying to clear up that
Jam Pony fiasco. You want to keep your job, don't you?"

"Yes, sir." The answer popped out before Otto could
stop it.

"Well, then, accept the responsibility of being part of this
op. Take the briefcase, and take this, too." White handed him
a photo and a sheet of paper with the drop point written on
it. "That's where this Dunphy will be at three A.M. tonight,
and a picture so you don't give five grand to the wrong asshole."

Holding the items at arm's length, by the tips of fingers,

like they were toxic materials, Otto finally asked, "What am I supposed to do until then?"

White's brow furrowed. "Run home. Take a shower. What am I, your mother?" Tossing a five spot on the counter, he got up and looked down at Otto, in several senses of the phrase. "Three o'clock. Call me when it's done."

Otto didn't like this at all, but he didn't know what to say either. He had no idea what he would do with his life if he lost this job.

"Yes, sir," he finally managed.

"Good boy," White said, and walked out of the restaurant, leaving Otto Gottlieb to ponder his future.

Otto looked at the photo of a forty-something Irish-looking cop. What a cliché, he thought. Redheaded with a few freckles, Dunphy had the red onion nose of an alcoholic and the hooded green eyes of a sociopath. The photo brought Otto no comfort whatsoever. Looking down at the remains of his scone and the cup of coffee, he realized he wasn't hungry anymore.

Having some time to kill, Otto caught a cab, went home and got on his computer. By one A.M. he knew everything there was to know about sector cop Brian Dunphy—forty-four, suspended twice for being overweight, with no money in the bank, an ex-wife who left him nearly ten years ago, a daughter he only saw on the weekends, and nothing to look forward to at the end of the road. No wonder this guy was looking to score any way he could.

Two hours later Otto found himself in Sector Eleven heading for the checkpoint with Sector Twelve. Not much happened out here on the edge of town, and he hoped to dump the money, get the imager, and get back home without any hassles. He parked his car a few blocks away and started to walk. He wasn't taking any chances that he'd be identified by having his car seen at the checkpoint. Still, he didn't much like walking down the street with a briefcase full of cash.

A light rain peppered the ground and Otto pulled his black topcoat tighter around himself. The night air had a chill, and he had a childhood memory of Michigan, which was similarly cold. He could see his breath as he neared the small shack that served as the checkpoint's guard post. Looking through the window of the shed-sized building, he couldn't see anyone inside. The light was on, but no one seemed to be home.

Moving around to the door, Otto opened it, walked in, and knew immediately that something was wrong.

The desk against the left wall held a coffeepot that was still on, a cup filled with steaming joe, and an ashtray with a cigarette burning in it, a pack of Winstons nearby. Everything was right where it belonged . . .

. . . . except for the sector cop.

A door in the back right corner led into the closet that served as a bathroom, but the door yawned wide open, the room empty.

Otto checked his watch—3:02. Brian Dunphy should be here.

But he wasn't. *Where the hell is the bastard?*

A five-thousand-dollar appointment wasn't something an underpaid sector cop would normally be late for. . . .

His own cop instincts twitching, Otto went back outside. The gate separating the two sectors was locked. He looked through the eight-foot chain-link fence, down the street into Sector Twelve, and still saw no sign of the officer. Then he looked back up the street in the direction he'd come and saw nothing there either.

The rain grew more intense, and for a long moment he considered calling White, then decided he better look around a little more. He considered leaving the briefcase in the guard shack to keep his hands free, and thought better of it.

An old factory neighborhood, Sector Eleven was mostly

run-down vacant buildings for blocks in every direction. Some had been taken over by squatters, who seldom ventured far at night, especially not on a rainy night like this one. Otto gazed down the street into Sector Twelve again and still saw nothing, the rain blurring anything beyond a few hundred feet anyway.

His heart fluttered, his stomach was in knots, and he had a warm, loose feeling in his bowels. Otto hated being scared, but something was terribly wrong here and he had no idea what it was. He withdrew a small flashlight from his coat pocket, turned it on, then struggled to hold it in his left hand along with the briefcase as he drew his pistol with his right from under his topcoat and started back in the direction from whence he'd come. His rubber-soled shoes moved silently over the concrete, his flashlight jabbing holes in the night, seeking any sign of the missing sector cop.

Halfway back down the block, an alley bisected the street. Otto was worried that if Dunphy had gone off to check on a prowler or something, the sector cop might be coming back down the alley, see the light and the gun, and wind up drilling Otto.

Wouldn't *that* be a son of a bitch.

Pushing himself flat against the brick building on the west side of the street, Otto moved back north. When he got to the alley, he first looked across the street to the east and could see nothing but rain in that direction. Feeling like a putz on the empty street, Otto peeked around the edge of the building, saw nothing, and risked shining the flashlight down that way.

Nothing.

He turned west in the alley, the flashlight and briefcase clumsily in front of him as he meandered ahead, careful to stay in the middle and aim the tiny pen flash at any shadows. Keeping his pistol ready, he moved forward slowly.

Five feet, ten feet, fifteen, twenty, nothing, the flashlight sweeping back and forth, the briefcase growing heavier by the second, his fingers aching, then stiffening, as the case wobbled back and forth.

Damnit, he thought. *Where is this asshole?*

Ahead, on his right, something tapped on metal in the shadows.

He swung the flashlight over and saw a dumpster. He couldn't tell whether the tapping came from the inside or from the far end, where he couldn't see. The tapping continued, slow, rhythmic—something man-made, for sure.

"Dunphy?" he asked quietly.

No answer—just the tapping.

Otto took a wider arc, so he could see around the far end of the dumpster.

Nothing.

The tapping stopped.

His gun coming up, Otto took a step forward, then another. Still no sound from the dumpster. He took a third step, and was now less than ten feet away. Taking a breath in through his nose, he blew it out through his mouth, just like he did when he was running.

The lid to the dumpster flew open, clanging off the wall, and a figure rose up from within the container.

Freaking at the noise, Otto dropped both the flashlight and the briefcase as he brought up the gun in a two-handed grip. The light stayed on, doing its job as best it could, shining crazily toward the foot of the dumpster.

The briefcase wasn't so lucky.

Money spilled out into the puddles in the alley, and the remaining cash got splattered by the rain. The crash of the lid scared Otto so badly he almost shot whoever-the-hell-it-was without getting a clear look.

Fumbling to keep the gun on the dumpster and pick up the flash, Otto stumbled, went to a knee on the wet pavement, and finally had the light and gun pointed at the new arrival.

"Freeze!" Otto yelled.

The figure looked up, saw Otto, the flashlight, and the gun . . . and screamed.

Then the screamer ducked back down into the dumpster, out of sight, but not out of mind.

Otto had only a glimpse to go on: the body shape had seemed male, but the scream was as high-pitched as a little girl's; and the person's hair was long enough that Otto couldn't tell whether he'd just cornered a man or a woman.

"Federal agent," he said, perhaps too loudly. "Put up your hands, then slowly stand."

No one stood, but Otto thought he could discern a soft whimpering from inside the dumpster.

"I'm not going to tell you again. Hands up and stand up slowly."

First he saw the dumpster dweller's hands, then the person slowly stood, the rain dripping off a disheveled mat of dark hair. "I didn't do nothin'," the man said.

Older man.

Otto shined the light on the guy's face—late fifties, kind of frail, wearing a lightweight navy windbreaker. The dumpster dweller had a scruffy beard and bad teeth that he managed to smile with. His way of showing he was on the up and up.

"What're you doing in there?"

"Gettin' out of the rain."

"You were making some kind of noise in there, a tapping—what was it?"

The old man's face went blank, then he looked down inside the dumpster. "Oh, that?"

"Oh, what?" Otto asked.

"Scrounged me a flashlight. Tried to knock it against the side, to get it to work. But the batteries is bum."

Otto came up to the edge of the dumpster, shooed the old man to the other end, then looked over the edge. He shone the flashlight in, and on the bottom caught a glimpse of metal. He homed in on it with the light, and when he finally figured out what he was looking at, his heart sank.

The thermal imager—beaten almost beyond recognition.

"Okay, old man—time to get out."

The dumpster dweller did as he was told, but not without bitching about it: "What'd *I* do?"

"Did you put that, uh . . . flashlight in the dumpster your-self?"

"No! It was there already, when I went fishin' inside. Honest. Swear to God."

Otto believed the old guy. The man didn't seem to be strong enough to have taken out a sector cop; and if he had, why was he down rooting in the dumpster?

"Go on, gramps. Take a hike."

The old man frowned. "Can I take the flashlight?"

"No."

"I found it. It's mine. You guys didn't repeal finders keep-ers, did ya?"

Fishing into his pocket, Otto pulled out a five and held it out to the guy.

"Bet it's worth more than that."

Otto brought the gun up and gave the guy a good look at it. The bum took the hint, and the five spot, climbed out and started to walk off in the direction of the briefcase.

"The other way, gramps."

The old man held up his hands. "You got it, boss! Other way it is."

When the old boy had disappeared around the corner, Otto finally took another breath. He shook his head—feelings of fear and anger gave way to relief. But uneasiness remained; what did the imager turning up mean? Where the hell was that greedy sector cop? Five dollars had bought what five grand was supposed to. . . .

Profanity running a race through his mind, Otto went over and stuffed the soaked bills back into the briefcase and carried it over to the dumpster, as if he were about to throw the damp money away.

Now it was Otto's turn to climb into the soggy filth to pull out the thermal imager. He took a quick look around, set the case on the ground, edging it behind the dumpster, and holstered his pistol. Using the edges of the container, he pulled himself up and over and inside.

The dumpster smelled—not surprisingly—of rot, decay, and, if he didn't miss his guess, human feces. Otto tried to bring to mind the time when he'd loved his government job, and as he shined the flashlight down and picked up the battered thermal imager, he realized he couldn't recall the last time he'd liked—let alone loved—his job.

He cast the beam over the imager and saw spatters of blood.

As sure as he was standing in garbage, he now knew Brian Dunphy was dead. That one answer led to countless questions. Where was the body? Who killed him? Why was he killed?

And was Otto's own life in danger . . . *right now*?

Again the urge came to call White. This time Otto didn't fight it. He pulled himself out of the dumpster, retrieved the briefcase, and headed back up the alley. He'd go to his car, dry off, call the boss.

At the corner of the street and the alley, Otto again looked up the alley across the street. The rain had lightened up just a touch, and he could see the old man he'd chased off, as well as several more street people, standing in a loose circle looking at a good-sized lump of something on the ground.

Without taking another step, Otto knew that he'd just found Brian Dunphy.

Pulling out his gun again, the NSA agent crossed the street and trotted up. The trio around the body split when they saw him coming, and the entire party disappeared into the shadows by the time he arrived.

Pointing the flashlight down, he saw something he'd seen before but had hoped to never see again.

The other time he'd seen a body in this condition, it belonged to that old-timer, Cal Hankins. Sprawled there, in a spreading pool of dark fluids, the bright red corpse that almost certainly belonged to Brian Dunphy gazed up at Otto with huge bulging eyes and a grotesque clown's grin in a caved-in skull with brains showing.

This made three murder victims who'd been skinned. All Otto knew of the second victim was that he was a cop. His info came strictly from the news, since he hadn't discussed that second kill with White.

But now he was looking at victim number three—the guy's uniform scattered around the alley, his gun and boots already stolen—and Otto had a chill. Was there a connection, beyond two victims being cops?

The car and getting dry would have to wait. Moving clear of the crime scene, Otto pulled out his cell phone and punched in the number for Ames White. The senior agent picked up on the first ring.

"Is it done?" he asked.

"Not really," Otto said. "And we've gotta talk."

For the next several minutes Otto outlined what he'd found, Ames White staying uncharacteristically mute.

When Otto had finished, White simply said, "Fuck."

"That about sums it up."

"You sure it's the sector cop? What was his name?"

"Dunphy. Pretty sure. He's been skinned, probably beaten to death with the imager, first. And there's pieces of uniform scattered around the alley—I haven't looked for ID or anything, but it's pretty evident that—"

"All right, all right—here's what you do. Get the hell out of there. You talk to any civilians at the scene?"

"Just the bum in the dumpster."

"Identify yourself to him?"

"No."

"Good. Bring me the money and the thermal imager."

"But, sir, the imager—it's almost certainly the murder weapon."

"I don't seem to give a shit, do I? If the cops get their hands on that device, you know damn well it's going to end up on the news, and then the transgenics will see it, and then it will be useless. Would that be a good thing, Otto?"

"That would be a bad thing."

"Right. Bring it."

"Yes, sir."

"Then, once you're safely out of the sector, make an anonymous 911 call and report the body."

"All right."

"And then I want you to get hold of Clemente."

That puzzled Otto. "The police detective?"

"Yeah. Let him know that it was you who phoned in the anonymous call, but that for national security reasons you had to leave the scene."

"Okay. . . ."

White's voice had delight in it. "Transgenics did this and now they're going to hang themselves. Tell Clemente what you saw and tell him that we have evidence the killer's transgenic."

"*Do* we have that?"

"We will, Otto. We will."

Otto didn't like the sound of that—the implication, however vague, was that evidence would be manufactured, if necessary.

"Now, Otto, after you talk to Clemente, bring me the money and pick me up at home. We've got work to do."

"We do?"

"This is going to turn into a PR war, Otto. We have a

demented serial-killer transgenic to tell the public about; if you think the rank and file are frightened of transies now, just you wait till the media gets their teeth in this. And which side of the PR war do you suppose has the most media on their side?"

"That would be ours, sir."

"Damn right," White said. "Now's our chance to use them too."

"Yes, sir."

"Got the drill, Otto? 911, Clemente, then get your ass over here."

Not liking this a bit—neither what was going down nor White's condescension—but realizing he had fallen in way over his head, Otto said the only thing he could think of, which was, "Yes, sir."

Hustling back to his car, his feet splashing in puddles, the briefcase pounding against one hip, the bloody thermal imager clutched in his other hand, Otto Gottlieb wanted nothing more than to be done with this awful night. At the car, he locked the imager and money in the trunk, got behind the wheel, started the engine and gunned it.

Time to get the hell out of there.

A few blocks down he found a pay phone, pulled over, and made the call.

"This is 911, how may I help?"

"There's a murdered sector guard in Sector Eleven, in the alley off Renton."

"Your name, sir?"

"Just check it out," Otto said, and hung up.

Knowing the police would try to trace the call, Otto wiped the phone clean of fingerprints and got back on the move again. As he drove toward White's house, he phoned the office, got the home and cell numbers for Detective Ramon Clemente, and looked for a nice secluded spot to pull over and make the call.

He pulled into the parking lot of an all-night restaurant near the King County Airport. Though the lights were on, the place looked vacant, and Otto figured he'd get the peace and quiet to make the next call.

He thought about it long and hard. If he went down this path with White, his career could be over; but if he didn't—his career could be over! Nice options.

Obviously, White was up to some bad shit here—Otto just didn't know what, exactly. He found it difficult to believe that the government's agenda was White's, that Washington was behind this antitransgenic crusade. But if he went in now and tried to rat out White, who would believe him? He had no evidence, and what did he have besides his own suspicions?

Suspicions of what? Evidence of what?

And what if Ames White's antitransgenic agenda *was* the government's?

As much as Otto hated to admit it, there seemed only one way to go. Shaking his head, listening to the cover-your-ass voice once again, Otto pulled out his cell phone and dialed Clemente's home number . . .

. . . once again, doing the bidding of Ames White.

Chapter Five
REALITY BITES

Most of the transgenics were deep asleep, catching the peace the waking world refused them, when the call came in from a guard post near the main gate.

But Max was awake—waiting.

She keyed the radio. "Say again?"

The guard said, "Got a guy approaching the main gate. Black dude with two white uniforms tagging along."

Looking up at the security camera, she saw Detective Ramon Clemente and two other officers at the gate. "Tell him I'll be right down," she told the guard.

"What's up?" Dix chimed, unrumpling his clothes as he came up the two stairs to his work area. He apparently slept in that half-goggle "monocle" of his; *Whatever*, Max thought.

"Light sleeper?" she asked him.

"Always. Gotta be, if you wanna make a habit of waking up in the morning. . . . We got visitors?"

"Time to start talking," Max said with a nod. "You got a discreet transmitter?"

The mashed-potato-headed transgenic looked injured. "Of course I do."

She grinned. "That's what I like about you, Dix—always ready."

"And willing, and able." He pinned a tiny microphone to the inside of her black leather vest. "This baby'll pick up both of you, easy deezy."

"Thanks, Dix." She started off, then had a thought. "Do me a favor?"

"As long as it's illegal, sure."

"Record this, will you?"

"You want the audio equiv of a paper trail, huh? No problem."

Max skipped down to the door, then snugged on a ball cap and stepped outside. Rain fell steadily, as if God was trying to calm the world, and the night felt damn near cold. As she strode toward the gate, she could make out Clemente, bundled in a dark overcoat, the two cops behind him looking like they would rather be anywhere else.

"You reading me, Dix?" she said easily.

"Loud and clear," came his voice in the minuscule earpiece she wore.

Max passed between two transgenic guards—fearsome critters designed to give the ordinaries pause—and approached the gate.

"You wanted me?" Clemente asked by way of a greeting.

The detective looked only slightly more rested and less stressed than the last time she'd seen him. He wore no hat and the rain ran down his impassive face like tears. His large brown eyes still appeared red-rimmed, and Max couldn't help but wonder what sort of debriefing the detective had endured.

"I missed you," she said, smiling at him.

The two people who had done the most to keep Jam Pony and its immediate aftermath from turning into a bloodbath faced each other with respect and perhaps a smidgen of affection.

He gave her a little grin. "I missed you too, Max."

"You're here because you want to be here?"

"Of course."

She didn't believe him for a second. "If we're going to make progress here, Detective, you're going to have to start telling the truth."

"It's the truth, Max. You know I don't want this to get any uglier than it has to—and that's not true of everybody on my side of the fence."

She knew who he meant: Ames White. And she knew too that White's influence might spread within the police department. That was why she had wanted Clemente as her police liaison.

Nodding, she said, "That's part of what I want to talk about."

"So, talk."

She shook her head. "Alone—you and me."

Now Clemente shook his head. "I have orders to maintain my bodyguards and stay on this side of the fence."

"Orders are always contingent upon field conditions, Detective. We talk alone—inside."

His expression revealed genuine frustration. "Max . . . I've got no power—this is way over my head."

"Don't underestimate yourself, Detective Clemente. You're here now, aren't you?"

"Obviously."

"And how did it go down? You're home asleep in your warm dry bed, and someone very important—the police chief maybe, possibly a general—demanded that you get your ass out of bed and haul it down here to the siege site."

He grunted a tiny laugh. "That's about it. Are you psychic, Max?"

"No—but I was bred to this kind of shit. I don't like it, but we can't choose our parents, can we?"

If so, she thought, *I wouldn't have picked a test tube.*

She gestured in a welcoming fashion. "Come on in out of the rain—*somebody* on the Seattle PD must be smart enough to do that, right? We'll get a cup of coffee and talk."

He gave her a long look. "If I come in, what about my guards?"

"The bookends stay out here in the rain. Just you."

Clemente eyed the two transgenic sentries. "*You've* got two guards."

"They'll stay here keeping your boys company. Just the two of us, Detective."

Nonetheless, Clemente looked uneasy.

Max stepped closer to the gate. "If I were going to kill you, Detective, you would have been dead Friday—think back . . . I had half a dozen chances."

His eyes tightened, acknowledging the truth of that.

"I need someone trustworthy on your side of this thing, and unfortunately for you, you're the closest candidate the Seattle PD has provided me, lately."

"And you trust me?"

"So far. You trust me?"

He thought about that. "You know . . . I think I do."

"Then you got two choices, Detective—come in, or leave."

Clemente wheeled, said something sotto voce to his two companions, then turned and nodded, curtly.

"You'll love it here," Max said, and pulled the gate open a little.

Clemente came cautiously through. Slowly, he scanned the twisted metal and derelict buildings rising around him, making ominous abstract shapes in the rain-streaked night.

"They're around," Max said, referring to the transgenics he was checking for. "But they'll leave us alone."

She led him inside a nearby building that had once housed a stem cell research facility. It was a low-slung brick structure and the glass door had long ago been shattered, but at least the roof didn't leak. The receptionist would have sat to the right. A door on the left led to what had once been offices, while another door in front of them went to the former labs in the back.

Inside what would have been the receptionist's cubicle sat a desk with a straight-back chair on either side. A single lamp perched on one end of the desk, and in the middle was a tray with a pot, two cups, two spoons, a carton of milk, and a bowl of sugar.

The walls were white, the floor dusty but free of clutter, and a window was to their right. Looking out the window, they could see the main gate, and would be able to make out any movement around it.

"I wanted you to have a nice view," she said. "But when I turn on the lamp, we won't be able to see outside."

"But your snipers will be able to see their target," Clemente said, "just fine."

"Then maybe we won't turn on the lamp," she said. "Doesn't bother me none—I have pretty good night vision."

Which of course was an understatement.

"Cozy is fine by me," Clemente said.

Max walked around the desk, and waved for the detective to take the seat across from her.

"You want that coffee I promised you?"

"Kind of late for me," he said. "I may want to get back to sleep someday."

"Whatever—but we may be here awhile."

He considered, said, "Make mine black."

She poured for them both. She had hers black as well.

Clemente sipped his coffee, and his expression had mild surprise in it. "Hey—this is good."

"We're multitalented. I'm sure the outside world would rather we drank blood or crushed insect guts. But we're people, Detective."

He drank some more. "Yes—people who are in a lot of trouble."

"You might be surprised how long we can hold out," she said. "We've anticipated this kind of situation for months. We've stockpiled food and water. We're well-armed."

This wasn't exactly true, though with Logan's tunnel supply line, they could indeed hold out for a good long time.

"Anyway," she said, "you're the one that's risking his health inside Terminal City. Ordinaries can't stay in here long—this is no-man's-land, a real biochemical bad trip for everybody but the transgenics."

"Are you suggesting that I tell the general who called me—it *was* a general, not the police chief, Max—and say all we have to do is back our troops out, and let you . . . people inhabit Terminal City?"

"We aren't negotiating yet . . . but why not? What good does Terminal City do anyone but transgenics?"

"Max, this is not going to end well."

She shook her head. "I don't see it that way. Call me an optimist, but I think this can turn out for the best."

He looked at her as if she were insane. "How in hell?"

"That's what you and I are going to hammer out."

Clemente patted the air in front of him. "Whoa, whoa. You think the two of us are just going to talk this thing out?"

Max sipped her coffee. "Why not?"

"We can't—"

"We already did it once—at Jam Pony."

He shook his head. "We didn't keep the peace there and we sure as hell didn't talk it out. You jumped White and his goons and kicked their asses."

She smiled.

"If one little victory makes you smile, fine," he said. "But us talking. . . . Max, I can't negotiate this. And nobody else wants to."

"You have to reason with them, Detective. Encourage your superiors to sit down and talk with us."

He looked into her eyes in the darkness. "You have two options, Max. One is put your hands in the air and walk en masse through that gate into custody, and hope that in the light of day, given due process and a full-scale public hearing, you'll get a fair shake."

"I can't wait till I hear the other option."

"It's a lot worse. Last time, we were lucky—only one person died. There's a hell of a lot more at stake now, and a lot more emotion on the outside. The media has people all stirred up, crying out, 'Kill the monsters.' Most of the military is up for just storming the place and painting the walls red."

She didn't break eye contact and her voice remained matter-of-fact. "You know that trying that would be a big mistake."

He stared at her for a long moment. "Do I?"

"You have the numbers, but don't forget—this is what we were trained for. Frankly, Detective, we'd wax your ass, then we'd disappear into the night, and you'd never know where we would hit next."

His expression was grave enough to indicate he'd taken that as the promise, not threat, that it was; but he said, "There's a far superior force mustering on the other side of that fence."

Shaking her head, she said, "They're not superior, Detective—there's just more of them."

And now, despite it all, he smiled. "You are one cocky little shit."

"I'm glad you didn't call me a 'cocky little bitch,'" she said, "'cause I woulda hated having to kick your ass."

His smile disappeared, but she chuckled and patted his arm. "Look, Detective Clemente—"

"If I'm going to call you Max, you call me Ramon."

"All right, Ramon. Look . . . I've been running since I was nine. Most of the residents of Terminal City will tell you the same or something very similar. I'm tired of running, we're all tired of it. We didn't bring this on—they made us, then they tried to kill us. All we did was defend ourselves. In that situation, anyone would have done as much."

"Most people aren't genetically engineered killing machines."

"From what I've seen, Ramon, the so-called ordinaries may not be genetically engineered, but they kill way more often . . . and for far less reason than the transgenics ever have."

"I can't argue that. But those ordinaries you speak of aren't going to be able to identify with you, Max—some of you have monstrous appearances, and all of you have super-human abilities that make you dangerous."

"We have to make them understand that we have hearts and minds and maybe even souls, too."

"So, how do we do that?"

She shook her head. "We're still trying to figure that out. I'm hoping we can get the word out, stop some of this media garbage that—"

"Wait, wait. Max, a battalion is waiting outside your door, and you want to stave that off with a PR campaign?"

"Ramon—I'm looking for answers. I need you to look for some, and seek allies within your ranks, cooler heads that don't have a hidden agenda served by the blood of my people."

He sighed. "Fair enough."

"It's going to take some time, and you've got to do anything you can to hold back the troops—keep them from storming our castle for a while . . . okay?"

"And if I try to accomplish that, do I have your word that the transgenics will stay inside?"

She gave him a decisive nod. "Those that are in will stay in. The others, the ones that are still out there," she said, and gestured toward the other side of the fence, "them I can't control."

"All right," Clemente said, and sighed. "How long do you need me to stall this thing?"

"I told you. We've got supplies for the next year—how 'bout you guys?"

"Max," the detective said forcefully, trying to brush aside her glibness. "Just how the hell long do you think I can keep them from attacking?"

"Ramon," she said, "this is my first transgenics-versus-the-United-States-military siege. I'm making this up as I go."

Clemente looked as if he were trying to decide whether to laugh or cry. Before he made any decision, his cell phone rang. He looked at her, and she said nothing. It went off again and he pulled it out and checked the caller ID.

"Fed number," he said.

"Take it—see what they want."

He touched a button and held the phone to his ear. "Clemente," he said, but the identification sounded more like an angry question.

Max watched the detective's face as the caller spoke. Ramon Clemente did not look happy.

"Yeah, I remember you," he told the phone, his disgust apparent. "Do you have any idea what fucking time it is?"

Clemente listened some more, his face shifting from pissed to serious.

Then the cop asked, "Where and when?"

Max felt herself growing uneasy—something wasn't right somewhere.

Clemente's expression was blank now, except for a fire in his eyes. "And *why* do you think a transgenic is responsible?"

A sick feeling oozed into her stomach.

"That's the opinion of your superior officer?" he asked whoever he was talking to. "You wouldn't happen to mean Special Agent in Charge White?"

Max rocketed to her feet. Wanting to rip the phone out of Clemente's hand, she started pacing behind the desk.

"You know I can't trust that son of a bitch," the detective said.

Did he mean White?

"I know he's high-ranking, but he's still a son of a bitch. . . . Where are you now, Agent Gottlieb?"

The caller said something—if the phone hadn't been pressed so tight to the detective's ear, Max would have been able to hear it—and Clemente's expression shifted back to pissed off.

"You left the scene of a *murder*?"

Now her stomach did a little back flip into the pool of nausea flooding her belly.

"You people never fail to amaze me," Clemente said. "We need to talk, and soon. . . . All right you tell *me* where and when! God knows I should defer to your high standards of professionalism."

Again the caller's response didn't help Clemente's mood.

"You better know in one hour, Agent Gottlieb, and you better call me back within that time span or I'll have a warrant issued for your goddamned arrest. The last I heard, federal agents weren't exempt from the laws of this land."

And the detective thumbed End.

"Murder involving a transgenic?" Max asked, stopping to lean on the desk. "What the hell is going on?"

She was doing her best to stay cool; she wanted to project power and control to this man. The half of that phone call she'd just heard raised too many questions, and she had a feeling she wasn't going to like any of the answers.

Clemente seemed to be working at controlling himself as well, though his anger and anxiety were clearly not directed at her. "A sector officer at the checkpoint between Eleven and Twelve was killed tonight."

Max tried to keep the rage out of her voice, with little success. "And Ames White thinks a transgenic did it."

Clemente nodded once, gravely. "And he's supposed to have proof."

"What kind of proof? That wasn't him on the phone; that was his stooge Gottlieb, right?"

"Right. As you probably gathered, Otto discovered the body but left the scene, so I don't know how the hell they secured any kind of evidence."

She drew a deep, slow breath; then she let it out and said calmly, "You do know that there's more to Ames White than just your typical government pain-in-the-ass scumbag."

"Well, he's definitely a government pain-in-the-ass scumbag. You don't have to talk hard to convince me of that."

"Ramon, if you just take a close look at him, you'll find out that there's a lot more going on than NSA duties."

Clemente's eyes tightened. "Such as?"

"White's—"

She stopped.

She knew that whatever she said was going to sound completely crazy, and she would lose all cred with the cop.

"Go on, Max. What do you know about White? Is he . . . dirty, somehow?"

"That hardly covers it."

"You have to tell me more."

Hell, she could barely believe the true agenda of Ames White herself . . . and she'd seen the agents of the cult firsthand. How could she hope to convince Clemente without the risk of losing his confidence completely?

"You just . . . need to take a good hard look into him," she managed.

"I can only look so hard."

"You're a detective, aren't you? Fucking detect!"

He gestured with open hands. "Max—if there are bad things to be found out about Ames White, what makes you think that either White or the government will let a local cop find them?"

"I found out, didn't I?"

"Then take the load off my shoulders—share what you know."

She sighed and sat back down, heavily; she wished the darkness of the room would just swallow her. "Look, you're not going to believe me . . . so I want you to check it out on your own. Seeing is believing, you heard of that?"

Intrigued, Clemente rubbed a hand over his chin. "What makes you think I won't believe you?"

Max rolled her eyes, shook her head. "It's too whack to be true. . . . It just *is*."

A tiny, teasing grin appeared. "Like the government making genetically engineered killing machines without the public's knowledge?"

She smirked at him. "Yeah, like that—only a whole lot weirder."

The detective's smile disappeared. He looked confused, and she could hardly blame him. At last he said, "You said you trusted me. Well, that goes both ways. Trust me with this, Max—trust me that I'll take you seriously."

And, so—taking a deep breath, and a leap of faith—she launched into the story of the ancient breeding cult whose snake-worshiping conclave of leaders manipulated events and people, and had for centuries; she pressed on, telling the detective how these crazies had been trying to breed genetically superior humans for the last thousand years or so, an objective that had eventually led to the modern-day creation of Manticore.

To some degree, they had succeeded in their attempt to build a "better" human. She had seen Ames White, who did the bidding of the conclave, perform acts of strength and daring that rivaled anything any transgenic could accomplish . . . with the added detail that White and the others like him could feel no pain.

When she had finished what even she knew sounded like

the most absurd of tall tales, Clemente looked even more confused, and a little bit like she'd punched him out.

But at least he wasn't eyeballing her as if she were a mad-woman. In fact, her gut instinct told her he believed her, or at least believed in her sincerity.

"Can you prove any of this?" he asked.

She shook her head. "Not really—anytime I've gotten any-thing, they've covered up, sort of a scorched earth policy. But that team that came into Jam Pony—you saw those pumped-up uber-humans—they didn't work for any government agency. . . . They worked for the conclave of the snake cult."

He said nothing for a long time. They just sat there in the darkness, with his eyes moving in thought, and Max study-ing him to see if she had outright lost him.

Finally, quietly, Clemente said, "You're right, Max—it does sound crazy."

Max's heart sank.

"But," he said, getting up, shaking his head and grinning wryly, "in this job, it doesn't pay to not look into things, just because they sound crazy."

A warmth for this man filled her, and she stood and ex-tended her hand; they shook, and she said, "Thanks, Ramon."

He checked his watch. "I've got to split . . . but I'll dig into this weird shit, as much as I can. Snakes, huh?"

"Snakes."

"Those I may not dig into."

She smiled a little. "Don't blame you."

"Why is White's agenda—the snake cult's agenda—anti-transgenic? Shouldn't all you genetic wonders hang together?"

"I don't understand it myself, Ramon. Still putting pieces together. The point is, White wants to wipe us out . . . and blaming murders on transgenics is a good way to win that PR war we were talking about."

"People don't usually die in PR wars."

"I don't mean anything light by that, Ramon. I'm sorry that the cop got killed, no matter who did it."

"Thanks, but getting killed wasn't the worst of it, not for him or your PR war—he was another skinning victim."

Max let out a long breath. "Skinned—how many does that make?"

"Three. One we found two nights ago . . . it was all over the news, you saw that, right? . . . Now this one tonight, and there was another a few months ago."

"All cops?" Max asked.

Clemente shook his head. "The first guy's prints came up on the computer that he was a shoe salesman, but there was something hinky about that one."

"Hinky how?"

Another head shake. "I've already told you way too much, Max. Now I'm outta here."

She walked along with him. "We'll talk again?"

"I don't know," Clemente said with a shrug. "This cop killing will be a priority, and if we *are* looking for a transgenic, well . . . you might not want to invite me back in."

"Ramon, this changes nothing about what we discussed; in fact, it shows we were on the right track—Ames White and others like him will try to use this to further inflame the public."

"Yeah, and it'll work."

"So find the real killer, why don't you?"

"Even if it's a transgenic?"

"It certainly won't be a transgenic from inside Terminal City."

"Are you saying it would be impossible for one of you to sneak out of here?"

That made her uncomfortable. "We are penned up, but . . . it would be possible, yes. So I tell you what—we'll look into this from this end too. After all, if the killer is a transgenic, we want him caught as much as you do."

The cop stopped to look at her. "You do?"

Max stopped and nodded. "Ramon, if we want to be part of this society, we have to prove to people that we're not monsters. If one of us is doing this, he needs to be stopped."

"Now that would be good PR," Clemente said.

"It's more than just PR—it's the right thing."

She escorted the detective to the gate, where the two transgenic sentries awaited. As he walked through, he turned back to face her.

"No one in, no one out—right?"

"Right."

Clemente started to turn away, but turned back. "And, Max . . ."

"Yeah?"

"We will talk again."

Her smile tight and sober, she said, "Good."

Clemente walked off into the early morning darkness, his two uniformed bodyguards falling in alongside him, heading for the National Guard barricade.

Her back to the gate now, Max asked, "Dix, did you get all that?"

"Oh yeah," came the voice in her earpiece.

"Call Logan, and transmit that tape to him. And, Dix?"

"Yeah?"

"Tell Joshua I need to talk to him right away."

"I'll get on it. Where are you gonna be?"

She started walking. "Coming to you."

Already waiting when she arrived, Joshua looked up when Max entered the media center. Dix, Luke, and several other transgenics manned the monitors, most of them concentrating either on the security screens or watching the TV news coverage. Dix sat up on his raised platform in front of his computer monitor.

"You get Logan?" she asked.

Dix nodded. "Got him online right now. You wanna talk to the boy?"

"Yeah." She climbed the two stairs up to Dix's work station. He slid aside so she could ease in front of the camera mounted on top of his monitor.

"Hey, you," Logan's face on the screen said.

"Hi—need your help."

"When did I ever say no?"

"Did Dix send you the conversation he taped?"

"I've got it."

"Good. When you check it out, you'll hear Clemente refer to a killing a while back. It was mentioned in passing on the news coverage of the cop who was skinned two nights ago."

"Rings a faint bell."

"It'll ring clearer when you listen to that conversation. What I need you to do is find out all you can about that first murder."

"Okay—get right on it. Are we trying to solve a murder? Do we have some sort of serial killer out there, skinning his—or her—victims?"

"All of the above and more. But mostly, know this: White's involved with this somehow. One of White's minions, Otto Gottlieb, called Clemente while he and I were confabbing."

"Does White suspect a transgenic? The TV newscast indicated that, remember. Or is this just antitransgenic media games?"

"I don't know," Max said. "But there's definitely something going on—typical Ames White manipulation and disinformation—and we need to know exactly what that is."

Logan said, "All right, Max. I'll find out what I can."

Relief flowed through her.

Somehow, having Logan working on this made her feel that it would all come out all right in the end. The other problems they'd met together had turned out all right, hadn't they?

Then she thought about where she was and the situation they were in and felt like laughing. Even surrounded by police and the National Guard, not knowing when an all-out genocidal attack might be launched on Terminal City, she felt everything was all right simply because Logan was on her side.

Max allowed that perhaps Original Cindy had been right in saying, "Boo, you are so whipped."

She couldn't help but smile; maybe she was.

"Something funny?" Logan asked.

She shook her head. "Just nice to know you're working with us."

"Nice to be appreciated. . . . I'll let you know when I have anything."

"Thanks," she said, wanting to say, *I love you*, instead saying, "I'll seeya."

"Yeah," he said, pausing, as if fighting his own urge to say something significant, but saying only, "Seeya."

And the screen went blank.

Max climbed down from Dix's perch and put a hand on Joshua's shoulder. "Can we go talk?"

"Sure, Little Fella."

They went for a walk, ending up again in the tunnel below the far end of Terminal City. Though it gave them privacy, the claustrophobic space also reminded Max of the basement at Manticore; and she found herself feeling uneasy about being down here, especially when she considered what she wanted to talk to Joshua about.

Finally, she just dove in. "You remember us talking about the others—the ones like Isaac."

"Yes, Max."

"I want to talk about them again."

"Okay." His canine brow wrinkled. "Something wrong?"

They took a few steps, the tunnel dark, their footfalls echoing very softly off the walls. Neither of them really needed the lights to see, and without Logan along, they didn't bother to turn them on.

"There . . . may be."

Joshua said nothing.

"You see . . . another policeman died tonight."

"And now Max thinks it was one of us too."

Max shook her head quickly. "No—it's just that Detective Clemente thinks there might be evidence that it was a trans-genic."

"Not good. Not good."

"Joshua, that doesn't mean it was someone from the Manticore basement, or even that the evidence is real . . . considering the source."

"Source?"

"Ames White."

A low growl escaped from Joshua and his eyes burned with hatred.

Though, like Max, Joshua sought only a peaceful life and a chance to fit in, a part of him longed to tear White into tiny pieces and watch him die very slowly. White had murdered his friend Annie—sweet Annie Fisher, a blind girl who had never hurt anyone.

Gentle giant or not, Joshua still wanted to exact a full mea-sure of revenge for this heinous crime. Max had kept Joshua from killing White that night at Jam Pony; but they both knew that if he ever caught up with White again, she would be wast-ing her breath, trying to stop the beastlike man that was Joshua from killing the manlike beast that was Ames White.

Max eased down the wall and took a seat on the tile floor. Though she was someone who needed to sleep only every few days, she felt like she could just curl up on the cool tiles. Joshua slid down and sat facing her, his back propped against the opposite wall.

"Because it's White," she said, "I've got to find out what really happened . . . and the more I know about our brothers and sisters on the outside, the easier it will be to deal with whatever 'evidence' White supplies."

Joshua considered this for a few moments, then said, "Father made many of us, but the others—the ones after Father—they didn't care about us. They hated us, the ones in the basement."

Nodding, Max asked, "What can you tell me about them, individually?"

The question seemed to perplex Joshua.

Taking a deep breath, Max asked, "You remember how you taught me about Isaac?"

"Isaac was easy to tell Max about—he was my brother, he was gentle. But they changed him."

"The others down there, you told me some of their names before . . ."

"Dill."

"Yes!"

Joshua looked surprised and a little scared.

"Sorry," she said, "I don't mean to startle you—it's just that that was one of the names you mentioned before. I want to know about them. Start with Dill."

Leaning back and closing his eyes, Joshua seemed to drift off for a moment. "He came after Isaac and me. Him and his brother, Oshi. After Father tried dogs, he moved to cats next."

"Dill and Oshi have feline DNA?"

"Uh-huh."

Of all the things in her genetic cocktail, the feline DNA had provided some of her most inconvenient if not biggest problems. She still battled going into heat twice a year—just one example of the kind of humiliating shit being a genetic test-tube baby could bring a girl.

"Any idea what kind of cats?" she asked him.

"Not sure for Dill. Oshi—a Siamese, I think. They hated being kept in cages, but because of the way they could run and jump, they were kept in the smallest cells. That was mean."

"Very mean, Joshua. And when they got out?"

Joshua shrugged. "Don't know."

"Didn't you mention a Gabriel?"

The snoutlike mouth smiled. "Joshua likes Gabriel. He comes from an ant."

"An ant?" Max asked, stretching her legs out in front of her. "No kidding—insect DNA?"

"Oh yes. Gabriel looks like Max."

That surprised her. "Like me?"

Joshua hesitated for a long moment. "Normal. Not like Normal at Jam Pony—normal like ordinaries. But Gabriel can lift six times his own body weight."

"Anything else out of the ordinary?"

"No. . . . Well, he has an extra pair of arms."

"He has an extra pair of arms, but he looks normal."

Nodding vigorously, Joshua said, "They come out of his ribs, so Gabriel just wraps them around himself. Gabriel looks chubby . . . but normal."

She studied her shaggy friend. "You know where Gabriel is, don't you?"

Joshua looked at the floor. "Not anymore. Not since I moved to Terminal City."

"He's in Seattle, though?"

"Gabriel was in Seattle."

"And you two were friends?"

Joshua continued to look at the floor. "Yes."

"You never mentioned him," Max said. Her voice was matter-of-fact, not hurt, though oddly, she did feel that way, a little. She thought Joshua was her closest friend, among the transgenics; and yet he had kept things from her, clearly.

"Gabriel was passing for human. I only saw him when he came to visit me in Father's house."

"So . . . he could still be out there."

"Yes. Still. Out there."

". . . Did they hurt him at Manticore?"

Finally looking up at her, he said, "They hurt us all, Max—you too."

She could hardly argue with that.

"The guards, they were scared of Gabriel because of his strength. They hit him with the prods whenever they went near his cell."

Max had tasted the electric prods of the guards herself, and knew firsthand how much it hurt.

"Guards try to keep Gabriel weak by always hitting him with them."

In the darkness, she shook her head. "I'm sorry, Joshua. I'm sorry to . . . dredge this all up."

"Nothing to be sorry for," he said. "*They* did it, we didn't."

She knew that, but like all victims, she suffered strange pangs of guilt.

They had all suffered immeasurably, and it wasn't a surprise that one of them might have gone rogue. To Max, the surprise was that the rest of them hadn't.

After a while she said, "I think you mentioned another one."

Joshua thought hard. "Oh! Almost forgot . . . Kelpy. 'Chameleon Boy,' the guards called him."

Max needed no explanation about Kelpy's DNA mix.

"Kelpy didn't work right," Joshua said.

"What do you mean, didn't work right?"

Joshua shrugged. "I just remember, guards and others, talking about what a waste of time Kelpy turned out to be."

"Was Kelpy beaten too?"

He shook his big head. "No, they said his power only worked when he was angry or scared or something . . ."

"Agitated," Max supplied.

"That's the word," Joshua said. "Agitated. When he was

agitated. So they didn't agitate him. They ignored Kelpy. Left him to die."

"No one to love him or help him," Max said.

"No one. Sometimes, Kelpy would just disappear into his cage."

Max knew that on some level all the transgenics felt that way. No one was going to help them, no one was going to love them. She'd learned different when she'd met Logan. Joshua had learned different when he'd met her.

"Was Kelpy still there when we came in?"

With a quick nod, Joshua said, "Yes—you even opened his cell yourself."

She shook her head. "I have no memory of him."

"I bet Kelpy has memory of Max. Later, Kelpy asked me your name and I told him, 'Max.' He said you were the only one who ever cared."

Someone she had never noticed. . . .

They got up and started walking back up the tunnel. She tried and tried, but she just couldn't seem to remember Kelpy.

As they climbed the stairs back up to the first floor of Medtronics, her cell phone rang. "Go for Max," she said.

"They're listening," a computer-altered voice said.

"Who's listening?"

"The ones outside the gate," the metallic voice said.

"Thanks, I already knew that," Max said.

The voice said, "The last time we spoke we were interrupted."

Clemente.

"Yes," she said. "We were."

Why was he calling now, and why all the secretiveness?

"Our mutual acquaintance supplied what looks like irrefutable information."

White had given him evidence that a transgenic was the killer.

"You do understand?" the altered voice asked.

"Yes. But that information . . ."

"Initially, damned near absolute. I've seen it. We'll talk later. Like I said we would."

The phone went dead in her ear.

"What is it?" Joshua asked.

"I think it was very bad news," Max said.

She thought about what Clemente had said last. *Initially, damned near absolute.* What the hell did that mean? Was that strange phrasing some kind of code? *Initially . . .*

But it wouldn't come.

Max looked at Joshua. "We better get back."

They stepped outside into the purplish light of breaking morning. The sun had barely dented the horizon, and she could already tell this was going to be another long day. They walked up the street in silence, Joshua lost in his thoughts, Max trying to figure out what Clemente had been talking about. . . .

Initially, damned near absolute.

Finally, as if coming toward her out of a heavy fog, she put together the detective's little code. Initially Damned Near Absolute. D-N-A. White had provided DNA evidence that the killer was a transgenic.

Now the next question was, why was Clemente telling her this?

There seemed to be only one reason for him to trust her at all: he didn't trust White any more than she did.

So maybe they did have an ally on the other side. She felt she had connected with Clemente, and that he had believed her, even including the absurd—but true—snake cult story.

Even so, that good news was heavily outweighed by the bad. Either White was manipulating evidence to make it look like a transgenic was killing cops or, even worse, there really was a dangerous transgenic loose in the city.

A serial-killer transgenic, at that.

Chapter Six
LAND OF THE FREE

Sitting in Dix's room to one side of his work station, finally getting some time to herself, Max sorted through mental files filled with the things she and Joshua had talked about. Even though it had been just this morning, that conversation in the tunnel seemed so long ago—perhaps because these facts, new to her, summoned old memories . . . of Manticore.

Even as Max had dealt with the daily task of just trying to hold the fragile truce together, what Joshua had shared with her weighed heavily. She sifted through everything again and again, over and over . . . and the conclusion never seemed to change.

These grotesque, terrible killings were—partially, at least—her fault.

After all, wasn't she the one who had turned the transgenics loose in the world in the first place?

She would have preferred not to feel responsible for the killings, to be able to rationalize them away; but the guilt, the responsibility, was hers. It had been her decision not to leave anyone behind at Manticore. Now, while hundreds, maybe thousands, of transgenics lived free and happy, a few failed living experiments were loose who would have been better off in captivity—better off for themselves, better off for the populace.

Max wanted to think White was behind these killings, and she knew him to be heartless enough to do such deeds, or have them done in the pursuit of the conclave's twisted agenda; but something deep in her gut told her that the evidence he'd presented to Clemente just might be real. . . .

A quick knock was followed by handsome, hazel-eyed Alec—in a blue T-shirt, Levi's and running shoes—filling the frame of the doorway. "You might want to take a look at what's going on outside," he said, jerking a thumb toward the hallway.

So much for some time to herself.

"What now?" she asked, not bothering to hide her weariness.

"Hey, I'm sorry to bother you—I know you're carrying the weight. . . . But you better come look."

With a deep sigh, Max rose and moved out to the media center. "Something good on?"

Luke, Mole, Dix, and the various monitor monitors all seemed tense.

"Not my favorite show," Dix said, and pointed at one of the security camera screens. "Some drunks on the west side are lobbing Molotov cocktails over the fence."

Max knew the nearest building was a good thirty yards in from the fence on that side, but as she moved to the monitor, she saw that the drunks were getting closer with each shot. And the building was a wooden structure, a two-story glorified shed that would not resist flames well at all.

Pointing at another monitor, Luke said, "And it looks like a TV crew's trying to get in, around the corner from the drunks."

Smirking, Alec said, "Is that the gentle whiff of a conspiracy I detect?"

"Where's the damn National Guard?" Mole asked, half a cigar bobbing in one corner of his reptile mouth. "They got the whole goddamn place locked down . . . and a buncha street-rabble drunks make their way through?"

Looking at Alec, Max said, "You take care of the incendiary substance abusers, and I'll take care of the media."

"Publicity hound."

"Why not? I'm almost as pretty as you are."

"Ouch," Alec said, joining her as she headed outside.

Soon they were behind the building that was serving as a target for the drunks and their firebombs.

"Stop them," Max said firmly, "but don't mess them up."

"Would I do that? Gentle soul like me."

"I'm serious, Alec. There's enough of the public against us already."

He shook his head as if he could hardly believe he was hearing this. "That's not John Q. Public out there, Max— that's some lowlife drunks who were probably paid to cause a distraction for that media crew."

"We don't know that. The news crew might just be taking advantage of—"

"Even so, do you *really* think I'm going to convert a bunch of drunks by talking to them?"

"Just don't mess them up, okay? That media crew would love to see you going transgenic on a bunch of ordinary asses."

"Fine!" Disgustedly, he took off into the shadows between two buildings.

Max waited two beats, then took off herself, in the other direction, to cut off the television team.

From twenty feet away, she watched the television crew fumbling on the other side of the fence. A short pudgy guy in a T-shirt and jeans hefted the camera while the obvious "talent," a too-tanned himbo in an off-the-rack suit, tried to look like a network anchor. In the meantime, a skinny guy in a windbreaker with the station's call letters and channel number emblazoned on the back tried to keep the wires from tangling.

Max eased forward, stopping at the corner of the building, staying in the shadows as she peeked around to see if Alec was talking to the drunks yet. As she watched, Alec sauntered out from between the buildings and approached the four inebriated men throwing firebombs. There still didn't seem to be any sign of the National Guard or the cops moving in from their barricade position.

"Gonna have to ask you fellas to stop doing that," Alec said to their guests.

The biggest of the drunks—a scruffy-bearded guy in frayed jeans and a MUTANTS GO HOME T-shirt, which included a bad, monster-movie-type image of dog-boy Joshua—stepped forward and yelled through the mesh: "Get stuffed, freak!"

The potbellied guy then heaved another bottle with a burning rag stuffed in its neck, this one in Alec's general direction. But the guy was so drunk though that Alec never moved and the thing still missed him by ten feet, shattering to spread a pool of fire that threw orange shadows on the blandly handsome planes of Alec's face, revealing a hood-eyed sinister quality that few ever had noticed.

"Look, guys," he said, his voice reasonable but with an edge, "you're half in the bag. Stop playing with fire before you get burned."

One of the drunks lit bottles for the other three and they all heaved them at once. Two landed on either side of Alec while the third sailed far over his head. Max watched as it crashed into the building and a splash of fire erupted on the wall.

This was going to get ugly. . . .

Alec turned his face toward where Max was hidden in the shadows—she guessed she shouldn't have been surprised that his transgenic-attuned senses would have betrayed her position—and he said softly, "Hey—I tried."

Then Alec jumped the eight-foot fence in a Superman single bound, landed in the midst of the four drunks and dispatched them with a blur of martial arts moves—assorted chops and kicks—before any of them even realized he was on their side of the fence. As the last one fell, Alec hopped back up the fence, pausing at the top to smile down at his arrayed victims, sprawled in bloody unconsciousness; then the X5 alighted to the transgenics' side.

Watching from the shadows, Max shook her head—so much for not messing them up; but in Alec's defense, he hadn't killed or even maimed them—a few missing teeth and a broken bone or two was about it.

On the other hand, the drunks had managed to spread their hatred in a literal manner, prior to Alec spanking them: the fire, courtesy of the one Molotov cocktail that had reached its target, made its way quickly up the wall, and soon the entire building was endangered.

Transgenics showed up, seemingly from nowhere, to fight the blaze with extinguishers and an old-fashioned bucket brigade—losing precious water—and in less than five minutes, the fire was under control at least, which was good news.

Only, news of another kind had also been made: Max had looked helplessly on as the TV crew captured Alec's attack on the drunks; but the camera also caught the fire, and the teamwork of the transgenics.

As the TV crew was recording the firefighting efforts of her brothers and sisters, Max had a moment of elation at the notion of the media showing something positive about the transgenics; then she noticed how the flames and smoke-streaked air played on those animal-tinged faces: her brothers and sisters, so many of them already condemned by appearances considered freakish by mainstream America, looked distorted, even more monstrous in the eerie lighting provided by the fire.

Max made her decision—she ran toward the fence, alighted atop it, then hopped over and landed in front of the cameraman, who nearly toppled backward when she filled his eyepiece. Stepping forward, she steadied him and in one swift motion ejected the tape and removed it from the camera.

"Hey!" the cameraman yelled.

"It's *her*!" somebody said.

Max gave the cameraman a stony stare, and he backed up a few steps.

The reporter with the smoothed-back hair, power tie, and too much cologne stepped forward. "*This* is why people hate you transgenics."

She spun toward him. "Why?"

"You can't interfere with freedom of the press."

"Actually," she said, "*this* is why people hate us transgenics."

And she grabbed him by the front of his cheap suit and, like she was plucking a flower, hauled him five feet off the ground. He looked down at her with terrified eyes in that tanned face, and was whimpering when she set him down again.

"You . . . you may not look like some of them," he said, trembling, "but you're a monster, too. . . ."

"We're monsters because you *make* us monsters." Wheeling around, talking to all of them, she said, "It's not freedom of the press when you set up a bunch of drunk dipshits to try to firebomb us."

"How dare you!" the would-be anchorman blurted. "Are you accusing me of manufacturing a story? I never—"

"Save it for the morning news," Max said. "You'll need the blather, 'cause you won't have the footage—I'm taking your tape. And you're lucky that's all I'm taking."

"You can't—"

"I already did." She turned and saw that the pudgy cameraman had plopped in a fresh tape and gone back to work, grabbing the tail end of this confrontation. "What's your name, bud?"

"Bud," the cameraman said, astonished by her apparent psychic abilities.

"Bud, tell me the truth. Did Wannabe Anchorman here bribe those drunks?"

The cameraman stood stock-still, the lens settled on Max's face. Finally, he asked, "Do I keep my tape?"

Through his teeth, the anchorman said, "Bud, I will fucking fire your ass."

"Thanks, Ben," the cameraman said, "for saying that on camera. The union will love you for it."

Max smiled. "I think you've answered my question, Bud—glad to see there's some integrity left, in certain corners of the modern media. Thanks."

She gave them a little one-fingered salute, and jumped back over the fence—like Alec, in one bound—and alighted in her catlike manner. Then she walked slowly toward where the wooden-frame building still burned. In the cool of the predawn morning, the heat of the flames on her face almost felt good, like a blush of pride. She knew Bud was still filming her, but she didn't give a damn.

Stepping forward, she tossed the tape into the flames.

Other camera crews emerged from the darkness to catch the dying fire on tape too, and she was sure that the anchorman would be spreading lies to his colleagues; but there was nothing she could do about that. Sooner or later she would talk to Clemente and try to explain it to him.

She hoped the detective would not consider her brief excursion over the fence—to defend Terminal City from flames and lies—as a violation of their agreement that she and the other transgenics remain within the boundaries of the toxic nightmare they called home.

Finally, trailing even the newspaper photographers, the police and the Guardsmen came rolling up. They talked to the anchorman with the attitude, and they interviewed Bud as well, and some of them helped up the drunks, who seemed to be coming around, one or two spitting a tooth like a watermelon seed. Glancing over at Alec, Max saw him working at suppressing a smile.

Watching the building burn, Max found memories swirling to the surface of her mind, dark remembrances of that terrible, wonderful night last year when Manticore had burned.

She wanted to think she'd done the right thing that night, freeing her brothers and sisters, even the failed experiments in the basement; but all this trouble—the deaths, from CeCe to the skinning victims—and with so many lost souls to worry about now, she could only wonder if she had done right.

The X5 also wondered if she would ever really know if she had done the world good or ill, or if she would always be haunted by the mantle of leadership and responsibility she had taken on herself.

Max was not alone among the transgenics who were haunted by memories of Manticore. Elsewhere—sleepless in Seattle—Bobby Kawasaki lay in his bed, remembering Max and how they had met and how she had liberated him. . . .

Kelpy had heard the commotion before it got anywhere near him.

The disturbance had started upstairs, and even through the floors and walls he could hear the yelling, the stamping of feet, and—scariest of all—the gunfire. His anxiety level rose, but inside his Plexiglas box, in the middle of the cell, there was nothing to blend in with. . . .

And so he'd stood there, petrified, rocking from one foot to the other. Lately, the doctors kept him in a straitjacket as well, over his clothes, which prevented him from stripping off those garments and trying to blend in on those few occasions they actually let him out of the box.

Joshua—the only one of them down here with anything resembling freedom at all—appeared in the small window in the door.

"It's going to be okay, Kelpy," the dog man's soft, reassuring voice had soothed. "Max is coming. . . . Then we blaze."

Before Kelpy could respond or ask who this "Max" was, Joshua was gone on to the next door.

Upstairs, the firefight seemed to grow in intensity, and Kelpy—just as he had countless times before—examined the lock mechanism of his Plexiglas prison in hopes of finding a way out. And just like those countless times he'd previously looked at it, he saw a device as cruelly indecipherable to him as the mystery of life.

Kelpy knew he couldn't have overcome that lock, even if his arms hadn't been pinned to his sides by the straitjacket.

When he heard the tumult break through the door at the end of the hall, Kelpy gave up and simply sat down, waiting to die, and not really minding the opportunity. Almost within seconds of the basement door bursting open, he could smell smoke. Realizing the building was on fire, Kelpy now actively hoped that one of the guards would step in and shoot him. The quick mercy of that seemed preferable to burning to death, or for that matter, surviving at all.

The sounds of the others screaming—whether from pain or fear, he couldn't tell—invaded the privacy of his skull. When it came to blending in with people, one of the secrets to success was empathy—and Kelpy had it; now he just wished he could turn it off.

The wails from the other cells felt like an army of demons inside his body trying to rip his soul to shreds. He curled into a fetal ball, trying to make himself as small as possible, and covered his ears with his body as best he could . . . but the screams still pierced, and the pain became unbearable.

Kelpy was about to start beating his skull on the plastic floor of his cage when the heavy metal door to his cell swung slowly open.

Sitting up, Kelpy searched for the sight of a guard or Joshua or someone . . . but no one came, and the screams suddenly shifted in volume. The door was only open a few inches, less than a foot—a smidgen provided by the release of the magnetic lock—but through that slit, Kelpy could make out motion.

He hoped someone was coming for him, either to kill him or release him. He really didn't care which, and was afraid to admit to himself which was his real preference.

No one stopped, though, the motion through the slit almost continuous now, and finally Kelpy realized that the others were free. They were running down the hall to freedom while he was still locked in the Plexiglas cage within his cell.

Suddenly it struck him that he really didn't want to die.

Struggling to his feet, Kelpy yelled; but he had a small voice, one that didn't stand out or draw attention, one that most certainly couldn't be heard above the cacophony in the hall. He shouted over and over, but he knew they didn't hear, couldn't hear. They were all running for their lives and didn't have time for him.

Tears ran hot down his cheeks and Kelpy resigned himself to burning to death, alone, his oven . . . and then his tomb . . . to be a plastic one, and eventually his remains would blend in with the mound of melted goo.

Then *she* came through the door!

Kelpy was so overcome, he simply stood still as she swept in.

How beautiful she was! Long black hair, luminous dark eyes, bee-stung red lips, and skin the color of the sugary caramels he was given at Christmas, all wrapped up in the black package of her attire.

"Don't worry," she said. "Everybody's getting out."

He watched silently as she ripped a leg off the steel bunk against the wall.

Stepping up to the cage, she said, "Stand back."

Kelpy backed up against the rear wall.

Raising the busted-off bunk leg, she crashed it down on

the lock, and the plastic around the metal mechanism seemed to vaporize.

The door opened, she reached in and helped him out onto the floor of the cell. She spun him and—from behind—he heard a rip as she tore the straitjacket to shreds, as if he too were a present and she was unwrapping him.

For the first time in days, Kelpy's arms swung free.

"Down the hall to the right," she said, her voice calm. "Follow the crowd, stay close to someone, and we'll all get out of here."

He nodded, struck dumb by her dazzling beauty, her commanding presence.

"Can you talk?"

He managed to say, "Yes."

"Good—you can help. Keep people moving, follow the crowd. Got it?"

He nodded again.

She smiled at him, and, for the first time in his very strange life, Kelpy was in love.

Before he could say anything else to her, she turned and sprinted out the door, off to help anyone who needed it.

Stripping off the remnants of the straitjacket, Kelpy in his prison gray immediately blended in with the gray walls of the cell. He knew that if anyone came in now—though he wouldn't be invisible exactly—he would be nearly impossible to see. He could feel his heart pounding in his chest . . . whether this physiological response derived from fear or the appearance of the black-haired goddess, he didn't know, and he didn't care. Either way, his adrenaline level was high enough that he blended in easily. He stripped out of his gray prisoner's uniform. . . .

Stepping out into the hall, the naked Kelpy kept to the sides, out of the way, and moved slowly among fleeing transgenics. While the rest ran pell-mell for their lives, Kelpy calmly searched for the dark-haired woman.

Of course, like the others, he did continue to move toward the exit; but he glanced into every cell, knowing she would be rescuing others, knowing too that—just as no one noticed him—his goddess would stick out in any crowd . . . let alone this one, where she was the only one who didn't resemble some sort of animal and the only one not dressed in gray.

Four cells from his, he found her, helping someone else; and he fell in behind her. She never knew he was right there, but he was close enough to smell her sweat and he knew no perfume would ever match her own scent. As she continued toward the exit, shooing some, cajoling others, checking cells for stragglers, Kelpy stayed as near to her as he could.

Finally—with nearly everyone out and the fire encroaching rapidly—Joshua shouted, "Max, come on! We've got to go!"

Max—so the goddess had a name, and her name was Max.

She took off running, practically dragging two transgenics as she went. He stayed right on her, her unseen shadow, protecting her without her even knowing he was there. She got the other transgenics outside, then headed back inside, Kelpy on her tail, hugging the wall. She sprinted down the hall and entered the control room . . . with Kelpy trailing.

The guard standing immediately inside the door caught a foot in the face from Max and went down in a heap. Amazed by her prowess, Kelpy watched from a corner as Max came up silently behind the seated blonde woman in a lab coat; the woman seemed to be in charge.

"Where's 452?" the woman, positioned before banks of monitors, demanded into a mike. "I'm not leaving without her!"

Grabbing the woman from behind, by the hair, Max said, "Good—'cause I'm not leaving without you, Sunshine."

Hammerlocking the woman, Max led her down the hall. All around them the fire greedily consumed the Manticore facility; but Max didn't seem to care—she apparently had something else on her mind.

Following the two women, Kelpy looked on, his curiosity
growing as he watched Max ignoring the danger of the burning building and leading the other woman down the hall,
then through some doors into some kind of lab.

"Where's the antigen?" Max demanded.

"I don't know," the blonde shrieked. "We've got to get out
of here *now*, 452!"

Standing off to one side, Kelpy looked at the walls full of
vials and small bottles of various colored liquids. Remaining
against the one solid wall in the room, he blended in and remained virtually invisible.

Swinging the blonde by the arm, Max slung her into the
steel door. The woman landed with a metallic thump, then
Max spun her around and slammed her into the door once
more. "My name is *Max!* Now . . . where is it?"

Max dragged the blonde around the room, bumping into
this and that, until finally the woman began screaming,
"Okay, okay, okay!"

The pair of females came to a stop, and the blonde jerked
a small bottle of amber liquid off a glass shelf.

Max wrenched it from her hand.

A guard in black beret and fatigues burst into the room
and raised his M-16 in the goddess' direction.

Kelpy took one step, but was too late.

The guard fired, but—amazingly!—the blonde swept Max
out of the way and two slugs ripped into the woman as she
went down.

Max came up fast, kicked a cart full of bottles, which
struck the guard, knocking the gun out of his hands. As the
cart caught the guard, Kelpy blended back into the wall, but
was ready to strike, should the guard make another move.

Hanging onto the cart, the guard looked stricken at having
shot his boss.

"I won't tell if you don't," Max said to him, and the aghast
guard beat a hasty retreat out the door.

Kelpy watched as Max leaned down over the bleeding blonde woman—was she dying?

"This virus thing you put in me," Max said, "how do I get rid of it?"

The woman managed, "You can't," and coughed blood.

"You just ate bullets for me—mind telling me why?"

Reaching up and stroking Max's face, the blonde said, "You're the one . . . the one we've been looking for."

Max gazed at the woman, astounded, uncomprehending.

"Sandeman," the woman said, her voice barely above a whisper now, Kelpy straining to hear her. "Find Sandeman."

The woman's hand fell away and she died.

Max wasted no time—how bold she was! How forceful!

Rising, she ran from the burning building, over fences, up the hill, with Kelpy behind her, out of sight. At the top of the hill she paused, grinning with obvious self-satisfaction as she watched the conflagration that was the Manticore facility.

Then she ran off into the woods.

Kelpy kept her in sight as he followed her through the brush and trees. When she piled into a van with some of the other transgenics, he had grabbed the bumper and jumped on the back.

He rode like that all the way back to Seattle.

Once in the city, Kelpy kept following Max, until he figured out that she worked at the bike messenger service, Jam Pony. Taking a cue from her, Kelpy knew he would need a new name. He heard a passing woman call her child Bobby and that gave him a first name. Looking around, he read the first word he saw. It was painted on the gas tank of a motorcycle: KAWASAKI. And now he had a last name.

Knowing it would take something extraordinary for him to find the nerve even to talk to her—let alone try to tell her of his love for her—the newly christened Bobby Kawasaki did the only thing he could, to stay close to his true love: he got a job at Jam Pony, as a bike messenger.

Though many months had passed, Max had still not recognized Kelpy—or rather, Bobby—even though she'd
looked right at him the night she'd helped him escape. Nor
had he forged a new relationship with her, as Bobby, not a
friendship, not even an acquaintance.

The closest Bobby had come was about six months ago
when Max had run into him, literally, coming out of the
bathroom. They bumped and she grabbed his arm to keep
him from falling down.

She looked him dead in the eye and said, "Watch it, bro."

He said nothing.

Max started to walk away, then paused and turned back.
"Do I know you from somewhere?"

"That's right, you do," Normal interrupted, handing Max
a package. "His name's Bobby, he's worked here for six
months, and you're both part of the great big wonderful Jam
Pony family. . . . Now get this package over to Sector Nine,
Missy. Bip bip bip."

"I *thought* I'd seen him before," she said, rather absently,
then turned and followed Normal, giving her boss some
shit—typical of her, what spirit she had!

Bobby was thrilled, but also—disturbed. She'd seen him,
and he got so excited he blended into the lockers and didn't
dare come out until everyone had gone home . . . only by
then Normal had locked him in.

It had been both the best and worst day of his life. She'd
noticed him . . . but, typically, he'd made no impression.

That day was the catalyst, the day Bobby's vision of what
he wanted his life to be had crystallized. He wanted to be
loved by Max and now, more than ever, he wanted to be
human—ordinary, like that Logan Cale person she seemed
so close to. Logan—she liked him; did she love him?

Bobby had already been using Tryptophan at that point,
buying, in fact, from the same Asian woman that Max
bought from. But if he was going to be really human, he'd

have to up the dosage; and in order to make ends meet he'd
have to find a new source.

It had taken a while to find someone affordable, but finally
Bobby found a new dealer at Harbor Lights Hospital. She
was a nurse and she seemed more than willing to give him
all the Tryptophan he wanted—and for next to nothing!

A tall, thin woman, Nurse Betty had short auburn hair that
barely covered her ears, big brown eyes, and thin lips that
were like a razor cut in an otherwise pleasant face.

"Why are you helping me?" he'd asked her.

The dealer smiled at him and said, "You look like you
could use the help . . . and I get the pills for nothing. So I'm
helping you, and I'm making a little money to supplement
my income. Win win situation."

He thanked her, but he didn't understand how she got the
pills for nothing. If she was stealing them—from the hospital
dispensary, maybe—sooner or later she would get caught;
and if she wasn't stealing them, where was she getting them?

In February his question seemed to be answered. She
hadn't shown for a scheduled meeting and his subsequent
phone calls had gone unreturned. Anticipating that she'd get
caught sooner or later, Bobby had another dealer lined up,
through his old street connections; but before he could call
the guy, his own phone rang.

"Hello." Bobby rarely received phone calls from anyone,
so his voice was tentative.

"Bobby?"

A male voice.

"Yeah, who's this?"

"I'm a friend of a friend."

Bobby had no friends, so he asked, "Are you sure you have
the right Bobby?"

"I'm talking about Nurse Betty."

Instantly suspicious, Bobby considered hanging up—the

guy kind of sounded like a cop—but decided to see what this
was about. "That so?"

"I know about your problem."

"Betty said I had a problem?"

"Yeah . . . and that if anything happened to her, you'd need
a new supplier."

"I've gotta go now."

"Wait," the voice on the other end said. "You don't want
to do that. I'm taking over Betty's customers. And I can
make you the same good deal she did."

"We didn't have a deal," Bobby said, his voice rising in
fright. "I'm hanging up."

"I'll give you the first hundred for free."

". . . Free?"

"Call it a good faith offer."

That easily, Bobby had a new Tryptophan supplier. After
the first couple of transactions, he never saw or even talked
to the guy again. They had a prearranged drop site. Bobby
went there, collected his pills, left payment in an envelope,
and went about his business.

Having already gotten his goals clear, he now needed a
plan. The first shopping trip had been an accident. Bobby
had been on his way home from a bar. Too many drinks
mixed with the Tryptophan had him feeling no pain and had
dulled his senses enough that he could barely walk a straight
line.

Two blocks from the bar, a guy fell in behind Bobby
and—when Bobby turned down a particularly dark street—
the would-be assailant made his move, up fast from behind,
arm outstretched, knife waving frantically in a shaking hand.

Even completely stoned, Bobby had heard the guy coming. Too wasted to blend, however, he simply turned when
the attacker got close, broke the man's hand, twisted away
the knife, knocked the guy to the pavement, and then
rammed the blade into the man's carotid artery.

Wrecked as he was, Bobby still managed to see his plan coming together. It seemed so clear he wondered why he hadn't seen it before. Although the mugger was smaller than him, he still liked the idea and did his best with his new project.

The mugger had even supplied a knife.

Looking back, that first shopping excursion had been a complete botch. By the time he was done, the material had been so tattered that it was worthless. He'd left the body in an old warehouse near his place. It was like the guy simply disappeared. No news reports of a missing man on either the TV or the radio. No one seemed to be looking for him and no one seemed to care if the guy ever turned up.

That had really got Bobby to thinking.

The first thing he did was stop drinking. For this plan to work, he needed to focus, to be strong. From now on the targets would have to be men who were larger than him—he'd learned that much from the first job.

A medium-sized guy couldn't wear a small-size T-shirt, right? Same principle. And he would have to work quickly, which with his transgenic abilities would be no problem.

When he started thinking of how to find bigger men, Bobby remembered that the Manticore guards were all bigger than him—that's why they'd had such an easy time of it picking on him.

Now, though—getting off the heavy dosage of Tryptophan on the weekend and letting Kelpy come out to shop—Bobby started thinking that he should be hunting men in uniform.

After everything the men like that had done to him at Manticore, they owed him . . .

. . . and, he knew just how to collect.

Chapter Seven
PASSING IN SCHOOL

Empty of vehicles, the lower floor of the parking ramp—
the building where the siege had begun—swelled with the
ragtag citizens of Terminal City.

Except for the handful on guard duty, the entire outlandish
contingent of transgenics showed up for the town-hall-style
meeting Max had called. Though the sun was rising, the
parking garage remained mostly dark and still rather cold.
May in Seattle—especially this close to the water—was
rarely warm. Though the morning chill had no particular effect on the transgenics, on the other side of the fence the
cops were certainly huddled in their cars sipping coffee and
slugging doughnuts.

With Joshua, Alec, Mole, Dix, and Luke in her wake, Max
swept into the middle of the crowd, and the din of conversation died away. Dressed in her customary black, Max stood
out from the disheveled if distinctive mess that was the
throng. Most had shown up here with little more than
shabby, scavenged clothes on their backs, and living in the
hovels of Terminal City did little to improve their appearance.

They may have resembled a Halloween ball for the homeless, but their Manticore-bred military discipline still held

and, to Max, they looked wonderful. The community was coming together, the rivalries and prejudices of the varying transgenics types—from ND X-Series, "beautiful" people like Max and Alec, to the ND Transhumans like Dix (a Nomlie), Mole (a second-generation model DAC), and Luke (a Mule)—forgotten, or at least put aside for the greater good. The unique populace of Terminal City did not want to spend their lives in a toxic ghost town any more than they wanted to spend them running; but this biohazard village was starting to look like a suitable alternative, at least for the short run.

Jumping onto a box so she could be seen as well as heard, Max called out, "I'm proud of all of you—we've taken a stand. We've shown we can live and work together, and that provides hope for the future—if we can get along with each other, winning over the ordinaries oughta be no big trick."

Her good-natured sarcasm went over well, grins flashing all around in every unusual face.

"But it's time for a reality check—time to stop patting ourselves on the back, and start dealing with the hand we been dealt, here."

The crowd stayed riveted on her every word.

"First, although we still have running water, it probably won't be long before they cut it off. We can smuggle in bottled water, but that's not going to serve the needs of a community this size. Ideas?"

Lightbulb-domed Luke stepped out of the crowd. "When we moved in here, we built our own generator. We're close enough to Lake Washington that we can build our own water system too."

With a quick nod, Max said, "Good—how close are you to completion?"

Luke frowned. "Well . . . we started on design when we moved in, but—" He shrugged. "—execution could take weeks."

Gazing out into the crowd, Max asked, "Any of you X2s and X3s got any engineering and construction skills we can tap into?"

A dozen or so hands were raised.

"Can you guys get with Luke and pitch in with the water problem?"

Some nodded, and started shuffling through the crowd toward Luke, to fall in alongside him.

Somewhere in the middle a voice shouted, "What about the cops? What about the soldiers?"

Voices erupted throughout the assembly, echoing off the cement walls of the parking ramp:

"We should attack!"

"We should go to ground!"

"Wait for them to come in—and slaughter their asses!"

The cries came fast and loud, and Max let them get it out of their systems for a while; then, finally, she raised her hands for silence.

"If we fight with these armies of the ordinaries," she said, "we will never win them over."

Someone cried, "Who cares?" Then followed shouts of "Fight!" and "Kill 'em!" For several frightening moments it looked as though the tightly packed throng of transgenics might turn into an angry mob.

Max held up her hands for silence again, and reluctantly the crowd quieted. Now, she had to shout to be heard over the rumblings of the crush of people. "This is *exactly* why they want to sweep us under the rug."

The grumbling subsided slightly.

"They think we are animals—monsters trained to kill. That all we want to do *is* kill. Is that true?"

The garage went tomblike silent now.

"Don't you have dreams? Desires? Am I the only one who wants a normal life?"

Heads started to nod in the crowd, accompanied by a murmuring of assent.

"What happens here . . . what happens now . . . is up to us. If we want to be a part of this society—"

"Why would we want to be part of that?" a voice yelled.

"Because that's the only real option," Max said. "We are soldiers, and we are special people, more special than those we call ordinary . . . but we are as small in number as our hearts are large. We are barely a city—not enough of us to form our own outcast nation."

The truth of that hung over the chamber, an awful cloud portending an inevitable storm.

"Like it or not, we are part of this land . . . a land that pretends, anyway, to be a haven for the tired, the poor, the huddled masses, the wretched refuse. . . . That's from a song they used to sing in America. Admittedly, you don't hear it much anymore; but those are the kind of words—words of freedom—that this country was built on."

Faces frowned in thought as emotion fought reason in these outcasts.

"You don't want to be part of that society out there, because the people are hateful . . . because they're afraid of us, and want to kill us without even knowing us. . . ."

Voices called out, "That's right," and other cries of agreement with this all too obvious notion.

Max continued, her tone doggedly rational. "Well, the only way they're going to get to know us, out there, is if we give them the chance."

Again the crowd quieted.

"And the only way for them to not be afraid of us is to get to understand us. That we are people, with hopes and dreams and families."

Heads again began to nod.

Max wheeled as she spoke, connecting with them all. "The only way to get the ordinaries to stop hating is to educate them in our shared humanity . . . but they think we only want to kill. Is that true? *Are* we bloodthirsty monsters?"

Someone yelled, "No," but the one voice seemed very small in the parking ramp.

Max's face tightened with determination, and she racheted up the volume: "I said . . . *is that true?*"

This time about half the crowd shouted, "No!" and "Hell, no!"

She raised both fists, high. *"Is . . . that . . . true?"*

"No!" they all yelled—many voices, one voice.

Relief flooded through her—Max had won them over again. Now, while she had them, she needed to get them involved in solving their problems. She lowered her arms, and her voice to a firm, resonable level: "We have some issues we need to deal with."

They all watched her attentively.

"In order to keep the police and National Guard from attacking," she said, "I had to promise one of their representatives that none of us would leave Terminal City until this is negotiated."

She saw several of them trading looks, and she knew what they were thinking: had they gone from being a nation to a gaggle of prisoners? But the reality was, many of them—most of them, in fact—had nowhere beyond the metal-mesh borders of Terminal City to go, anyway.

Oh, a few looked like they wanted to bolt now; but if they were truly united, the others would help persuade them.

She made a mental note to smuggle in some cigars to keep Mole happy.

Again she spoke, her voice ringing off the cement rafters. "They're also claiming that one of us on the outside is killing ordinaries."

"So what?" an X3 toward the front blurted.

Max shot him a look that silenced him. "Some of you have seen the news reports of a murderer who is skinning his victims."

Nods and murmuring were the only response.

"That's just the sort of crime the antitransgenic forces would love to lay on Terminal City's doorstep."

"Are you asking," an X5 near the front asked, "to turn in one of our own?"

"If we have a maniac among us, yes—for our own safety. If we are a nation, a city, we need to live by the rule of law—and if we have a murderer in our midst, it is no betrayal of ourselves to see him brought to justice."

The reptilian Mole asked, "Our justice? Or theirs?"

"I don't have an answer to that yet. That's something we will decide as a group—it's day at a time, people. We are learning to walk, here . . . so be careful not to run."

Nods again, even from Mole.

"For now, come to me if any of you know anything about this—particularly if there is one of us on the outside so troubled that these atrocities make a terrible kind of sense."

Again she wheeled around as she spoke to them.

"Remember—the last thing we need right now is for the ordinaries to prove we are the fiends they say we are." She gestured to her little council of advisors—Alec, Joshua, and Mole—and added, "If you can help, if you know anything, please come to us."

No one moved, no one spoke; but she had expected as much—that anyone here who came to her with information would do so only after long, private thought.

"Thank you for your courage," she said, "and your patience—we're doing the best we can and we'll make sure that this turns out the way we all want it to."

The crowd slowly dispersed, conversation echoing off the cement walls . . . but calm conversation; this was no mob, rather the concerned citizens of Terminal City. It made Max feel proud; still, she knew what she had accomplished in the meeting was all too tentative. The compound remained a powder keg.

Max, Joshua, Alec, and the others headed back to the makeshift headquarters of the media center, and were just entering when Max's cell phone rang.

"Go for Max."

"They're still listening," the computer-altered voice warned.

Clemente.

"I thought you might call," she said.

"I thought we had a deal."

"We do."

"I've seen the news tape—you know which one I mean . . ."

The detective was referring to Max and Alec leaping that fence to deal with the drunks and the media.

"Yes, I know the tape you mean."

"And it shows our deal being broken."

"Technically, perhaps—but we were merely defending our borders. There was no choice. You should see that, too."

"And which side of that fence were you on?"

"I told you we had no choice. You know damn well we were merely defending ourselves from arsonists."

"And terrorizing the press? Is that any way to win the PR war?"

". . . I hear you."

"I hope you do. But you're not winning any points for trust, right now."

The phone went dead in her ear.

Max settled in to watch tapes of news coverage of the transgenic siege.

And while she did, Joshua tugged Alec by the sleeve and—when Alec only frowned, in confusion—the dog man latched onto his friend by the wrist and led him into the hallway.

The iron grip of the gentle giant always surprised Alec, who gingerly reclaimed his hand and shook it a little.

"You don't know your own strength, big guy," Alec said.

Sheepishly, Joshua said, "Sorry. It's important."

"What is?"

Joshua began to sway back and forth, agitated. Alec could tell already that this wasn't going anywhere good. . . .

"I think I know something."

"I'm sure you do, buddy."

"I mean . . . something that would help Max."

"Well, that's fine," Alec said, still having no idea what they were talking about, but rather used to Joshua's torturous routes to what he had on his mind. "You should help her if you can."

"Help Max if I can . . . but Joshua can't."

Alec said, "Oh . . . kay. . . ." As usual, he and Joshua not only were not on the same page, they weren't even in the same book. "You can help, but you can't."

Grinning, an eager puppy now, Joshua said, "Yes. You've got it, Alec! I knew you would know what Joshua should do—what should I do?"

"Whoa, boy." Alec blew out air while he ran a hand through his hair; then he shook his head. "Explain it to me first. How *exactly* can you help Max?"

"I . . . know a guy."

That was a start.

"Okay," Alec said. "And?"

"And . . . the guy is passing."

Alec nodded. He understood—a transgenic passing as human. "Lot of those around. And this helps Max how?"

"Guy might know who's killing on the outside."

Alec perked up. "*How* would he know?"

Joshua looked at the floor, then up at Alec. "They knew each other at Manticore."

"They?" Alec asked. My God, this was like pulling teeth—and Joshua had some big teeth. . . .

"The guy," Joshua said, "and Kelpy."

Alec frowned. "Kelpy? Is that a name?"

"It's a name: Kelpy—Chameleon Boy."

Alec felt like he needed a map to follow the conversation. "Chameleon Boy?"

"Kelpy . . . he could be the one."

"The one?"

"The one . . . taking skins. Killing."

Finally, Alec felt like he was in the same conversation as Joshua; and this was indeed important. "Kelpy's on the outside?"

"Yes—Max freed him, like she did me, and so many of us."

"Where on the outside?"

"That Joshua doesn't know. But . . ."

Again, Alec could discern the drift. "You think this guy you know might know where Kelpy is?"

Joshua nodded vigorously.

"Great. Good job, Joshua. Now—let's go tell Max."

Pawlike hands went up, as if in surrender, and Joshua's eyes flared. "Can't!"

Alec, about to head back into the media center, froze. "Can't?"

"He's passing for human. If I tell Max, and she tells that detective . . ."

"You're afraid this guy's cover will be blown."

"Cover blown?"

"People will know he's transgenic. He won't be able to pass, anymore."

"Yes, Alec! Yes—guy's cover blown."

Alec shook his head. Leave it to Joshua to have a moral dilemma about this; anyway, Alec sure as hell wouldn't. "You know Max, Joshua—she won't blow your friend's cover."

Joshua shook his head. "No way. Joshua promised guy."

"All right—then you and I'll slip out, and just . . . talk to your friend."

"Can't!"

Figuring he understood Joshua's hesitance, Alec said,

"We'll find a way out of here without being seen. Then we'll talk to your friend, and we'll find this Kelvin, and talk to him too."

"Kelpy."

"Kelpy, Kelvin, whatever." Alec placed a hand on Joshua's big bony shoulder. "We'll find a way out, buddy—take care of business and be back before anyone notices."

The big mane shook from side to side. "Can't go! Max said so."

"She didn't mean us," he lied. "We're part of the inner circle."

"Inner circle?"

"Yeah—she meant all the others, you know, at the big meeting. She said if anyone had any info, to tell us— remember?"

Joshua thought about that, nodded.

"So when they bring info to us, we're supposed to do something about it, right?"

"Right—like tell Max."

"Yeah, but we can't tell Max. You don't want to blow your friend's cover, remember? So we gotta handle this ourselves."

"Ourselves."

"Right. And if we can solve these murders, we'll be heroes."

Joshua's eyes brightened. "Heroes?"

"Yeah, yeah," Alec said, getting into it now. "We'll be heroes, Max'll be happy, and we'll all get the hell out of Terminal City."

"Max happy?"

"She'll be ecstatic if we can find out who this skinner is. All we have to do is figure a way out of Terminal City."

Joshua shrugged. "Tunnel," he said.

"We don't have time to dig a tunnel, bro," Alec said.

Joshua stepped closer, grabbed Alec by the sleeve. "Already *have* a tunnel—Joshua's in the *inner* inner circle! . . . Come on."

Half an hour later, the handsome X5 and his caninelike friend stood on the street beyond Logan's building. Joshua wore a motorcycle helmet that covered most of his face, and they both had on loose, anonymous jackets. The cops were all looking toward Terminal City, so Alec and Joshua just quietly walked away into the cool overcast Seattle morning.

"Where's your friend live?" Alec asked.

"Far."

Alec nodded. "Of course he does. We wouldn't want this to be too easy, would we?"

Joshua frowned in confusion. "Why not?"

"Just jokin'."

"I see. Alec likes to lighten up even serious situations."

"Yeah. I'm a laugh riot. Well, come on, big guy—we'll work on our little transportation problem."

Alec longed for his motorcycle, but figured that was a lost cause. The cops had probably impounded it as soon as Normal told them who he was; and though Normal seemed far more tolerant toward trangenics now, he would still be cooperating with the cops.

So, they'd have to steal a car. Such contingencies were not a problem for Alec, who was a pragmatic, situational-ethics kind of guy. What with the siege at Terminal City, there were fewer cops on the Seattle streets, but—having watched the news with Max—Alec knew that those fewer cops were also shooting more and chasing less.

They would have to be careful.

Alec considered calling Logan Cale for a ride; but Logan hadn't been in his new Medtronics pad when they'd exited, and Alec didn't have Cale's cell number with him. Anyway, Alec knew that Logan would've talked to Max about them all staying within the fence line, and Logan just might rat them out for being outside—the guy was totally pussy-whipped by Max, after all.

Safer to steal a car, Alec decided.

Three blocks later, Alec saw what he wanted: a gray Catbird parked against the curb, with no one around. Five minutes or so after that, he and Joshua were riding in style—a GM, the Catbird was one of those new ones with four-wheel drive, room for eight, and—if they were lucky—it would have a nice selection of movies. Gray seemed such a nice, nondescript color, plus Alec had switched plates with a sky green Olds.

For the first time since they'd left Terminal City, Alec felt safe and in control.

"Okay, bro—where's your friend live?"

Joshua said, "Queen Anne."

Alec counted the checkpoints between here and there. Getting through them would be tough anytime, and even harder doing it in daylight. "This guy, does he work?"

"Guy has good job."

"Yeah?"

"Janitor," Joshua said with a envious smile.

Alec made a mental note to explain to Joshua the difference between a job and a good job. "Does the guy work during the day?"

"Sure," Joshua said.

"So, then—he won't be at home now, he'll be at work."

"Yeah, right."

Back to pulling teeth again. "Do you know where he works?"

"Works at school."

"Joshua—do you know *which* school?"

The big guy looked lost for a long minute, and in the meantime Alec drove around aimlessly, avoiding checkpoints and adhering to the speed limit.

"Suzuki," Joshua said at last.

Nodding, Alec asked, "Ichiro Suzuki Elementary?"

"Yes! Suzuki Elementary."

Alec allowed himself a smile. Named after the legendary Japanese immigrant baseball player, Ichiro Elementary was one of the few public schools that had stayed open, post-Pulse. The beauty of Joshua's friend being there, instead of at home, was that now the transgenics in the stolen car would pass through only one checkpoint, not five.

Pleased with how this was turning out, Alec sped off toward that checkpoint.

The line waiting to pass through was mercifully short and they sat for only a couple of minutes before the checkpoint cop—an athletic young man with brown hair and a ready smile—waved them forward.

"Good morning," the cop said.

Alec said, "Morning. Jam Pony messengers." He held up his ID, hoping to hell the guy just glanced at it and didn't check it through the computer, where it might be flagged.

The cop's smile disappeared. "Thought you guys rode bikes."

"We do, or anyway we probably will again. But after the hostage thing with those damn transgenics, boss made us team up and take cars. Safety in numbers kinda deal."

"Makes sense. You can't be too careful with those freaks running around."

"Hell no," Alec said firmly.

Leaning down, the cop looked through the window at Joshua sitting in the passenger seat in his red motorcycle helmet. "What's his story?"

With a quick grin, Alec explained, "He's worried about getting hit in the head."

"Yeah, head," Joshua mumbled through the helmet.

"Had a bad run-in with a mugger with a brick, last week." Alec leaned out and his tone turned intimate. "God only knows what another head shot would do to him."

The cop nodded. "Guess you guys do hit some rough neighborhoods."

"Yeah—me, I wear a cup."

"Don't blame ya," the cop said with a chuckle. "Get movin', fellas."

"Yes, sir," said Alec as he pressed the gas pedal and got them slowly, steadily the hell out of there.

The school, long, low, and brick, crouched in the middle of a huge, surprisingly well-tended green lawn. To Alec, sitting in their car parked across the street, the building looked like a museum piece, a postcard from a past he'd seen only in photos and on video.

"So," Alec asked, "you know where he is in there?"

"Never been to school," Joshua said ambiguously, as they both got out of the car.

"No matter," Alec said, "we'll find him. How many places can there be to look? What's his name, anyway?"

"Hampton." His motorcycle helmet still perched on his head, Joshua came around the car to the driver's side. "Maybe Joshua should go alone."

Alec tried to figure out where the big guy was headed with this one. "Why would you think that?"

"Alec might scare Hampton."

Alec managed not to laugh in Joshua's face. "You're kidding, right?"

"Hampton is *passing*, Alec. You show up, an X5 . . . that might scare him. Make him blow his cover."

"What about havin' you make the scene, big guy?"

Joshua's eyes went wide. "Hampton knows me."

"Only you never dropped by school here before, did you?"

"You think having Joshua show up would scare him? Maybe I should leave the helmet on."

"Definitely leave it on. But we're both gonna go—all right?"

Alec took Joshua by the arm—no more inane discussion—

and they crossed the street, strode through the front door, and Alec immediately realized that this job could be a lot tougher than they thought. A corridor ran perpendicular to the door— it seemed to go on endlessly in either direction; looking both ways, he saw entrances to hallways that ran perpendicular to this main one. He guessed that this main hall probably had a twin at the other end of the building.

This was going to take a while.

Directly across the hall from them was a door marked OFFICE.

"Should Alec go one way and Joshua another?" the dog man in the helmet asked.

Alec knew a bad idea when he heard one, and turning Joshua loose on his own devices was definitely one. The real question was which was riskier, separating and maybe finding Hampton sooner, or staying together and risking exposure by being in the building longer.

"We should stay together," Alec said.

"Which way, then?"

The questions never got easier. Sighing, Alec said, "Wait right here—I'm going into the office. Maybe they'll know where Hambone is."

"Hamp-*ton*."

"Whatever. I'll be right back."

Joshua nodded and hugged the wall, trying to make his six-foot-six-inch frame look inconspicuous.

Alec crossed the hall, opened the door and walked into a long narrow room halved by a counter. To his left, as he came in, empty chairs lined the wall and, to his right—just past the end of the counter—a closed door beckoned, the top half pebbled glass with the words VICE PRINCIPAL painted in black letters on it.

To his far left, laid out in the same fashion, he saw that door's twin with the word PRINCIPAL stenciled on it. Beyond the counter, as if guarding the wall of cubbyholes behind

her, a huge woman at a small desk sat in a tablecloth of a flo-
ral dress, her gray hair piled high on her head, the ghost of
some long-ago trend in hairstyles.

"May I help you?" she asked in a high-pitched small voice
that didn't suit her body type in the least.

It was Alec's opinion that these ordinaries could do with a
little DNA tampering themselves.

"Jam Pony messenger. I'm looking for a Mr. Hampton. I
believe he's a janitor here."

The woman nodded, making various chins collide, forced
herself to her feet and trundled toward the counter. "I don't
see a package."

"My partner has it outside."

She looked unimpressed. "Employees are not allowed to
receive personal items here at the school."

"Ma'am, I don't know anything about that. If you could
just tell me where to find him—"

"You'll need to sign in first, then sign back out when you
leave." She glanced toward a clipboard with a pen chained to
it. "And Mr. Koopman will be informed about this."

"No skin off mine," he said, picking up the pen and looking down at the graphed paper. Beside *Name* he wrote
"Reagan Ronald," put down delivery as the purpose of his
visit and "Janitorial" as his destination.

"Janitor's room is down the main hall. Take a left up the
first hall, then he's the third door on the right. If Mr.
Hampton is not there, I don't know where he is."

"Thanks for being so helpful," he said, in a manner so
faintly sarcastic, he hoped she'd be thinking about it for a
long time.

Outside, Alec waved at Joshua and the big guy fell in step
next to him.

"And I thought Manticore was bad," Alec said, not liking
the school experience much so far.

"School people tell you where Hampton is?"

"Where he probably is." Alec didn't bother to tell Joshua about the woman's negative reaction to Hampton getting a personal delivery. Some things were better left unsaid.

Walking briskly, the duo turned left down the shorter hallway. Most of the doors were closed, so no teacher or pupil faces looked out to see them. The third door on the right stood ajar. They could see a man Alec's size with dark hair and a tidy goatee—another X5.

Not surprising—pretty easy for X5s to pass.

The guy was bent over a sink, filling a bucket, completely engrossed in what he was doing.

The sink occupied the right wall of the tiny room; brooms, mops, buckets, and the like stood like a rack of rifles along the back wall. You could take the boy out of Manticore, but you couldn't take Manticore out of the boy.

When Joshua said, "Hello, Hampton," the guy nearly jumped out of his skin.

Joshua—now a step into the cramped janitor's room—removed his helmet. "It's okay, Hampton. It's me—Joshua."

The X5's brown eyes were wide with shock and displeasure. "What the hell are you doing here?"

Hampton stepped past Joshua and tried to pull the door closed, but smacked it into Alec.

Nostrils flaring, Hampton demanded, "And who the hell is this asshole?"

Joshua said, "This asshole is Alec. He's another friend. X5."

Hampton's anger gave hard edges to his sarcastic smile. "Great! Happy to see you, bro—come on in. Let's have a party."

"Thanks," Alec said, and stepped in, pulling the door closed behind him.

Turning his attention back to Joshua, the janitor said, "You know I'm trying to pass. What the hell's the idea—"

"That's why we came," Joshua said. "So no one would know."

Hampton looked at Alec for help.

Alec said, "We figured you'd rather talk to us than the cops or maybe the feds."

The janitor's frown dug deep grooves into his handsome face. "What the hell's this about?"

"Take it easy," Alec said. "Just hear us out."

Hampton let out a deep sigh, forcing himself to calm down. "Okay, fellas—just make it quick, okay?"

Joshua looked at Alec, prompting him to take the lead, and the janitor turned his attention toward Alec too.

"Here's the deal, Hampton," Alec said in a rush. He knew the guy didn't want them there one second longer than necessary. "You've seen the tube—somebody's killing people. And skinning them."

The janitor nodded. "Couple of 'em cops. Sure. What the hell's that got to do with us?"

"Could be Kelpy," Joshua put in.

Hampton's face turned long and pale and sad—as if Joshua had just told him his brother had died. "Oh, damn. . . . You sure?"

Alec shook his head. "No. But the cops think a transgenic's responsible, and Joshua thinks this Kelpy might be . . . disturbed enough to be doing this weird shit."

"Men in uniforms," Joshua said, "were mean to Kelpy in the basement."

"I bet," Hampton said dryly.

"We need to find him," Alec said. "And at least talk to him."

Looking up at Joshua, Hampton said, "And you boys thought I'd know where to find him."

Joshua said, "Yes."

"Guys, I'm sorry. Haven't seen him for a while."

"How long?" Alec asked.

"A month, maybe two. And he was getting pretty bizarre at that."

"Bizarre how?"

Hampton shook his head. "Being human was all he could talk about—the only thing that mattered to him anymore."

"Passing for human?" Joshua asked.

"No—*being* human."

"We are human," Alec said.

"Not exactly," Hampton said.

"Anyway," Alec said, picking up the prior thread, "you say you have no idea where he is? Can't you give us a lead, anyway?"

Shrugging, the janitor said, "Kelpy had an apartment over in Queen Anne."

Alec said, "Isn't that where you live, Hampton?"

"Yeah, on Sixth. Bobby's place is on Crockett."

"Bobby?"

"Yeah. He uses the name Bobby Kawasaki. Only a few of us know about Kelpy."

"Bobby Kawasaki . . . you're shitting me."

"No," Hampton said, frowning, "I'm not. Why?"

"Nothing," Alec said.

But really it was something: *Alec knew the name.*

It belonged to a Jam Pony messenger. He'd heard Normal call out for the guy before; but for the life of him, Alec couldn't put a face with the name.

"Can you give us Kelpy's—Bobby's—address?"

Hampton did.

"Thanks," Alec said, and turned back to his towering companion. "Better put your helmet back on, Joshua."

But before Joshua could take that advice, the door to the small room swung open.

Alec turned to see a skinny man in his late fifties, in shirt and tie, his hair short and gray, his brown eyes huge with fear as he stared up at Joshua's helmetless head.

"Oh, my God," the man squeaked. He tried to shut the door but Joshua came running out, knocking the visitor aside. Alec turned and immediately punched Hampton in the face, and the janitor crumpled to the floor in a heap. Joshua stood in the hall, aghast, as Alec slipped into the corridor as well.

The guy in the tie snatched a walkie-talkie off his belt and held it up to his mouth. "This is Vice Principal Koopman—they're *here*! The freaks are here—they must be trying to grab the children!"

Alec ripped the radio out of the guy's hands and threw it against the brick wall, smashing it into a thousand pieces. Then he and Joshua sprinted up the hall, into the main corridor and out of the building.

Once the car was a safe distance from the school, Joshua asked, "Why did you punch Hampton?"

"To protect his cover. They'll think he was fighting us. He'll be all right."

Joshua nodded. "That went sideways."

"Yes, it did."

"FUBAR."

"FUBAR, indeed," Alec said.

The X5 knew that once this made the news, Max would be righteously pissed, and there would be hell to pay. The only way to make this better was for them to find Kelpy or Bobby, or whatever the hell he was calling himself now.

The sector cops would be looking for them, and having to go to Queen Anne meant five more checkpoints to clear, which meant the smart money was on stealing a different car. In a grocery store parking lot, Alec traded the gray Catbird for a maroon Ford. They passed through the checkpoints with no real trouble and finally got to the address Hampton had given them for Kelpy.

The odd couple climbed the stairs to the eighth floor, and found Kelpy's door seventh down on the left. No light was visible under the door, but Alec was through taking chances for the day. Using the old Manticore hand signals, they came up with a plan. Alec slid to one side and pressed himself against the wall. Still wearing the helmet, Joshua stood in front of the door and knocked.

"Pizza," he said.

There was no response from the other side.

Knocking a second time, louder this time, Joshua repeated, "Pizza."

Still no one came to the door.

"Fine," Alec said. "We do it the hard way."

"Hard way?" asked Joshua.

Easing his friend aside, Alec used burglar tools—two picklocks—on the door. Soon the two were standing within a small studio apartment, as silent as it was dark.

Alec hit the light switch, but the dim forty-watter overhead did little to improve the gloom inside the tiny flat. "Not exactly living high, wide, and handsome, is he?"

Joshua said, "Not high, not wide," clearly not knowing what he was saying.

Alec dispatched Joshua to start on the kitchen side, while he handled the other. They took their time, moving ahead slowly, hoping not to miss any bit of evidence that would either prove Kelpy was the killer or exonerate him. After checking the stove, Joshua opened the refrigerator door and stood, staring.

"What have you got?" Alec asked.

"Tryptophan in the fridge," Joshua said, holding up a white bottle big enough for five hundred or so doses.

"Take it."

"That's stealing, Alec."

"Take it!"

Joshua stuffed the bottle in his pocket. In the bathroom, in a cupboard under the sink, Alec found a canvas bag. Inside he found the wallets, pistols, stun rods, and badges of two sector cops and an NSA operative named Calvin D. Hankins.

"Not exactly the jackpot I was hoping to hit," he said.

Ducking into the bathroom, Joshua looked at the items and frowned, and his voice quivered as he asked, "Kelpy . . . Kelpy is skinner, isn't he?"

"Looks that way. . . . Sorry, big guy." Alec loaded the evidence back in the bag. "We've got to get this stuff to Max, ASAP."

"Okay. But Alec—she won't be happy. We won't be heroes."

"No, but she'll be pleased we found this before the cops or Ames White. Did you find anything?"

Joshua shook his head.

As they walked out into the main room, Alec noticed a door next to the one they'd busted in. A closet, had to be. "Did you look in there?" he asked.

Joshua shook his head. "Didn't see it."

Glancing from Joshua to the door, Alec turned the knob and opened it.

Inside they saw something even their Manticore hardened eyes were unprepared to process.

A dress mannequin stood on the floor, wearing a Frankenstein patchwork, an incomplete garment, whose sections were various tones, ranging from brown to off-white, depending in part upon their relative freshness.

The garment in progress consisted of the stitched-together flesh of Kelpy's victims.

"Crazy bastard's making a human suit," Alec said.

"Why, Alec? *Why?*"

"To be human, I guess. Somewhere in his Manticore-fried brain, he came up with that hot one. . . . Wait . . . what the hell . . . ?"

Hating to touch the thing, Alec swiveled the mannequin slightly.

On the blank head of the thing, Kelpy had pasted a photo

of a white face with spiky hair, wire frame glasses, and a serious save-the-world look.

Joshua said simply, "Logan's picture. Alec—why is Logan's picture on that statue?"

"Not good," Alec said. "Not good."

Walking down the eighth floor hall, Bobby Kawasaki knew something was wrong.

He could almost smell it. At his apartment he paused and saw the faint glow beneath the door.

Someone was inside!

Not wasting a moment, his fear spiking, Bobby stripped, tossed his clothes down the hall, and blended into the wall.

Not thirty seconds later, his head covered by a motorcycle helmet, Bobby's old friend Joshua stepped into the hall. A young man who appeared to be an X5 followed, the canvas bag of goodies hanging from his arm.

They took a few steps in the opposite direction and Kelpy attacked.

Reaching into the bag, Kelpy pulled out a stun rod before the X5 could react. He touched the X5 with the rod, and the young man yelled as he shook violently.

Growling, Joshua spun toward Kelpy, but not in time. . . .

Snatching up the second stun rod, Kelpy hit Joshua in the chest even as the beast man lunged forward with a lionlike roar that turned into a shriek. Kelpy hit both of them again, and left them twitching but unconscious.

He dropped one of the stun rods, keeping the other with him. There was much to do now and very little time to do it. The cops would probably be on their way, if any neighbors had heard and reported the ruckus. That meant getting his project, and getting out of there, as fast as he could.

Kelpy would have to move his plan up now—he would need to work faster.

But that was all right: the sooner he finished, the sooner everything would go his way. He removed his project carefully from the mannequin and packed it in a suitcase. He dressed quickly, once again becoming Bobby Kawasaki, bike messenger. Slinging the suitcase's strap over his shoulder, Bobby took one last look around the rathole. He wouldn't miss it a bit.

Leaving the apartment—forgetting to collect his Tryptophan in the fridge—Bobby picked up the canvas bag, felt the weight of the pistols inside and thought about killing Joshua and his intrusive playmate, still lying helpless in the hallway.

Then he heard sirens, the elevator buzz, and decided discretion might well be the better part of valor. Turning, he walked to the stairs at the far end of the hall and disappeared . . . in that way that only Bobby/Kelpy could.

Chapter Eight
PLEDGE OF ALLEGIANCE

TERMINAL CITY, 10:59 P.M.
TUESDAY, MAY 11, 2021

Pacing, Max asked, "Where the hell are they?"

Dix shook his lumpy head. "Haven't seen them since the meeting this morning . . . and I can't find them on any of the video feeds."

Lizard-man Mole offered, "Terminal City is a big place."

She whirled at him. "You're not in on this, are you?"

Mole's cigar almost dropped out of his mouth. "No! Hell no—in on what?"

"I wish to hell I knew," she growled.

The X5 had a sick feeling about this; as much as she valued Alec—as much as she secretly liked the guy—Max was well aware of his self-centered, guileful ways.

They were in the media center, waiting for the eleven o'clock news. Max prowled restlessly, while Dix and Mole sat here and there in the room, the crew watching the monitors hugging the screens.

"If they are up to something," Mole said, "what pisses me off is they *didn't* invite me."

Max shot him a look. "Don't whine—it's not becoming."

Mole shrugged, leaning back in a spring-sprung easy chair no self-respecting thrift shop would accept. "Hey, it's not like it was my idea, them jumping the fence. I'm just sayin'—"

She raised an eyebrow and the big tough lizard man piped down, sucking his cigar like a pacifier.

"Anyway," she said, flopping into another shabby easy chair, "we don't know for sure that they've gone anywhere." This was said without much conviction.

Mole started to open his mouth again, probably to ask where the hell she thought they were, but the ugly frown etched on her lovely features encouraged him to keep his questions to himself.

"All right," she said, heaving a sigh. "We've got plenty of other things to worry about. Let's get back to work."

And she hauled herself out of the chair, without even having really settled in.

"Wait!" Dix said, "News is starting." He turned the volume up some.

"Would it be asking too much," Max said dryly, "that the lead story not be Alec and Joshua?"

The news anchor was a blonde woman with manicured hair, suspiciously energetic blue eyes, and a long, thin face. She looked as though she hadn't had a cheeseburger since before the Pulse.

"In our top story tonight," the blonde said, "transgenics invaded the Ichiro Suzuki Elementary School today . . ."

Mole spoke for all of them: "Holy freakin' shit. . . ."

"We go now to our reporter on the scene, Ben Petty."

Petty stood tall, straight, and wore a nearly identical suit to the one he'd worn the night before, when he'd bribed the drunks. "Thank you, Liz."

"Hey, Max, isn't that your pal?" Dix asked.

Max shushed him.

Petty was saying, "Today, two transgenics invaded Ichiro Elementary, apparently intending to kidnap children."

"Kidnap children?" Mole asked, half out of the easy chair, dangling cigar stuck to the saliva of his lower lip. "Why in the hell would they do that?"

As if speaking directly to the lizard man, Petty said, "Local police have refused comment, but a high-ranking federal government source has speculated that the transgenics hoped to barter a deal to end the Terminal City siege by using school children as hostages."

"Ames White," Max said, spitting the name like an epithet.

The shot widened to show a man with a bandaged nose standing next to Petty. "Janitor Hampton Rhoades successfully fought off the transgenics, though one of them did, before fleeing, manage to break the janitor's nose."

One of the monitor crew sat up, a slender female, gesticulating, yelling, "Hey, I *know* him—he's a second-gen X5!"

All of them turned toward the source of that comment, an X5 whose name Max didn't know—typically pretty, with short brown hair, doe eyes, a pug nose, and a red-lipstick blossom of a mouth.

Dix asked, "Where d'ya know him from, Kade?"

"Not the streets—Manticore. His name was Stoop. He was a squad leader. If he got his nose broken, it's 'cause he let somebody do it."

They all traded looks, obviously wondering why these "transgenics" would invade the school . . . and, beyond that, why one of their own would fight them.

Were the two Alec and Joshua?

On the tube, the janitor was being interviewed by Petty.

Rhoades was saying, "I don't think they wanted trouble."

"Then how do you explain them breaking your nose?"

Shrugging, Rhoades said, "They were scared. I discovered them in my supply room—probably just looking for stuff, you know."

"You're being heralded as a hero," Petty said, "for saving these children."

"I don't think—"

Petty turned toward the camera. "There you have it—a

pair of transgenics, chased off in fright by a grade school janitor."

Max shook her head. This just kept getting better and better, didn't it?

"Keep a tape of that garbage," she told the monitoring crew. "But for now, I've seen enough."

She was on her way out of the room when the phone rang. She answered with her standard, "Go for Max."

"It's me," Logan said in her ear, and just the sound of his voice soothed her.

"Hi. Anything?"

"I may be making some progress. Can you stop by?"

"New place?"

"Yeah. Now would be good."

"I'm on my way."

She hung up, relieved at the thought of being in Logan's presence. This leadership gig was the pits. . . .

Walking toward the back fence of Terminal City, she watched as the community settled in for another night. A helicopter thrummed overhead, its searchlight probing their home like a prison beam searching for escaping prisoners; but at least it kept moving, stopping to hover for only a moment, at various points. The tension level in their toxic little town was high enough already, without choppers and firebombs, and she had to wonder if Clemente's control outside the fence was any less tenuous than her own, inside.

Here and there she saw transgenics bedding down. Some, she knew, like Dix, had real beds and real rooms, however shabby they might be; many, though, had only whatever scraps they could make into a bed, with a hollowed-out building to serve as shelter. Sooner or later this situation had to break. Other than Clemente, though, no one on the outside seemed interested in talking. She could only guess the authorities—and this included Ames White, but also more responsible types, without snake-cult hidden agendas—were patiently waiting to starve the transgenics out.

That was a plus, since the outside world was unaware of their Medtronics tunnel supply line.

On the minus side, her slender grip on the Terminal City reins seemed to be slipping. If she couldn't even get her closest comrades—Alec and Joshua—to follow her orders, how did she expect to get any of the others to?

Arriving at Medtronics, she slipped through the door, down the stairs, and into the tunnel. She trotted easily to the other end, went upstairs and found Logan bent over his computer, hard at work.

The office looked only slightly neater than the last time she'd been here, and a third desk had already been added to the cluttered two. Three different monitors displayed images, and Logan seemed to be tasking between all three.

"Hey, you," she said.

"Hey," he answered, his attention still on the computer stuff, but just enough warmth in that one word to make her feel better. The disappointment of Joshua and Alec's betrayal might have degenerated into self-pity, had she not known that Logan was still there, steadfast.

She tried to look over his shoulder without getting too close. If she leaned in to read, and even a stray virus-infected hair touched him . . . well, she didn't want to think about that. "Progress, you said?"

Logan nodded but kept working. After a few seconds of punching keys, the image on the middle monitor changed. "No kidding," he said to the monitor.

"What?"

He glanced at her. "That tape you gave me of you and Clemente?"

"Yeah?"

"Clemente talked about prints in the computer coming up as a shoe salesman on the skinner's first victim."

"That's what he told me," Max confirmed with a nod, "but also that something was hinky with the ID."

"Hinky is right," Logan said, tapping some more keys.

"Don't tease—what do you have?"

"The victim's name, according to the fingerprints, is Henry Calvin."

"Okay."

"Only, the shoe store where Henry supposedly worked went out of business six months ago."

"Making the late Henry an unemployed shoe salesman."

"Well, his being out of work might explain why he lived on a vacant lot—'cause that's what his address checks out as."

"Sure about this?"

He gave her the "puh-leese" look.

"How'd you do that?"

Small shrug. "It was easy, really. The file was designed to stand up to a cursory viewing. The government, as usual, never thinks that anyone will dig any further."

Max took a step closer, still careful to not get too near. "So the guy's ID is fake."

"And if he's a fake shoe salesman, in a government file— what is he in real life?"

"Someone who works for a government agency—a covert one, maybe?"

Logan swung around in the chair. "I think that's a reasonable assumption."

Excited, Max said, "The NSA, then—White!"

He favored her with a grin. "Interesting thing, though. I hacked into the NSA files and there's no file for Henry Calvin."

"Why, does that surprise you?"

"Not really—so I kept digging, and it turns out that on the same day that Henry Calvin died, an NSA agent named Calvin Hankins retired."

"Retired?"

"Yeah . . . and another odd thing is that his partner, only twenty-seven years old, left the NSA the same day, on full disability."

"You mean, he retired at age twenty-seven? Disability for what?"

"Good questions, and maybe we should ask the agent himself." Logan swung back around and tapped the keys some more.

A picture popped up on the screen. The man was young, slender, good-looking in a nondescript way, with dark hair swept straight back and brown eyes that made him look wiser than his years.

"Sage Thompson," Logan said by way of introduction. "Hankins' partner."

"It would seem," Max said, "a reasonable assumption that his leaving the NSA had something to do with his partner's death."

"Maybe he had a full-bore mental breakdown over his partner being murdered and skinned . . . maybe this all went down when the two were out in the field together."

"Meaning Thompson knows something about that first murder."

"Again—a reasonable assumption."

"Any idea where we can find him?"

"He's in the phone book," Logan said.

Max smirked darkly. "That's encouraging. With White involved, the guy could be on the bottom of Puget Sound."

"I called his house and got no answer. Then I got Asha to do a drive-by, and she said the place was vacant . . . and there's a For Sale sign in the yard."

Asha Barlow, a friend of Logan's, ran with the revolutionary S1W, an underground cell almost as wrapped up in saving the world as Eyes Only. Despite her initial jealousy of Asha, Max had learned to trust the woman and knew that if Asha said Thompson was a ghost, a ghost he was.

"You'll find him for me, Logan? You know, my hands are tied here. I promised Clemente I'd stay put."

"I'm looking," he assured her. "I'll do what I can."

"Track him down, get whatever you can—using Asha's a good idea, with me on the sidelines. We're under enough pressure here without Ames White making a transgenic poster child out of a serial killer."

"What if that serial killer really *is* a transgenic?" Logan asked.

"Then we're going to need all the media magic Eyes Only can muster."

Her cell phone rang again.

"You're a popular girl," Logan said.

"I shouldn'ta listed myself with that dating agency." After the second ring, she punched the Send button. "Go for Max."

Dix's voice blurted, "The cop's back at the fence! You better get up here. He doesn't look happy."

Shaking her head, she said, "On my way."

"What?" Logan asked.

"Clemente's dropped by—seen the news lately?"

Logan nodded. "I figured that was just typical Ames White disinformation."

"I hope to God it is—Alec and Joshua went over the fence this morning."

"Oh hell. . . ."

Max let out a sigh that started at her toes. "No one knows why. And we've heard nothing from them. Can you beat that, Logan? I ask this band of outcasts for one thing—stay put till this is negotiated—and two of my closest confederates ignore my request."

Pushing away from the computer, Logan said, "Leadership is getting someone to do what they don't want to do—to achieve what they want to achieve."

"Who said that?"

"Tom Landry."

Max just looked at him.

"Football coach—Dallas Cowboys."

"If you say so. But by that yardstick, I failed."

"No—they probably failed you. But you also haven't heard their side of it yet. And you owe them that much, right?"

She said nothing at first, but as his eyes unrelentingly bore in on her, she finally said, "Right. . . . How do you stay so positive?"

"Because the alternative is despair. And when that happens—the Ames Whites of the world win."

Max looked at him long and hard, knowing that her love for this man had blossomed from an admiration that somehow still grew.

"Thanks," she said. "I needed that. . . . Now I've really gotta go."

She didn't want to leave Logan's side, but she turned away and headed for the tunnel back to Terminal City.

Clemente was waiting at the main gate when she got there and, what a shock! He looked pissed off . . .

. . . not that she could really blame him, after the day's fiascoes.

"You took your sweet time," he said, his voice edgy and cold.

Max ran a hand over her face. "Ramon, I'd love to tell you that you're my only problem right now . . . but you're not."

He sucked in a breath, then nodded. "All right—I can accept that."

"What can I do for you?"

"Come with me for a while," he said.

She smirked. "Yeah—right."

Clemente's eyes locked with hers. "Trust is a two-way street, Max . . . and right now yours is looking like a dead end."

"Well, that's cute, Ramon, but—"

"I need to talk to you in a secure location. Can you appreciate that?"

"Yes."

"Should I trust you?"

"Yes."

"Then are you willing to come with me, on the assurance that I'll allow you to return to Terminal City?"

"Yes," she said, thinking that Clemente was living up to that Tom Landry definition of leadership damn well.

Turning toward one of the security cameras, Max made several hand motions.

"What was that about?" Clemente asked.

"Just telling the gang what to do if I don't come back."

The transgenic sentries, at her bidding, opened the gate for her.

Clemente led Max through the blockade of squad cars, around the officers who glared at her, unmasked hatred in their eyes, and past the National Guard trucks, the troops scattered along the perimeter. Moments later she was following the detective into a seven-story office building.

The first floor had an atrium lobby with a bank of three elevators to the left and, at the right, the restaurant that was their destination. Sitting in a booth next to a huge plate-glass window, Max could see the Terminal City main gate and the large military presence on this side of it.

She wondered if part of the exercise was for her to see just what she and her people were up against.

The restaurant itself was more like a lunch counter with a dozen booths lined around two outside walls. Back in the pre-Pulse days the place probably did great breakfast business as all the medtech people stopped in on their way to work. The back wall of the counter area was mostly a huge mirror surrounded by shelves that held coffee cups, water glasses, malt glasses, and sundae bowls. The red Formica counter held stainless steel napkin holders and sat in front of silver stools with red tops.

It felt strange—comforting and a little surreal—to be out in the real world again.

The booths were still comfy, the tan Naugahyde worn but clean. Usually open until eight or nine, the place had been commandeered—Clemente explained—as the officers' mess during the siege. At the moment, other than one anxious-looking middle-age waitress, the place seemed vacant.

Arriving with coffee, the waitress poured two cups, set one in front of each of them, then set the pot on the table too.

When the waitress left quickly—too quickly—Max's smile disappeared. "Secure location, huh?" she said, her voice cold. "Get 'em out."

"What?" Clemente seemed confused.

"You get them out or I'll do it for you."

"What are you—"

"Cut the crap, Ramon. Show of trust? You've got three SWAT guys playing hide-and-seek behind the counter. I can see them in the damn mirror."

Reluctantly, he turned and saw what she meant. "All right—you heard her. Up and out."

The three SWAT team members stood, sweat beading their faces. Max wondered how long they'd been crammed down back there. For the first time today, she wanted to smile; but didn't. The SWAT officers looked as irritated as they did embarrassed, and she saw no reason to antagonize them further.

"The two in the men's room, too."

The detective's eyes were wide with amazement. "How did you—"

"I didn't," she said. "You just told me."

He sat back in the booth, rubbed a hand over his face and let an exhausted smile leak out. "Johnson, Carlesimo," he yelled, not bothering with the walkie. "Come on out!"

Two more SWAT officers emerged from the men's room, weapons in their hands, confusion on their faces.

Clemente thumbed toward the door. "Go ahead—it's okay. Everybody out."

The entire SWAT contingent trooped out, the waitress, too.

"How the hell did you figure that?" the detective asked, his face betraying no trace of embarrassment at being caught with his pants around his ankles.

"With only three behind the counter, you'd want backup. The only place out of sight was the bathrooms. You wouldn't want me stumbling into your guys in the Women's, so that meant they had to be in the Men's."

"And you knew there'd be two because . . . ?"

"SWAT guys can't pee by themselves. You breed it into them. They're like pigeons—they mate for life."

Clemente nodded. He seemed chagrined. "Neither one of us has been very trustworthy, have we?"

"I've at least tried. I didn't hide shooters behind a lunch counter. And that waitress is a policewoman, right?"

His face turned stony. "Maybe—but you just helped two transgenics leave Terminal City."

"Not true."

"What about that elementary school? I know you're monitoring the news—you saw it."

"I told you before, Ramon, not all the transgenics in this city are inside our—"

He cut her off. "But these two were. I got detailed descriptions from the school staff. These two I saw with you that first night, saw them myself."

"You could be wrong," she tried feebly.

"I might have believed that if we hadn't taken them into custody earlier."

Detective Clemente tossed two photos on the table in front of her, and Max felt her stomach do a back flip—and land badly.

She looked down at the pictures of Joshua and Alec—they were on a floor, their eyes closed, their faces peaceful.

Trying not to betray the emotion she felt, she asked, "Are they dead?"

Shaking his head, the detective said, "No—but they had a hell of a close call."

"What *happened* to them?"

"They were attacked by someone who almost electrocuted them."

"What?"

"With stun rods."

"Where did this happen? When?"

"An apartment house of squatters in Queen Anne—over on Crockett."

Max tried to make sense of it, but couldn't add anything up. "What were they doing there?"

Clemente studied her. "You're asking *me*?"

"Yes I'm asking you!"

"You really don't know?"

"They were gone for hours before I even found out they were on the outside."

"Are you saying they'd already gone over the fence when you told your people to stay put?"

She drew a deep breath, let it out. "I wish I could tell you that. . . . No. They knew about my order."

Max stopped short of telling the cop that these were two of her closest comrades.

"Shit," Clemente was saying. "I was hoping you'd know something."

She glanced around. "Is this location really secure?"

"Yes. Swept it for bugs this morning. And there's been no sign of White or his people."

"Ramon—why were you hoping *I* would know something? You're the one on the outside. What's your problem?"

The detective reached beside him, into a briefcase, and pulled out more pictures, arraying them around the table.

Max looked them over as he spoke. "The stun rod you see in these photos . . ."

"Yeah?"

"It belongs to one of the murdered officers who was skinned."

Max rocked back in the booth as if she'd been punched.

Clemente bore down on her. "Any idea why they went to the school?"

She shook her head. "None. I'm telling you, I don't even know why they left Terminal City." She sat forward, almost pleading. "Could you take me to them? Could I see them?"

"No. Anyway, they're still unconscious. They're in a hospital—safe . . . and they're going to be all right."

"You have to let me look into this," Max pleaded.

"No way. No way! If you can help us from inside, fine. Otherwise this is a police matter and we'll take care of it."

"My guys did not kill those officers."

Clemente put a hand out and touched hers—a shockingly intimate move meant to reassure her. Which it did.

"I know that," Clemente said. "In fact, my guess is, somehow they either found . . . or stumbled into the killer. Whoever it is, he's the dangerous one. I mean, Max—this guy got the drop on . . . and nearly killed . . . two transgenics."

"Which is why you should let me hit the streets and find out what is up with this!"

"No—Max, the bottom line here is, this is a police matter. You have to go back inside and be the leader those people need right now."

She sighed. "Yeah. . . . Yeah, I know. People I trust keep telling me that."

"And I'm one of them?"

"You're one."

"Then I hope you'll take this the right when I say . . . I've got more bad news to share with you."

Max again locked eyes with him, wondering if she could take any more.

"Someone," Clemente said, "has pulled some strings."

"What now?"

"A clock has started ticking. We've got till Friday. The feds say, if we locals can't settle this within a week, they'll come in and take over."

"Ames White," Max said.

Nodding, Clemente said, "My best guess, too. But who pulled the strings doesn't matter—all that matters is, if this standoff isn't settled by Friday, the Army will move in on Terminal City—tanks'll come rolling right through those fences."

Max said nothing.

"So how do we settle this thing, you and I?" Clemente asked.

"We find that killer."

"I'll find him—but I see your point. As long as the media is filled with a transgenic Jack the Ripper, negotiating with Terminal City gets lost in the alarmist shuffle."

"Well put. Where are you with the investigation?"

With a shrug, Clemente said, "We've searched the apartment where your friends were found. It's been cleared out. It's a squatter's flat, like I said, so we have no name, and the neighbors didn't ever remember seeing the guy. We got some skin cells from the shower drain, could be the killer, could be skin from one of the victims. We won't know for a while."

"What about the DNA evidence White gave you?"

Clemente started to say something, then seemed to change his mind. "I won't bullshit you. How did you figure that White shared DNA evidence with us?"

"It wasn't exactly the Enigma code, Ramon. You guys wouldn't have put the word out that this was a transgenic killer if you didn't have something . . . and White would be eager to provide that, I'm sure."

Nodding, Clemente said, "White's team got skin cells off this piece of top secret equipment that the killer took from his first victim."

"Oh, you mean the shoe salesman?"

Clemente took the bait. "Yeah—the shoe salesman . . . who really worked for the NSA, only I never told you that."

So, Logan had been right: the first victim was one of White's people.

Max asked, "Why didn't White give you this key piece of evidence immediately?"

Clemente gazed at her with respect. "You'd have made a good cop, Max. That was my first question too."

"And the answer?"

The cop shrugged. "White said the killer stole the piece of equipment, and it had only been retrieved recently."

"Retrieved?"

"White was a little vague on that part," Clemente admitted.

"You believe him?"

"Don't really have a choice. Anyway, under a press-blackout restriction, he did give me possession of that gizmo for twenty-four hours. It was smashed up, and covered in blood—the victim's blood—and it matched up perfectly. The lab also found more skin cells from the killer, and we ran our own DNA tests and the killer is definitely transgenic."

"According to evidence provided by Ames White," she said.

He shook his head. "If this evidence is faked, it's head and shoulders above anything I've ever come across. I've seen the government try to cover shit up before and they suck at it. Your little community across the street comes to mind as an example."

"Point taken," she said. "What about fingerprints?"

"None anywhere. Not at the scenes of the crimes, none on that piece of equipment, none on the stun rods, and none in the apartment."

Frowning, she asked, "How is that even possible?"

Clemente sat back in the booth. "I have no idea."

Max decided that the best way to show her sincerity would be to level with Clemente. "Suppose I told you I already knew that the first victim worked for White?"

"How?"

"By putting the pieces together from what you told me, and the computer work of a friend. And I also know that our dead NSA 'shoe salesman' had a young partner who left the agency at the same time—with full disability."

Clemente was sitting forward, scribbling this in a small notebook. "What's the partner's name?"

"You're not going to find him. He's gone to ground."

"Tell me anyway, Max. I have my sources, my ways to find people. This guy's a material witness in a homicide."

"I'll tell you his name, Ramon, because I want to build trust. And in the days ahead we'll need that. If we're going to get this fixed before the tanks roll in, we have to promise to tell each other the truth from now on."

The detective studied her, his face serious. "You have my word."

"Mine too. But here's the thing. If you do a big high-profile manhunt, then Ames White will get to your witness first, and then neither of us will ever get to talk to him."

"I can protect him."

"The police can't protect him from White."

Clemente's eyes narrowed. "I didn't say the police. I said, 'I can protect him.' "

She considered that; then she took the leap of faith, of trust. "His name's Sage Thompson."

She gave him the agent's last known address as well.

Clemente scribbled the information in his notebook. "If you've been inside Terminal City, how do you know he's not home?"

A half smile played at the corner of her mouth. "Well, I

have my sources, too—including a nontransgenic friend, who visited the house and said it's vacant and for sale."

"I'll find Thompson," Clemente said. "Now, we better get you back inside. Here's my cell number." He handed her a slip of paper. "You find out anything, you let me know."

"You'll do the same?"

"I'll do the same."

They walked slowly back to the gate in silence. The night had turned chilly again and Max saw no stars. By tomorrow it would be raining again. Sometimes she wondered why she'd left L.A. in the first place, earthquakes or not. She was tired of being cold and wet. When this was over, she promised herself, she and Logan were going somewhere warm for a while.

In spite of herself, she smiled.

"What?" Clemente asked as she stepped through the gate.

Turning back, she asked, "You ever been to Florida, Ramon?"

He nodded. "In my Army days."

"Warm there?"

Now he smiled too. "Most of the time."

"Be nice to see the sun again," Max said, then she trotted away.

Otto Gottlieb sat in his car and stared out at Puget Sound in the darkness.

Discovery Park was vacant at this hour, the West Point Lighthouse poking holes in the blackness as it swept back and forth. Agent White and the detective, Clemente, were in the middle of some kind of pissing contest, which White of course was determined to win. Toward that end, White had talked Otto into being evasive with the police about how, when, and where the NSA had come back into possession of the imager.

The deceit had gone so deep that a fed-up Otto had finally

come to believe that White had gone rogue. There didn't seem to be any other viable explanation, and Agent White's perfidy had now broadened in scope to include Otto Gottlieb as well.

Otto pounded the steering wheel. He'd gotten so caught up in trying to save his ass, he'd forgotten to cover it . . . and now he was about to be hung out to dry. Sooner or later the truth, whatever that was, about White's clandestine activities would come out . . . and who was going to be there to take the blame?

Otto.

Shit.

There had to be someone he could talk to, someone he could go to . . . but who? White was well insulated. Otto knew that his partner had friends in Congress, if not higher. His own predicament was simple—could he trust anyone in the NSA?

The answer, of course, was no; not his peers, not his superiors . . . no one.

Otto considered other agencies at the federal level, but who? The FBI? Probably not. CIA? Ditto. Though he knew people in both, he had no idea who might be tied to White. The state authorities were out of the question, as well—White had the governor in his pocket, and God knew who else.

Only Detective Clemente had stood up to White, and Otto wondered if a local cop could accomplish anything more with White than providing a source of minor irritation. Still, it seemed like the most viable of the not wonderful options available.

The problem was, what would he say to Clemente? What proof did he have that White had gone rogue?

Taking a deep breath, Otto sat back, listened to the mournful cry of the foghorn, and tried to build his case. White had used that transgenic, X5-494, to chase down other transgenics. That had seemed like a bad idea to Otto to begin with, but White overruled him, and in the end they lost 494 as well.

When that operation went south, Otto had been forced to help in its cover-up, and he had no remaining proof that White had used 494. The few other agents who'd been there, who might corroborate his story, all seemed firmly in White's pocket.

Of course, they probably thought the same thing about him. . . .

White had bred both trust and distrust among his own team all along. Though the agents all appeared to be loyal, to Otto's eye that loyalty seemed more aimed at White than at the NSA, and he didn't feel comfortable trying to win over any of the others to his side. Odds were, even if he mentioned his suspicions to one of them, that agent would turn around and tell White.

The fiasco at Jam Pony and the deliberate obstruction of Detective Clemente's homicide investigation had only intensified Otto's suspicions. And the conversation with White this evening had been the final straw.

Otto had been driving White home at the end of the day, his boss pissed off because once again Washington had ordered White's NSA unit not to get involved with the siege at Terminal City. When White received that word, he'd gone ballistic; but by the time he got in the car with Otto, White had simmered down to mere anger. Driving as fast as he could without looking obvious, Otto sped toward White's house, anxious to get the man out of his car.

"They don't trust me, Otto," White said, turning his gaze out the passenger window at the houses they passed.

"I'm sure they do, sir. They just have a plan for Terminal City that doesn't include us."

"The transgenics are our job," White said, his voice rising. "We should be allowed to do our job."

Otto didn't know what to say to that, so he said nothing; he was well-practiced at providing eloquent silences.

"They're going to screw it up, and she's going to get away."

" 'She,' sir?"

"452—the one they call Max. She's the key, Otto. They all band around her. Kill the head and the body will fall."

"Maybe that's the plan."

"What?" White seemed surprised Otto had contributed a thought.

"The plan—to capture her, and bring the alliance of transgenics down. If she is the leader."

"She's more than the leader, Otto. And if she's captured. . . ."

"Sir?"

White turned from the houses to look at Otto. Glancing over, Otto caught his boss's gaze and recognized the fiery glow that always preceded one of White's odd choices.

"You should go on vacation, Otto. Take the next week off, starting tomorrow."

"I've used my vacation for the year, sir."

"I'll clear it with Washington."

"But, sir—"

White's gaze turned hot. "Do what I tell you, Otto. You're not cleared for what's going to go down here."

"Like at Jam Pony, sir?" Though no overt sarcasm tinged the words, Otto instantly regretted saying them.

Rubbing a hand over his face, White was clearly attempting to hold in his temper. When he spoke, his voice sounded icy and robotic. "Yes, like Jam Pony. Drop me off, go home, don't come to the office for a week. Do you understand?"

Otto looked over at his boss and saw the face of a madman. Worried that White's next step might be a bullet to the back of his head, Otto said, "Week's vacation sounds good, sir."

Five minutes later, Otto had dropped White in his driveway and sped away. He'd driven aimlessly for a couple of hours before winding up here, at Discovery Park. Now he wondered if he dared go home. And if he didn't go home, where *could* he go?

Suddenly, Otto Gottlieb realized he was a man without a country. He needed to tell someone something. He just didn't know who to talk to or what the hell he would say that wouldn't make him sound like a lunatic.

Clemente suddenly seemed like too small a fish to do battle with a shark like White. Then Otto thought of the one thing that White seemed to hate as much as the transgenics: Eyes Only!

Otto needed to get to Eyes Only. They'd tried to track the hacker down for months, and though they'd narrowly missed him once, that was the only time they'd gotten even a sniff of the guy. Now that he needed help immediately, Otto wondered how exactly one contacted an underground cyber journalist. Smoke signals, maybe?

Maybe he should just let White do whatever it was he was going to do at Terminal City and stay out of it. They were only transgenics, after all. . . .

Only transgenics.

The phrase chilled Otto. He remembered seeing historical videos where one racist after another had used the same defense to cover his own stupidity and rage. "They're only Negroes." "They're only Jews." "They're only Mexicans."

And now words had formed in his own brain: *They're only transgenics.*

Otto stared out at the sound and thought about his life, why he'd chosen government service in the first place, and as he made up his mind about what he would do, he heard himself saying, "With liberty and justice for all."

And as he thought that for the first time in his adult life, he actually knew what those words meant.

He put the gun that had been in his lap back in its shoulder holster and drove home, with a reason to live.

Chapter Nine
CRASH LANDINGS

JAM PONY, 8:02 A.M.
WEDNESDAY, MAY 12, 2021

Original Cindy missed Max.

Things seemed to be slipping back into numbing regularity at Jam Pony. Where the bike messengers were concerned, Normal was pretty much back to normal—which was to say, obnoxiously pushing them on and putting them down—and neither he nor anyone else seemed to want to talk at all about what had happened here just five days ago.

It was as if not talking about it made the hostage crisis never have happened—though the shellshocked look in everyone's eyes said otherwise.

Original Cindy hadn't spoken to Max, her best friend, her sister, since they'd parted company Saturday evening; and, though she was going through the motions at work, Cindy was on edge, worry boiling in her stomach, like an untended pot of greens on a back burner.

Sunday had been spent curled up in the apartment, trying to withdraw into herself, seeking sleep as refuge; instead, she found herself watching mental movies of her recollections of Max.

Everywhere she looked, something set off another flood of memories—the kitchen, the sofa, the table where they ate—even the damn bathroom triggered another torrent of emotion.

It was as if she were eulogizing her friend, and she kept telling herself to stop thinking of Max in the past tense. Max wasn't dead . . . but Cindy couldn't keep from adding *yet*.

And when Cindy did manage to drift off to sleep, Terminal City invaded her dreams, the siege turning into a pitched battle that—as the dreams became more and more nightmarish—always ended with Max lying lifeless. . . .

Monday had come as a relief. Jam Pony held Max memories, of course—good and bad—but being around Sketchy and the others seemed better than being alone at home.

Bullet holes still pocked the exterior, and crime scene tape sagged around the door like ghastly prom decorations still hanging the day after. Entering, Original Cindy walked past where CeCe died—the floor scrubbed too clean in that spot—and wandered back to where the messengers were gathered in the slapdash employee's lounge. Normal stood in front of the group, a clipboard clasped in both hands like a life buoy he was clinging to.

"Come on in, missy," Normal said. "Just show up whenever you're ready. It's not like we keep regular business hours here."

A few messengers sat in the scattered chairs, while most stood, their eyes bouncing back and forth between Original Cindy and Normal.

Though his words carried their usual sarcastic edge, Normal's tone did not, and she took small solace in the fact that even Normal—who saw himself as the model of stoicism—remained a little off balance.

She stepped up next to Sketchy and stood quietly, her only response to her boss a barely audible, "Whatever."

Normal winced—apparently noting her atypical lack of wit—and picked up where he'd left off. "As I was saying, the police have finished their investigation and have said that we can reopen. So, today we're starting over—starting anew."

They all looked at him, dead-eyed, saying nothing. Typical

of Normal's idea of a pep talk, it was long on talk and short on pep. Ignoring their indifference, he pressed on.

"Looks like we're going to be a little short-handed here for a while," he said, with a glance at his clipboard, "and so there will be overtime for those that want it—nothing mandatory."

They all looked at each other in confusion. The words "mandatory" and "overtime" had always come out of Normal's mouth as one long compound word. To hear him say that overtime wasn't mandatory was the Pope casually stating that birth control was cool with him.

The announcement seemed to trigger a mass short circuit among the messengers. They didn't respond with an "All right!" or a "Yeah!"—they all just stared at their leader, numb.

"That must be the good twin," Sketchy said under his breath to Cindy, beside him.

Cindy might have laughed at that, if the suggestion that the real Normal had been kidnapped hadn't struck her as reasonable.

"I'll check the basement for a pod," she whispered.

"Anyway," Normal was saying, "best way to keep your mind off the unpleasantness is to work hard. Do that, and we'll all get through this together."

With that rather remarkably human comment from their usually tight-assed boss, life had started on the road back to the everyday.

Now, on Wednesday, life at Jam Pony was mundane again, as if the past week's events were nothing more than a bad dream. Standing alone in the locker area, Original Cindy—in black slacks, gray turtleneck, and orange quilted vest—looked over at Max's locker. Her gaze held for only a few seconds before she had to look away.

She felt she was letting her Boo down—and, in a way, that her Boo was short-changing her, as well. The idea was that

Original Cindy would be working for Max and the besieged transgenics here on the outside . . . but no orders from Terminal City headquarters had been forthcoming.

Sketchy came up, handed her a paper cup of coffee and gave her a big forced smile. Dressed in his usual jeans and T-shirt, he looked all right from a distance, but closer examination revealed red-rimmed eyes, his blond and brown locks hanging weedlike in his face, like they hadn't been combed since he'd left Terminal City.

"Heard from her?" he asked quietly.

Original Cindy shook her head. "You?"

The phony smile faded. "Nope."

She saluted him with the coffee. "And what did I do to deserve this?"

"Nothin', just. . . . You look kinda lonely."

"Do I look lonely enough that I would need the company of a fool like you?"

He thought about that, then said, "Yeah."

And Original Cindy did something she hadn't done for days: she laughed.

"I miss her too," Sketchy said. "I wish to hell we'd hear from her—we were supposed to be out here, on this side of the fence, *helping*. . . ."

"I know. I'm afraid maybe Max jus' wanted us outta there, jus' to protect our asses. I mean, we can't hang around that toxic shit *too* long—Original Cindy don't wanna grow no extra eyeballs or nothin'."

He let out a mirthless chuckle. "I was . . . I mean, she's . . ."

"Spit it out."

"You were right, Cin—what you said at Crash that night, after . . . you know . . . after I found out about her. That she was . . . special."

Original Cindy knew Sketchy was referring to that day in the not-too-distant past when he'd caught Cindy pilfering

Max's and Alec's records from Normal's files, to keep the documents out of the hands of government agents. Even Sketchy had been able to put together that Max and Alec were transgenics.

Sketch said, "You know what? Max is the best person I know . . . and she is the best friend I've ever had."

Cindy nodded. "True that. Same for this one."

"You know, I been thinking back on all those lunches with you and Max, Herbal and me, and I . . ." He swallowed. "I just wanna say . . . well, I . . ."

She kissed him on the cheek. "You said it nice and clear, Sketch."

Sketchy's face turned a lovely shade of fuchsia.

Normal strolled up to them. "You leaving the sisters of Sappho for this lump, Cynthia?"

Turning to their boss, Original Cindy said, "I'm not turning to the dark side, no—but if I did—" And she ran her fingers through Sketchy's hair. "—my brother Sketch here would not be the worst catch."

Brightening, the lanky messenger seemed to grow a couple of inches, in at least one direction.

"I'll do my best to form no mental images," Normal said. "Enough banter."

He handed an envelope to her and a package to Sketchy.

"Bip bip bip," he said.

Normal flashed the pair a quick grin, then put on a frown and went off to hassle the short-timers.

"Hmmm," Sketchy said. "Is it my imagination, or does Normal seem to be softening here?"

Original Cindy shook her head and made a tsk-tsk noise. "That's some scary shit, ain't it?"

"More than my tender nerves can take." Sketchy held up the package. "Well, I better get bip-bip-bipping. . . . If you hear from our girl, you'll let me know?"

"Bet your pasty white ass."

"You know, you liking me doesn't seem that different from when I sickened you."

"It's a fine line," Cindy admitted.

Sketch smiled, shook his head, and headed outside to his bike.

Turning back to glance at Max's locker one last time, Original Cindy looked farther down the aisle and saw that kid no one ever seemed to notice. What was his name? Bobby Suzuki? Tommy Nagasaki? Kid had less personality than Normal in his sleep.

Sitting in front of his locker, the kid glanced around, and apparently didn't catch her watching as he pulled a bottle of pills out and unscrewed the lid. It looked identical to the bottle of Tryptophan pills that Max kept in her locker to control her seizures.

Slowly moving closer, careful not to be spotted, Original Cindy watched as he shook two pills out into his hand. He screwed the lid back on the bottle and stuck it in the pocket of his vest. She caught only a glimpse of the pills in the kid's hand as they headed to his mouth, but that was enough for her to see the pills were just like the ones Max took.

Sliding up next to him, she asked, "Hey, Tommy boy—you stealin' my girl's meds?"

The kid shook his head emphatically. "No, no. I'd never hurt Max. . . . And it's Bobby."

"So, if I check my main girl's locker I'm gonna find her meds still in there?"

Now the kid nodded with equal enthusiasm. "Go ahead and look. I swear I didn't take anything!"

Eyeballing the guy—God, what a nonentity!—Original Cindy moved over in front of Max's locker and dialed the combination lock.

Opening the door, she looked inside and saw Max's bottle perched on the top shelf, where it always sat, safe and sound.

She picked it up, shook it, found it to be maybe three-quarters full. That seemed about right.

"All right, Robby," she said. "My bad."

"It's Bobby. . . . Can I go now?"

"No—not till you tell me why you're takin' Tryptophan."

"It just relaxes me. It's over-the-counter med."

"Not in that quantity. Listen, Timmy—maybe you weren't around durin' the party we had the other day. . . ."

"The hostage crisis? I was here. Don't you remember?"

"Yeah, sure. Anyway—if you was here, you should know where I stand on a certain controversial issue."

"I do. You're Max's friend."

"And you're . . ."

They both looked around to make sure no one was watching.

"Isn't it obvious?" he asked.

Normal strolled by, like a hall monitor trolling for trouble. "You two still here? This is not Club Med, people. There's work to do—get moving."

They walked outside together and mounted their bicycles. She looked at the kid in the morning sunshine. For some reason, she felt like this was the first time she'd really seen him.

Why did she think of him as a kid? He could be twenty . . . or thirty . . . or . . . ? Whatever, he was of indeterminate race, with full lips and black curly hair that reminded her a little of her own. Like Max, he appeared to be a mixture of all people, only his features seemed almost blurred compared to Max's well-defined face.

Looking closer, though, he might have some Afro blood in him. . . .

Together, they rode away slowly, her envelope stuck inside her vest, his package in a bag over his shoulder.

"I never told Max," he said, "but, yes, I'm a transgenic, too."

They rode side by side in the street.

"How long you been passin'?" she asked.

He shrugged one shoulder. "Since Max got us out of Manticore."

"That's not all that long. . . . You seem to be fitting in okay."

"That's no problem for me."

"You and Max are friends?" Funny, she thought, that Max would have a friend at Jam Pony that Cindy didn't also know.

He nodded. "If it wasn't for Max, I'd still be there. At Manticore."

"But Manticore was burned."

"I'd just be some more ashes."

"I gotta say, man, you seem so regular, I woulda thought you were on the outside as long as Max."

They paused at a light.

He shook his head. "I'm supposed to seem regular—that's what I do."

She shook her head. "It's still not safe for you out here by yourself."

"Ain't that the truth," he said with a sad smile. "But they're all in Terminal City and I'm stuck here. What am I gonna do—march up to the gate and ask to be let in?"

Cindy thought about that. "There's other ways."

"You think?"

"I'm here, ain't I?"

"Yeah."

"Well, you saw what went down Friday."

"Sure."

The light changed.

"I was with her when she left, right? And we all ended up in Terminal City."

"And you got out?"

"What do you think, chump? Do I look like a mirage to you?"

"Come to think of it, Sketchy went along with you and Max, too, didn't he?"

She nodded.

"And that friend of Max's—Logan?"

"You know him?" she asked, a little puzzled now.

"Seen him with Max before. Stops by Jam Pony sometimes."

That was true.

"Yeah," she said, "Logan went, too."

"Did all of you leave?"

They were riding slowly through the light traffic.

"Well . . . you saw Sketch at work, right?"

"What about Logan?"

She frowned. "Why are you so interested in Logan?"

"Well, it's just . . . I wondered if he was transgenic, too—'cause that's the only way he could stay in Terminal City, right? I mean, ordinaries get sick if they stay too long."

"Well . . . you're right about that. That's why Max got us out of there—me and Sketch and Logan."

"If she got you out, could you get me in, the same way?"

Something felt way whack about this to her. If this mouthbreather was a transgenic, why hadn't Max or Alec ever pointed him out? And why in the hell was he so worried about the three ordinaries? Last, but not least, she reminded herself, was the fact that now he suddenly wanted to know the route she'd used to get in and out of Terminal City. . . .

They were at another light.

"Look, Teddy," she said slowly. "It's not that I don't trust you—it's just that I need some kind of . . ."

"Proof," he said. "I've been a human the whole time you've known me . . . with no sign of transgenic ability . . . then I start in with all these questions."

She nodded, liking the fact that he got it so fast. "That's a big bingo, Barney. Why don't you whip up a little super somethin' for me?"

"Can't do it," he said, almost sadly. "The drug—the Tryptophan you saw me taking earlier?"

"Yeah?"

"It's an inhibitor. It works to keep my abilities from taking over my life."

"That's not how it affects Max . . ."

"We're all different. You know what an X5 is? I'm not an X5. I'm more like Joshua."

"You ain't no dog boy."

"No—and I can show you what I am, later . . . when the dose has worn off. But not now."

"Works for me," she said, suddenly nervous. "Look, I better get my shit in gear—Normal'll fire my ass."

"I want your help, Cindy."

"Maybe we could hook up at Crash later, Benny, and when nobody's lookin', you could show me your stuff, then."

"Sure."

Original Cindy nodded at the guy and pedaled away.

That weirdo was way too interested in Max. . . . Cindy felt like she'd nearly, if accidentally, betrayed her best friend. No way in freakin' hell would she show that strange character— soul brother or not—the tunnel into Terminal City.

After pumping a few times, Original Cindy glanced back and he waved. She faked a smile and waved herself. Then, once she'd gone two blocks, she looked back again and he was gone.

She heaved a sigh of relief, the whole exchange with that kid having weirded her out completely. She made a mental note to call Sketch as soon as possible and warn him—right after she warned Max. Reaching into her pocket, she pulled out her cell phone.

Glancing to her left, she saw the kid riding easily right next to her. In her surprise, the phone slipped from her hand, crashed to the street, and shattered.

"Even on my meds," he said calmly, "I still have my transgenic speed."

Her mouth dropping open, Original Cindy veered right, trying to get away from the guy; but her wheel clipped a crack in the pavement and she went down hard, the bike tumbling over her, her head smacking hard off the pavement.

As things slowed and grew very quiet, she felt a dull throb in her head, the bike seeming to fly away from her unbidden, and she looked up to see the strangely unformed face of her fellow Jam Pony bike messenger, looking down at her just as her world turned colorless, then dark gray, then black.

"And it's 'Bobby,' " she heard him say, just before all consciousness left her. "For now, anyway. . . ."

Less than forty-eight hours to negotiate a settlement before the tanks rolled in . . . and the residents of Terminal City weren't any closer now than they'd been when the police followed them into the parking garage last week.

Sitting in the media center, exhaustion weighing her down like her bones were made of lead, Max rubbed a hand over her face and wondered what she and her mutant band could do to stave off a full-scale army invasion.

Dix and his crew sat arrayed around the monitors, the room quiet, almost funeral, as they went about their business. Rubbing her forehead with the tips of her fingers, Max pondered her missing friends.

Alec and Joshua remained incommunicado in Clemente's custody, assuming the pair was still alive. Thinking back to her own hospital adventure—she'd been shot trying to save a kid's life, only to have a nurse try to administer a prescription of poison—Max wondered if Ames White had gotten to them yet.

She knew Logan could find out what hospital they were in; but even so, the risks of a rescue would be great. If White had located them, Alec and Joshua might already be dead, or moved, or simply used as bait for a trap to lure her. And if Max left Terminal City to go break them out, she would break faith with Clemente and put everything and everyone at risk.

If the only risk were her safety, she'd already be on her way. But now she had to take into consideration the effects of her actions on others.

Damn leadership, anyway—a pair of handcuffs.

Mole strode in, dropped his shotgun on the table and lit a cigar. He shook out the match and sat down across the table from her. "You okay, kiddo?"

"Peachy. Anything going on out there?"

He shook his lizard head. "Ever see them old war movies? 'Quiet—too quiet.' " He took a long drag on the cigar, then blew so much smoke out, it was like fog rolling in. "Cops ain't movin'. They seem content to just wait for the big boys to get here with their tanks and shit."

"Yeah—won't be long now. The whole damn circus will be in town."

"Our people, though . . ." His voice trailed off ominously.

"What?" she asked, sitting up.

"Mood's changing. They're worried out there, Max— maybe even scared. Look at the compound monitors."

Dix turned from his monitor. "Yeah, we got little pockets of somethin' or other, all over the place."

Max and Mole went up and looked over his shoulder. Almost every camera showed cliques of transgenics around the compound. Three or four, sometimes six or eight to a group, they all just seemed to be talking among themselves.

"What are they jawin' about, anyway?" Dix asked.

"They're planning," Max said. "In case we're not."

Mole puffed on his cigar. "Why? Don't we have a plan for when the Army gets here?"

She wished she had a good answer to that; but all she could give him was: "I'm still hoping it won't come to that."

"Yeah, I'm kinda hopin' my complexion clears up, too," he said, rubbing his reptilian cheek. "But just in case our dreams don't come true—" He waited for Max's eyes to meet his. "—might also make sense to have a plan in place."

Trouble was, there was no spin she could put on the notion of doing battle with the combined forces of the U.S. Army and National Guard within Terminal City that made it more palatable. "Tomorrow we'll put our heads together on that."

Sitting heavily on the edge of Dix's desk, the lizard commando said, "Anything you say, Scarlett O'Hara."

Not wanting to take this conversation any further, Max went back down the two stairs to the main floor. "Gotta check a couple of things. Be back."

Mole waved absently and Dix sat forward, eyes on his monitor, all his concentration focused on watching the splinter groups.

Stepping out into the sunshine, Max walked aimlessly for a while, allowing herself some quiet time. As she passed the groups they had seen on the monitors just a few minutes ago, some of the transgenics looked up at her expectantly. She smiled and tried to exude a confidence she didn't really feel. Most of them allowed her some space, but at the fourth group she passed, one of them—probably an X6, judging by the young man's features—separated himself and approached her.

He wore his brown hair shaved except for long braids set on each corner of his skull. His jeans and T-shirt both looked like they hadn't seen the inside of a washing machine for months. Thin-faced, he had wide-set brown eyes, a small, straight nose, and full lips.

As he fell into step beside her, a smile creased his face. "How ya doin'?" he asked.

Returning his smile, she said, "Good. You?"

His smile disappeared. "Kind of . . . worried, actually."

"I can understand that."

"Rumor says the Army's comin' soon and that they have orders to kill everybody. I even heard there might be an air strike."

"Doubtful," Max said. "The media blade cuts both ways. We have a few protesters supporting us, you know."

"Really?"

"Yeah—they got their own signs, 'Save the Transgenics,' 'Stop All Animal and Human Testing,' that sort of thing. Not a huge group, but it indicates support we can build on. What's your name?"

"Travis."

"Travis, it's going to be all right."

He frowned in thought. "So, the Army's not coming?"

"I didn't say that. I just don't think they're coming today."

"But when they *do* come . . . ?"

He was keeping up with her as she walked the compound.

"We'll be ready."

Now he found another smile. "Thanks. Can I tell that to my buddies?"

"Sure—tell everybody and anybody that whatever happens, we'll face it together."

The smile faded. "Frankly . . . that isn't much comfort, when you're worried that you're going to be . . . slaughtered. . . ."

Max stopped and so did the young man. She looked unblinkingly into his eyes. "That's what this whole thing is about, Travis. It's not about whether we win or lose or tie. It's about facing this together, not alone. The Army wouldn't have any trouble with just one of us, would they?"

Travis shook his head.

"But what about hundreds of us? Thousands?"

He saw her point and grinned. "I'll spread the word," he said.

As she watched him leave, with some spring in his step,

her cell phone chirped. She pulled it out and flipped it open. "Go for Max."

"Hey, you."

Logan.

She smiled. "Hey."

"I thought I should let you know—I'm going to be gone for a while."

"How long a while?"

"Most of the day probably," he said. "I'm meeting Asha at Crash. I think I've got a lead on Sage Thompson . . . and I need to talk to her about checking it out."

"Logan . . . it's getting tense here. I just talked to a young guy named Travis. He doesn't want the Army to come in and kill us all like animals."

"Can't blame him."

"What kind of name is that? Travis?"

"Well, Max . . . there was an officer at a famous battle in Texas, a long time ago, named Travis."

"What battle was that?"

"The Alamo."

"I haven't run across that in my reading, yet. How did it turn out?"

". . .Great. Everybody was a hero."

"That's something, anyway. Hey . . . be careful."

"I will. You too."

She disconnected.

Logan Cale sat at his desk looking at the phone for a moment.

Max sounded exhausted, and he wished there was more he could do to help her. She took so much on her shoulders, but now there was nothing to be done about that . . .

. . . except, maybe, get to the bottom of the skinner mystery, and see if clearing that hateful story out of the headlines could help ease the tension on the transgenics' situation in Terminal City.

Rising, Logan gathered his cell phone, his keys, and headed for the door. His car was parked near the end of the exit tunnel, and within ten minutes he was speeding toward the bar.

Crash, the favorite hangout of the Jam Pony gang, was nearly vacant at this hour of the day, the big video screens with the racing and other sports footage playing to a mostly nonexistent audience. Brick archways separated the Crash's three sections: the bar, the game room, and the restaurant area, with its tables and chairs. The jukebox, which usually screamed with metal-tinged rock music, stood mercifully silent; the occasional knock of pool balls from the back and the news on the television at the far end of the bar were the prominent sounds. A small lunch crowd would be in, in a half hour or so; but for the time being only the bartender and Asha were at the bar.

Logan came down the stairs and took a seat next to the blonde freedom fighter.

"Hi," she said.

"Hi, Asha."

A cup of coffee with cream sat in front of her. If it was her first, he wasn't that late. She'd taken only a few sips and the liquid still steamed.

The bartender, a skinny, tattooed guy with long, greasy, black hair, shambled toward them from the TV. His name was Ricky and he usually worked nights; judging from the bags under his eyes and the frown etched into his face, morning duty didn't suit him. He brought Logan a cup of coffee and shambled off again.

"He doesn't say much in the morning," Logan said.

Asha smiled. "He doesn't say much more at night. Now, tell me what the rush is."

"It's about that NSA agent we were looking for."

"Thompson," she said quietly.

He nodded. "I may have found something."

"Yeah?"

"Eyes Only has tracked him to the Armbruster Hotel."

"I know the place."

"Well enough to watch my back?"

"Oh yeah."

Daylight sliced across the bar, and they both looked up to see the silhouette of a man standing in the doorway. The sun blinded them and they couldn't see him clearly, but there was something about the guy that seemed familiar. The tail of the man's overcoat waved once more, then the door closed.

Blinking furiously to readjust his eyes, Logan peered up at the man, who was already halfway down the stairs: black hair slicked back, tight dark eyes, and an olive complexion; dark suit with a white shirt and conservative striped tie.

Logan turned casually to Asha, but his words were as urgent as they were quiet. "Go—he's White's man."

Asha slipped off the stool and meandered toward the back. She was a memory by the time the man came up and stood next to Logan, showing him a badge.

"I'm Special Agent Otto Gottlieb. Can we talk?"

Logan simply shrugged.

"May I sit?" Gottlieb asked, gesturing toward the stool.

"Free country."

"That's the theory," Gottlieb said as he hopped onto the stool. "Your friend sure left fast."

"Not my friend. I think she was a working girl, got a glimpse of you and thought, 'Cop.'"

"She wasn't wrong, was she? . . . Mr. Cale, I need to talk to you."

So he knew Logan's name.

Ever casual, Logan said, "I'm listening."

"Not here. We need to go somewhere else."

Smiling, Logan said, "You'll pardon me if I don't jump at the chance, Agent Gottlieb, but that's not the most enticing pickup line I've heard in a bar. . . . People who go 'somewhere else' with government agents, these days, have a tendency to disappear for good."

Gottlieb looked shaken, a bead of sweat trailing down one side of his face, like a teardrop that lost its way. "Look, Mr. Cale—you work for Eyes Only."

"Actually, I'm self-employed."

"I need to talk to him."

Logan smiled broadly. "Why sure, no problem. He's an underground cyber journalist you feds have been after for years . . . and now by simply asking me, you'll get a direct line to him, no questions asked. . . . And what would you like for your other two wishes?"

"Mr. Cale, what if I can give you an assurance that—"

"I don't work for Eyes Only. I share some of his distrust of the government, but it ends there. So maybe you better just leave."

Gottlieb didn't move. His attitude shifted, subtly. "As someone who doesn't know Eyes Only, Mr. Cale, can you tell me why your fingerprints were all over the apartment where we traced his last broadcast to?"

Logan started to rise, but Gottlieb put a hand on his arm. "I'm not here to arrest you. In fact, I have a gift for you—a show of good faith."

Withdrawing a manila envelope from his overcoat, he laid it on the counter between them.

Sitting down again, Logan asked, "What's this?"

"All the fingerprint files from the apartment. White never saw them."

Logan studied the agent; the man's face had a tortured sort of sincerity etched on it. "What about the NSA fingerprint people?"

"They're no problem," Gottlieb said. "They delivered the print identification just as they were supposed to . . . to me. Agent White lost interest in Eyes Only when the situation at Jam Pony came up. I give them to you now as a sign of my sincerity."

"These prove nothing," Logan said. "This could all still be in a computer anywhere."

"I've dealt with that. They're gone."

"Well, hell—what more assurance could I need than that?"

"Listen, Mr. Cale! Just hear me out."

Ricky the bartender wandered up. The agent shook his head and the bartender went back to the TV. Logan wanted to bolt, but after slipping the envelope inside his jacket, he turned to face Gottlieb. "So talk."

"Can't we go somewhere?"

"No—this place is empty and not bugged, unless you've bugged it. Tell me here or not at all."

After mulling that for a few seconds, Gottlieb kept his voice low and asked, "The name I mentioned earlier . . . the man I work for. You know him?"

Logan nodded.

"I think he may have gone rogue."

Laughing out loud, Logan said, "No wonder the NSA snapped you up—you don't miss anything. Anything else hot off the presses? Any word in yet about whether Nixon's a crook?"

Gottlieb's eyes fell, his face turning crimson, as he said, "I tried to give him the benefit of the doubt. We're supposed to be on the same team, after all, he and I."

"Ames White is on a team, all right," Logan said. "But not the one you're playing on, or any team that's trying to help this country."

"I figured that out."

"Good for you, Agent Gottlieb! Now, why don't you go

talk to your superiors about it?" Logan rose, tossed a bill on the bar, and took a step.

Gottlieb grabbed onto Logan's arm. "I can't talk to my superiors, or to anyone else in the government. White's got ties everywhere—I couldn't trust anyone. My friends in the government may be *his* friends. There's no way to know."

Logan let the hand rest on his arm as he nodded. "You're right about that much. But why Eyes Only?"

"If you can't trust your friends," Gottlieb said meaningfully, "who's left but your enemies?"

That was a good point.

"All right, follow me out," Logan said.

Then he climbed the stairs and headed outside. The sun had grown warm and felt good on his face. With Gottlieb stepping up next to him, Logan heard the cock of a gun and wondered if he'd been suckered . . .

. . . until he turned to find Asha standing behind them, her pistol aimed at Gottlieb's skull.

"Maybe we should find somewhere more private," Logan said as he lifted Gottlieb's pistol from its holster.

The three of them turned down an alley, trooping far away from the street and into the shadows, Gottlieb leading the way, but Asha prodding. The alley smelled of decaying food and urine; somewhere, a cat cried out. Slipping behind a Dumpster, the three of them stood out of sight of the traffic on the street, though Gottlieb still peered around nervously, looking for prying eyes and eavesdroppers.

"Tell us what you know," Logan ordered.

Otto Gottlieb gave them his story—all of it.

Logan had suspected much of what Gottlieb had to report, and had actually seen the assassins outside Jam Pony; but he knew they needed more.

"Do you have proof of any of this, Otto?"

Gottlieb shook his head. "There never is any—White calls it 'plausible deniability.' "

The phrase had an all-too-familiar ring to Logan. "Where *can* we get proof?"

"If I knew that, I wouldn't have come looking for Eyes Only."

Logan decided to change course. "Where's Sage Thompson?"

Looking as though he'd just been punched, Gottlieb asked, "How the hell do you know about him?"

"Because Eyes Only found out about Calvin Hankins."

"I can't believe it. . . ."

"Otto, do you know where Thompson is?"

"No! But if I did, he might be able to corroborate some of what I've told you."

The smell in the alley was as unpleasant as it was thick; Logan—ready to find a new office—said, "If you're on the level, Otto, you'll have to do exactly what I tell you."

Gottlieb sighed. "I'm good at that."

"You got a car?"

"Sure—just around the corner."

The three of them marched to the vehicle. Asha got behind the wheel, Otto sat on the passenger side, and Logan got in the back.

"Hand me your cuffs, will you, Agent Gottlieb?"

"Make it 'Otto.' " He fumbled around behind himself and got them out, then held the cuffs up over his shoulder.

"Right hand," Logan ordered.

Gottlieb frowned. "What?"

Asha stuck the gun in his ribs, and the agent's right hand went behind the seat.

Locking the bracelet over that hand, Logan said, "Now the left."

Gottlieb obeyed, awkwardly extending his other arm around the seat, and Logan cuffed him with his arms pulled behind him.

"What's this about?"

Logan got out and Asha rolled down the passenger side window for him to lean in. "Show of good faith or not, I can't trust you, Otto. So, you're going to have to trust me. Asha will watch you—she'll take you to a safe place. I'll join you as soon as I can. If I find Agent Thompson, we may be able to help you. If you're lying . . . well, I think you can fill in that blank, yourself. Do we have an understanding, Otto?"

Looking very scared, Gottlieb nodded.

Logan shook his head slowly. "I hope you're telling the truth, Otto. A lot of people are depending on you . . . and if we don't find Agent Thompson, they might all be in serious trouble."

And right now Otto Gottlieb looked like he knew all about what it was like being in serious trouble.

Chapter Ten
NO PLACE LIKE HOME

Alec opened his eyes to terrible, harsh brightness, and immediately shut them again. He tried to move his arm up to shield his face, but found the limb restrained, the other one too. Keeping his eyes closed, the light warm on his face, he tried to move his feet; they too were tethered.

"You're not going anywhere, 494," a familiar caustic voice said.

Alec's gut tensed: *Ames White*.

The X5 did not move, eyes shut, as if opening them had just been a twitch, a flutter in his sleep. A hand settled on his face, thumb under his chin, fingers and palm on his cheek, a chill snake-belly touch. The fingers began to tighten—White had the strength to crush a man's skull, even a transgenic like Alec.

"Open your eyes, 494," White said. "Or would you rather I close them forever?"

Alec opened his eyes and stared into the face of the cold-eyed NSA agent, who removed his hand from the X5's cheek, though the man still hovered over the right side of the bed like a vampire caught in the act. The agent—in his typical dark suit—had the sick pale look of a bloodsucker at that, his skin an unnatural white brought on by the fluorescent lighting.

Alec's head was swimming. "Is this . . . prison?"

"Don't be silly," White said, a small smile playing on thin, cruel lips. "It's a hospital. You're getting the best of care—your furry friend, too."

His head was settling down. "How did I get here?"

"The police. A friend of mine on the department whispered in my ear—something about your friend's dog snout that made some people think you two might be transgenic."

Restrained though he was, Alec was able to survey the small hospital room—it was empty but for himself and White. "I don't see a police guard. Is there one in the hall?"

"Maybe you'd like a map of the building? How else can I be of service? . . . The guard is federal, 494. Transgenics are the NSA's jurisdiction—but surely you know that?"

Alec smirked back at the man. "And you haven't killed us yet, because . . . ?"

"Why, I'm hurt, 494—you transgenics are citizens like any American."

"That's funny—I seem to remember you telling Congress we're a bunch of homicidal freaks."

"Aren't you? You stumbled in on the road show of *Silence of the Lambs,* didn't you? Courtesy of one of your own?"

"What the hell do you want? Why am I alive?"

The jokey mask fell and the emotionless, dead soulless son of a bitch Alec knew White to be was revealed in all his antiglory. "Because, 494—we're going to have a little talk, you and I."

Alec shook his head. "Could you have a nurse turn me over? So you can kiss my transgenic ass?"

A little half smirk colored the dead-eyed face. "Your choice—this is America, after all. You can die fast, or you can die slow, or—here's another option—you can die very fucking slow."

"How about none of the above?"

"No—not on the docket. Bottom line is, 494 . . . you and I are going to talk . . . and when we've explored our various areas of discussion, you'll be dead. Quick and painless, or slow and drawn-out—one from column A, or one from column B."

Alec spit in White's face.

Slowly, White wiped the saliva glob away with a middle finger, and flung it back in Alec's face.

"And while your body begins its inexorable journey to putrefication, I'm going next door and have the same chat with Dogboy. He should be easier—a chew toy, a little Alpo, and he'll be howling at the moon."

Alec managed a smile. "If Joshua ever gets his paws on you, White, you'll learn a whole new meaning for 'chew toy.' "

"I don't think so. I think he'll spill his canine guts and then we'll take him over to the pound—afraid we'll have to put the pooch down. Pity, isn't it?"

Taking a quick inventory, Alec decided that other than aching all over, he seemed to be pretty much all here; the conversation with White had given him time to gather his wits, and his mind felt clear.

He seemed to be wearing only a flimsy, sleeveless hospital gown, and he could sense the bandage from his bullet wound still covering his left shoulder. Straining against them, Alec realized he was cuffed to the bed, the metal bracelets jangling a little when he relaxed.

The X5 had a vague recollection of seeing a stun rod swing toward him, but that was his last memory.

Standing over him, making sure Alec saw every movement he made, White slowly opened a straight razor and seemed to savor the way the light caught the blade and winked.

"One of the many ways my people are superior to transgenics," White said conversationally, "is that we don't feel pain—simply don't experience it. Transgenics, on the other hand . . . when you prick them, they bleed."

"You're the prick who's gonna bleed," Alec snarled, fighting against the cuffs holding him down; but they wouldn't give. The metal dug into his wrists, the pain somehow calming, giving him strength.

"Where shall we start? . . . How about with your friend 452?"

Pulling against the cuffs with everything he had, Alec said nothing.

White slowly moved the blade back and forth, watching the light dance on steel. Against his will, Alec found himself watching the blade as well, as if it was a hypnotist's watch, trying to lull him into a terrible trance. The restraints continued to dig into his flesh, but he kept up the fight. . . .

"I want you to tell me how I can get to her."

"Climb the fence at Terminal City and whistle, dickweed."

"You and Lassie 'climbed the fence,' 494—and yet no one saw you do it. That compound is under close surveillance, but there must be a way out—and in—that no one knows about."

"Click your heels together and say, 'There's no place like home.' That should do it."

"A sense of humor. I like that, 494. I have one too . . . watch. . . ."

White leaned down close, his face only inches away from Alec, their eyes locked, then the agent made a narrow two-inch slice in Alec's right shoulder. Gritting his teeth against the pain, the young transgenic said nothing.

"I'm so pleased you're not cooperating, right away," White said. "You see, for all my strengths, I have one weakness . . . I do hate transgenics. . . ."

He opened the slice another inch.

Alec strained harder against the cuffs, his gaze still on White, the blood warm as it seeped from the wound and ran off his arm, the pain only spurring him on.

"I'll ask again, 494. How can I get to 452?"

"Go to hell and take a left."

White walked around the bed, his eyes never leaving Alec's. "I certainly hope you're enjoying this as much as I am."

"How could I enjoy it as much as a sick sadistic shit like you?"

The razor carved into his other arm, below the bandage covering his bullet wound. White made this cut about the same length as the first but a little deeper, the wound weeping tears of blood.

"There's a back way into Terminal City," White said. "I need to know what it is—you see, I want 452 in my own personal custody, before the Army swings through having their fun."

Alec, blinking away tears of pain, had to wonder: "Why?"

"Maybe I want her head to put over my fireplace—what concern is that to a dead man? Now, why don't you tell me the truth and I'll speed this up for you."

The door creaked open, and White spun. Alec, like White, threw his attention to the doorway, where a young, pretty African-American nurse stood, her mouth agape, hands flying up to cover it.

"What in God's name!" she cried.

Razor in hand, dripping rubies, White lurched forward and barked at her, "Get out! This is federal government business!"

The nurse—who apparently did not find this typical behavior from a federal law enforcement officer—shrieked bloody murder, and—with White momentarily distracted—Alec summoned all of his remaining strength to pull against the cuff around his wrist. With a shrill whine, the metal tube of the bed frame snapped and Alec's hand burst free.

As White spun back toward him, the razor rising in a wide arc, Alec swung his fist with everything he had behind it, catching White in the sternum, sending the agent sprawling, tumbling backward across the room and smacking hard into a wall, the razor flying out of his hand.

The nurse screamed again, turned and fled.

Alec knew he only had seconds now.

Jerking the bed frame on the left side, he broke that and slipped his left hand free. White had slid down the wall, and sat there in a rude pile, his eyes bleary, his mouth sagging open, sucking air in and out like a leaky bellows. The man might not feel pain, but physical damage nonetheless slowed him down.

From out in the hall, Alec could hear approaching footsteps. Sitting up, ignoring the blood running down his arms in narrow scarlet ribbons, he yanked off the bottom rail of the bed and slid it out, freeing his feet.

White used the wall to prop himself up and get back to his feet, his free hand disappearing inside his jacket, toward his pistol.

Alec leapt from the bed and ran over, blurringly fast, to pummel White with a right, then a left.

The agent hit the wall again and slid back down into his dazed sitting position, his gun clattering to the floor.

Sweeping out with his foot, White caught the backs of Alec's legs and sent him sprawling, as two more men in black stormed in, guns drawn. They hesitated for a moment, taking in the sight of their fallen leader. Rolling back under the bed, Alec came up and out on the other side, the bed now between him and his thoughtful visitors.

"Kill the bastard!" White bellowed.

The two swung their guns toward Alec, but the X5 was ready for them: he picked up his side of the bed and lifted, the whole thing coming up in front of him like a shield. Barreling forward, he felt bullets punch through the bed and exit, slowed, on either side of him. He heard the pistols' further reports just as he slammed the thing into the two agents and knocked them to the ground.

White was rising now, but Alec dove, and they reached the pistol at the same instant. As they wrestled for control, the two agents under the bed started moving and Alec heard shouts in the hall.

Only seconds remained.

Head-butting White, Alec knocked the agent senseless, grabbed the gun, and found the cuff keys in White's jacket pocket. As he spun, the two agents were clawing, climbing out from under the bed, both searching for their lost pistols.

Alec kicked the first one in the head, sending him promptly to dreamland, then spun and caught the second one under the chin with the butt of the pistol. He too went down for a long nap.

Stepping into the hall, Alec saw agents coming from both directions. He fired at both groups—aiming high, wanting to scare and back them off—and they scampered back around the corner, leaving the hall, for the moment, to Alec.

He sprinted to the door to the right of his room, opened it . . . and saw an empty bed. That made sense—White would keep the room next door vacant for security purposes.

Then he quickly ran to the door on the other side of his, on the left, and ducked inside. White had referred to Joshua being "next door"—Alec hoped that was literally true. The room was dark, the curtains drawn, no one in here but the patient in the bed.

If this wasn't Joshua's room, he knew he'd never get his friend out. He could hardly search the building, and would hate to have to abandon the naive dog man.

He looked quickly toward the big figure under the sheet. "Is that you, Joshua?"

". . . Is that you, Alec?"

Now, he—they—had a chance.

Sticking his head back out into the hall—still no men in black—Alec fired a couple more rounds in either direction, just to encourage the suckers to keep their distance. Moving to the bed, he uncuffed Joshua's right hand and gave him the keys.

"You all right?" Alec asked.

"I feel good—why are we in the hospital, Alec?"

"Okay, uncuff yourself, big guy. We gotta go. Ames White and his bozos are after us."

Scooting back to the door, Alec peeked out. The agents were making their move, hugging the walls and pushing tall stainless steel carts that held the food trays in front of them, as mobile shields.

Alec emptied the clip at them, bullets whanging off metal, and turned back to Joshua. "You ready?"

Joshua jumped off the bed. He too wore only a hospital gown, looking not a little absurd in it. "Let's blaze."

"Through the window," Alec said.

But when Alec went to it, the thing was firmly locked.

"Alec needs to stand back," Joshua advised.

And, in two steps, Joshua was standing in front of the wall-mounted television. Wrenching the box free, he pitched it, the glass of the window shattering as it flew through, the curtains jerking off the wall and going along for the ride. A few seconds later they heard the TV crash onto the concrete in a glass-shattering explosion.

Joshua looked out the now open window. "We're up high, Alec."

"There's a ledge. Move it! Go!"

Joshua climbed through the broken window, skillfully avoiding the teeth of glass waiting to bite him; soon he was out onto the ledge, and Alec quickly followed.

They were a good six or seven floors up, with a concrete expanse of parking lot beneath them. His back to the building, Alec could see something down in the parking lot, off to his right—a dumpster maybe?

Already sliding along the ledge, Joshua headed toward the window of Alec's room. Looking in that direction, Alec realized that White had opened the window in hopes they'd come that way.

"No!" Alec yelled.

But it was too late.

As Joshua neared it, Ames White leaned out, pistol in his hand.

Reacting instantly, Joshua grabbed White's gun arm and pulled. White came flying through the window. He squeezed the trigger, the shot going wild, into the sky. Sunlight off the window blinded Alec for a second. Then he heard White's yell of rage—not fear—as he fell.

Regaining his vision, Alec looked down to see White sprawled like he was making a snow angel in a dumpster full of garbage bags.

Turning to Joshua, Alec yelled, "Jump!"

"Jump?"

"Now!"

Gunshots exploded from the rooms on either side of them, and they both leapt into the afternoon air.

When they hit, even though the bags were soft, it felt like concrete. It took Alec only a few seconds to gather himself, and as he rose, he caught a whiff of the dumpster—medical waste disposal was pretty casual, in these post-Pulse times—and felt the sudden urge to vomit. From above, he heard no more gunfire—the agents were probably coming down after them—and he knew they had to shake it.

"Joshua!"

His large friend rose from the muck with Ames White tucked under his arm in a headlock.

"We've got to go," Alec said. "Kill him or drop him, I really don't give a shit."

Yanking White's face up by the hair, Joshua thrust his leonine countenance into the agent's barely conscious, slack features.

"You should die for the things you've done," Joshua said.

"But if I kill you, Max says you win—you make us look like monsters. But you're the monster."

White's upper lip curled back in an awful grin. "Freak."

Joshua punched the agent once, knocking him out.

"Soon," he said to the slumbering agent. "Soon you'll pay for Annie."

"We've got to blaze," Alec urged, "gotta jet," using the Max idioms that would get Joshua moving his hairy ass.

The two friends in hospital gowns climbed out of the dumpster and took off at a run, their bare feet slapping against the pavement as they went.

Alec knew how much Joshua wanted to destroy White for killing Annie Fisher, Joshua's one friend among the ordinaries, a blind girl who hadn't cared what the dog man looked like, and who could "see" past Joshua's stunted social and intellectual growth to the sensitive, intelligent being just starting to blossom after a lifetime of Manticore abuse.

But Alec knew Joshua had no desire to disappoint Max, and she'd kept him from killing White once before. The big fella wouldn't go against Max's wishes.

And if Joshua knew how Alec had manipulated him into leaving Terminal City—very much against Max's wishes—Joshua would be angry as hell . . . though Alec knew his friend would forgive him. He always did.

As they made their way through the streets, their gowns flapping in the breeze, Alec realized they had to get back to Terminal City, and fast—and they had to tell Max they now knew the identity of the killer.

The problem was, they were miles away, with no transportation, and—in broad daylight—the normal-looking Alec was running along next to a seminude six-foot-six-inch 240-pound dog boy. And, of course, both were wearing hospital gowns, not exactly a current fashion trend.

Alec almost laughed at the absurdity of it. Of all the contingencies that Manticore had trained their test-tube soldiers for, this particular one had never come up.

His arms didn't hurt, but the now-dried stripes of blood on his arms might draw attention as fast as them running with their asses hanging out of the gowns. They had to get off the damn street, toot sweet.

The neighborhood they were sprinting through looked vaguely familiar to Alec, and he realized suddenly—when Joshua made a right past a grocery store—that the big guy knew right where they were and where he was going. They had been held at County General less than two miles from Joshua's old pad—"Father's" house.

So they should be able to easily make their way to the large Gothic home that had belonged to Sandeman, their Manticore creator—about whom they knew little—before the man—the only benign presence at the project—had disappeared. *Better to be lucky than smart,* Alec thought. They both had clothes on hand from when they'd lived there together, and the phone had been reconnected once Logan had taken over. Should still be working. . . .

Cars were sparse in the neighborhood in mid-afternoon, and the sidewalks were all but empty. Then, in the distance, Alec spotted a car coming toward them, a dark model that just might be government issue.

"Joshua," he said. "Car!"

But Joshua seemed to be ahead of him. The car, stopping in the middle of the next intersection, was a little over two blocks away when Joshua pulled off a manhole cover and climbed down out of sight. The vehicle now only a block away, Alec followed Joshua down and pulled the manhole cover back in place only seconds before he heard wheels rolling over it.

The aroma down here wasn't any more pleasing than the dumpster back at the hospital. Standing in dirty brown water that came almost to his knees, Alec shivered in the foul, frigid stuff; but Joshua didn't seem to mind or even notice. Alec took off walking after his towering friend, who knew these tunnels as well as anyone in the city.

In the months since Max freed Joshua from Manticore, the sewers had served as a mini-underground railroad for the big guy, allowing him to move around the city without detection. Alec figured the sewer system was how Joshua had managed to stay in touch with the janitor, Hampton, without anyone knowing that he was ever gone.

Twenty minutes later, they dried off and changed into their own clothes in the run-down house, the interior of which had been taken over by Logan after the trashing of his penthouse; no sign of Logan right now, though.

Joshua's wardrobe ran exclusively to T-shirts—size XXXL—and jeans, while Alec had left little more than that behind himself. While Joshua never made inconspicuous company, getting the big lug out of that hospital gown was, Alec knew, a good start. . . .

Picking up the phone, Alec dialed Max's cell. In the silence before the ring, his transgenic hearing picked up a low frequency hum, and he knew someone—the NSA? the National Guard?—was trying to trace the call.

He slammed down the receiver.

Should have thought of that. He'd seen how many times Max had used her cell, so of course the government would have the number and be tracing all incoming and outgoing calls. Another reason to get back to Terminal City, to tell her to ditch the phone.

But how to get back?

It was miles away and would take them hours, even if they did use the sewers to avoid being seen.

He needed someone on the outside, and neither Original Cindy nor Sketchy had wheels; still, they were the only two people he knew that he could trust, so he started dialing.

Original Cindy's cell went unanswered; Alec didn't know

what to make of that. He had no time to spare to ponder it, though, and he dialed Sketch.

"A car?" Sketchy asked when the greetings were out of the way. "I guess I could borrow a car."

"We need you to pick us up at Joshua's house," Alec told him.

"What are you doin' on this side of the fence?"

"Not now, Sketch. Just get the car and haul ass over here. I'll explain everything on the way back to Terminal City."

"Fifteen minutes," Sketchy said. "Half hour, tops."

Forty-five minutes later, they were still watching out the window when a beat-up van pulled to a stop in front of the house.

"I gotta get myself a better support system," Alec said.

"Yeah," Joshua added. "We gotta blaze."

They climbed in the old van and Sketchy hit the gas. But soon they were lumbering through heavy traffic, and Alec explained what had happened, and who the killer was.

"Bobby Kawasaki?" Sketch said, suddenly very white. "From Jam Pony, you mean?"

"Yeah—he's a transgenic, passing. . . . You okay, Sketch?"

But Sketchy's eyes were wide and woeful. "Christ! I think I saw him this morning, with Original Cindy. I'm pretty sure they left together. Then I didn't see either one of them the rest of the day. Never reported back from their first deliveries—Normal was really pissed."

Alec looked at Sketch and the van went dead quiet.

"Sketch—you better step on it."

Bobby Kawasaki sat in the worn wing chair and watched the crappy signal on a TV produced in some third-world shithole back before Pulse. The cheap motel room was dusty and dingy and had seen few customers on more than an hourly basis for most of the last ten years; but the desk clerk,

a tiny Asian man with thick glasses and thinning hair, asked
only one question: "You got cash?"

Bobby's project hung safe in the closet on a hanger—he'd
had to leave the mannequin behind—and Original Cindy lay
on the sagging bed with a compress on the nasty bump on
her head. He had meant to scare her, but when she'd taken
that tumble off her bike, the woman took a much nastier spill
than he'd anticipated. Glancing over at her now, he wondered
if she would ever wake up.

After her crash, he'd left her bike lying in the street,
loaded her onto his own bike and pedaled straight back to
the motel, with her riding in his lap, her legs tossed up over
the handle bars. From a distance she would have looked like
she was having a joy ride, her face pressed into the cheek of
her boyfriend. It wasn't the greatest ruse, but people minded
their own business in Seattle, and it had gotten them back
here to safety and seclusion.

Taking her to a hospital was out of the question. He'd lose
control of her there, and be right back where he started. That
was also the risk of keeping her here. If she died, she would
be of no help to him, which would be a pity, after all
the trouble he'd gone to. The trap he'd laid for her this
morning—letting her see him take the Tryptophan—had
worked like a charm.

Well, at first it did, anyway. Bobby had gotten the woman
talking, and she seemed about to help him of her own voli-
tion, when something he'd said seemed to make her wary.
Though he'd run the conversation over and over in his head,
he still didn't know where he'd made the mistake.

It didn't matter now anyway. If she died, he'd dump her—
her skin was the wrong shade and size to be of use to his
project, after all. If she awakened, she would help him. If she
didn't help him, he would kill her.

Bobby watched her ample chest as it rose and fell in shallow breaths. She was still with the living—the question was, for how much longer? Turning back to the television, he watched the Satellite News Network, looking for stories about Terminal City.

Though the national news still covered it, the siege seemed relegated to the back burner as earthquakes and other catastrophes started shoving at each other for space on the little screen. The local news still seemed largely focused on the siege, however; interestingly, a few protransgenics protesters had also shown up—FREAKS ARE PEOPLE TOO, one sign said, and BAN TRANSGENIC TESTING, said another.

Original Cindy moaned, and Bobby went to check on her. Slowly, as if every centimeter of movement caused excruciating pain, she moved a hand up to the washrag on her forehead. She touched it gingerly and her eyes fluttered, then opened wide.

Looking up at him, she managed to say, "You—Bobby."

He smiled a little. "You remembered my name. I'm flattered."

"What . . . what happened?"

"Your bike took a tumble. I picked you up and brought you here." He could tell by her eyes that she didn't remember clearly, yet, and what he was saying made little sense to her.

"Where's . . . here?"

"Just a motel."

She tried to sit up, but the pain obviously forced her back, her hand again going to the lump. "This bitch hurts."

"Probably a concussion," Bobby said.

"Why did you bring me to the No Tell Motel? If you think you're gettin' some, you ain't been payin' attention to Original Cindy's predilections—short form: you ain't gettin' none. Concussion or not, I'll kick your scrawny ass."

He smiled. "That's not what I want from you."

Confusion tightened her eyes.

He went on: "I just want to join the others."

She still didn't get it.

"At Terminal City, I mean."

"That's right," she said slowly, her voice thick with discomfort. "You're a transgenic."

He watched her wrestling with that. If she remembered what had freaked her out this morning, they'd have to do it the hard way. If she didn't remember, then she might still help him on her own. Her eyes cleared slowly; from the look of her, she didn't remember a thing.

"I should probably get my beautiful booty over to the ER," she said. She tried to sit up again, but had no more success than the first time.

Helping her lean forward, he propped up the pillows behind her. "Aren't there doctors in Terminal City?"

Her eyes tightened again, this time mockingly. "You shittin' me, right? They make doctors out of any of you Manticore men? You killin' machines, not healin'."

"I don't know—a lot of the X5s and X6s have medical training."

"Maybe so, but I don't know if I can make it over there— can I rest for a while first?"

He didn't like that, but she'd been cooperative enough, so he said, "A while longer, Cindy—then we've got to go. Or do we need to wait till dark?"

She studied him. He knew what she was thinking: if she trusted him, and Bobby turned out to be a spy for the feds or something, she might be endangering everybody inside those fences.

Finally, she said, "No—I can get us in, during the day. No problem."

"Great—but you better be quiet and rest, because I'm really anxious to join my brothers and sisters."

Lying back, she closed her eyes.

Original Cindy was tired, and still woozy from the probable concussion. But as she began to drift off to sleep, she suddenly remembered why she'd crashed. . . .

It had been him—Bobby Kawasaki—he'd scared her.

So tired, so tired, but she thought something about his wanting into Terminal City so badly was . . . whack. She didn't know what that was, exactly—it was her gut, and Original Cindy listened to her gut, it was a goddamn eloquent instrument, and she knew this nondescript little brother was *wrong* . . . and she had to buy as much time as she could until she figured out a way to warn Max.

In what seemed like seconds—which was a little over an hour later—she felt hands on her, as he shook her awake.

"Come on, Cindy—rise and shine! Time to go."

Groggy, she managed to sit up; but the pain filled the whole side of her head, ran into her neck, down her shoulder and into her arm. It might only be a concussion but, damn, girl! *Everything* hurt.

"I've got to call them," she told him, "to tell them we're coming."

"No—no calls. Come on. Get up. You need my help?"

"They . . . they won't let us in."

He shook his head. "If they're not maintaining radio silence, they should be, and I'm not going to be the one to break it. We'll worry about getting in when we're there. Come on."

"How . . . how are we going to get there?" she asked. Her legs were rubbery. "My head's poundin' like a bitch. I can't walk."

"We'll flag down a cab."

He let her lie there while he pulled out a large suitcase and laid it open on top of the dresser. She watched as he pulled something big and tan out of the closet and gently folded it inside the case. The object looked like leather, a patchwork garment, very amateurish, even primitive; but she couldn't be sure what she was seeing, exactly. Between her fuzzy

vision and the duskiness of the room, it could have been almost anything. . . .

Bobby put a small flashlight in one pocket, tucked a long
knife and scabbard into his boot, and carried a stun rod
under one arm.

She noted this, the knife and the stun rod reasonable pre-
cautions for a transgenic . . . but that intelligent stomach of
hers was sending warning signals. . . .

Once Bobby had packed up, he none too gently led her
outside. She recognized the neighborhood, once they exited
the motel. The only good thing was that in a slum this
dumpy, it would take them forever to get a cab, even in the
middle of the day.

Unfortunately, he'd been kidding about the cab. The first
car they came to, he broke into, tossed her inside in the front,
put the suitcase in the back, and hot-wired the car.

As they drove, she focused all her energy on trying to
think of a way to warn her sister.

Max was worried, and wishing she could trade this leadership gig in on kicking the crap out of some bad guy, any
bad guy.

Alec and Joshua were still missing, Logan had been gone
for some time now and she hadn't heard so much as a peep
from him, and when she tried to call Original Cindy, her
Boo's cell phone had this odd buzz to it, and no dial tone.
Stomping into the media center, she tossed the phone on a
table.

"Any ideas?" she asked Dix.

His half smile was only technically a smile. "Cell phone
ain't working, is it?"

She shook her head angrily.

"None of 'em are," he said. "Looks like the feds are taking the gloves off. Instead of just monitoring our transmissions, they're jamming them now. They cut off the power

into the area, a couple of hours ago. By now they've figured out we have our own generator."

Luke walked in, an empty glass in his hand. "They just cut the water."

"Is our system up?" she asked.

Dix shook his head. "But we're close—fifteen, maybe twenty-four hours, we'll be up and runnin'."

"Hope we've got that long," she said.

Those who were the closest to her—the inner circle of Logan, Joshua, and Alec—were now all outside the perimeter, and she could no longer contact any of them. Well, at least she could talk to Clemente. Who woulda thunk that cop would be her new best friend?

She said, "I'll be back," and strode out of the media center.

Max bounced down to the fence line and found the Guardsmen and police officers huddled behind the cars in tense silence. "Hey, guys! Where's Clemente?"

Several of them shrugged, and a couple said, "Don't know."

Across the way, Colonel Nickerson came out of the restaurant where she'd met Clemente. She watched as he marched over, ramrod straight.

"Colonel, I need to talk to Clemente."

He shook his head. "Detective Clemente's on assignment and can't be reached."

"Well, reach him anyway."

"No." He frowned in such a way that it encompassed his whole body. "Detective Clemente's off the front lines. You may have noticed, we've turned off the power and water and jammed communications in and out. This is going to end, 452. It's going to end soon."

She thought about leaping the fence, kicking his ass, then jumping back over. *Can't do it*, she told herself. *Gotta be mature. . . . Damn leadership, anyway.*

"Thanks ever so," she said, and turned back toward the compound.

Time to call a meeting.

Half an hour later, the whole mess of them had gathered again in the garage.

"There's no water!" someone yelled.

Dix stepped forward. "We're working on it. One more day at the most."

The crowd grumbled at that.

"We've got bigger things to talk about," Max said, taking over again.

"Is the Army really coming in?" one of them called, and several others more or less echoed the question—literally, in the cavernous garage.

"That," she said, "is the threat."

Contradictory shouts erupted everywhere:

"We've got to go!"

"Fight 'em!"

"Fight with what?"

Max held up her hands but it did no good. The crowd—this outcast mix of the beautiful and the grotesque—was only a heartbeat away from chaos.

Stepping forward, Mole raised his shotgun, aiming it up the ramp into the next level. He glanced at her for permission—and Max nodded her go-ahead: the cops couldn't possibly think they were being fired upon, neither could the crowd, and cement dust wouldn't come raining down on them if he fired it straight up into the roof.

Mole fired once and, when the roaring echo had died, the place went eerily silent. He had gained their undivided—if somewhat momentarily hearing-impaired—attention.

"A week ago," the lizard man yelled, circling as he spoke, "I wanted to run!"

A voice shouted, "You were right!"

Mole looked in the direction of the voice as he pumped another round into the chamber—the pumping of the shotgun was a small sound that seemed very loud. "Shut the fuck up. It's *my* turn to talk."

No one argued.

"I wanted to run," Mole said, "and Max made her speech about not living in fear anymore . . . and it was a goddamn good speech, that all of us heard, and took to heart . . . and yet here you all are, a buncha candy-asses ready to run as soon as the goin' gets a little tough."

They were all listening attentively.

"Well, not me!" He chewed on his cigar, wheeling around, seeking any face that might disagree. "This place is a shithole—and some of us have been here a hell of a lot longer than a week—but it's *our* shithole . . . and I think that no matter what comes, it looks like this is our home."

Some of them nodded.

"Every pioneer carves his home out of the wilderness. . . . Well, this is our wilderness, and this is our home. And I'm ready to fight to protect my home, if it comes to that. If there's a peaceful solution, fine. If not," he raised the shotgun over his head, "they can bring it on."

Scattered cheers erupted, and began to grow. Applause followed, and built into an echoing simulation of machinegun fire, over which could be heard chanting: *"Term-i-nal City . . . Term-i-nal City . . . Term-i-nal City!"*

Max waited, enjoying the enthusiasm, the esprit de corps; finally she stepped forward and raised a fist.

The room fell silent; and fists were thrust high.

Max said, "We will do everything we can to end this peacefully! . . . But Mole is right. Terminal City may be nothing to brag about, but it's our home . . . and we're not running anymore."

Luke came in carrying the flag Joshua had made. He handed it to Max and she waved it overhead as the crowd cheered.

Like their surroundings, it wasn't much, but it was theirs, and if they had to defend it, they would do so to the death.

Chapter Eleven
DYING TO MEET YOU

After what seemed like hours in snarled Seattle traffic, Logan Cale finally pulled up to the well-worn seven-story brick structure that was the Armbruster Hotel—at one time, *the* place to stay in the Emerald City . . . of course, those days had ended not long after the Gold Rush of 1896. The canvas awning over the front door, once forest green, had long since faded into a limp pastel pup tent, while the grand entrance—wide smoked glass that had at one time been clear—was attended by winos, not liveried doormen.

Logan punched numbers into his cell phone.

Asha picked up immediately. "Yes?"

"It's me. I'm finally here—with the price of gas, you wouldn't think traffic jams would be a problem. How's our guest?"

"He's been a very good boy."

"I wonder if he's for real," Logan said.

"If he isn't . . ."

"Asha will spank. Okay, start the clock. If you haven't heard from me within half an hour, you know what to do."

"Roger that," she answered, and the line went dead.

Entering the lobby, Logan was greeted by an aroma that was a cross between one of Mole's cigars and a YMCA men's locker room. Ratty carpeting and shabby furniture were overseen by an elaborate cut-glass chandelier that loomed like a reminder of better days; and, off to the right, the front desk remained impressive, too: it looked like an oak bar from a western movie. When this place was torn down someday, the chandelier and that oak piece would be about all that anyone would bother to salvage.

Behind the counter, seated on a high stool, was a lumpy-faced sixtyish guy so white that Logan would have mistaken him for an albino Manticore experiment, if the man's eyes hadn't been so dark, like a couple of raisins adorning a dish of ice cream. The desk clerk was hunkered over a magazine—*Barely Legal Teen*—which, Logan realized as he drew close enough to get a look at the cover, was neither about the law nor aimed at a teenage audience.

The white-haired clerk made no effort to hide the porn mag when Logan got to the counter, nor did he look up.

"Excuse me," Logan said.

Finally tearing himself away from the photos of naked girls, the clerk glanced up at Logan with eyes that were deader than rap music.

"You have a guest here named Thomas Wisdom. Could I have his room number, please?"

"No."

"No?"

"We don't just hand that information out to anybody who asks. Don't you think our guests deserve their privacy?"

Logan glanced at the magazine. "How much is a subscription to that fine periodical?"

The clerk's eyes narrowed. "It's a monthly. Cover price is eight ninety-five."

"But you save money when you subscribe."

"Still . . . probably run fifty bucks."

"I see. And it'd come in a plain brown wrapper?"

The clerk got Logan's drift and nodded. "Sure. Nice and discreet."

From his billfold, Logan withdrew a crisp fifty dollar bill. "Which room did you say my friend Mr. Wisdom was in?"

"417, sir."

Logan placed the fifty-dollar bill over one of the nude photos. "Enjoy," he said.

A tiny yellow smile appeared in the lumpy white face.

Then Logan reached out and grabbed the clerk's wrist. "You know what I hate, though, when I subscribe to a magazine?"

The dark eyes were large now. "No—what?"

"When they call up and ask me to resubscribe. On the phone?"

"Why don't I hold all of Mr. Wisdom's calls for you?"

"Would you? You're a dear."

By way of contrast with the lobby stench, the elevator smelled like urine. As the floors dinged by, he wondered if he was walking into an Ames White trap. Though tracking Thompson had been tough, the computer techniques he'd used could easily be anticipated by White, who knew of Eyes Only's techno bent. If Otto Gottlieb was either lying, or a pawn, then. . . .

As the doors slid open on the fourth floor, Logan decided the pistol snugged behind him should stay put—if he approached Thompson with gun in hand, the wrong signal would be sent, and things could go violently awry. Anyway, no point letting his paranoia get the best of him. On the other hand, paranoia had kept him alive more than once, in the Eyes Only game. . . .

Every surface in the hall appeared to be some shade of gray, from the cheap carpeting to the peeling paint on the walls; even the wall-mounted lights, hung every six feet or so, seemed to be covered with a patina of age-old smoke. As he walked down the corridor—the room he sought was down around the corner—the urine smell gave way to Lysol.

Logan approached the door marked 417 cautiously, then stood to one side and reached over to knock.

No response—and no noise within the hotel room, either . . . not a radio or TV, or someone getting up from a chair; nothing.

Logan really needed Thompson to be home—and his gut told him, despite the silence, the man was on the other side of that door. Thompson was hiding out, burrowed in; damnit, he was here—he *had* to be. . . .

Stepping closer, Logan knocked again. Still nothing. A third knock was also answered with silence.

Or maybe his gut was wrong. Logan wondered if the porn-loving desk clerk had known Thompson was out when he sold him the information. . . .

In frustration, Logan spoke to the door, loudly: "Mr. Wisdom—Mr. Wisdom! I need to talk to you." Then he leaned in and listened to nothing at all. Finally, he nearly shouted: *"Mr. Thompson—"*

The door snapped open, to a wide crack, and Logan found himself staring into the gray snout of a Glock barrel.

"Keep your voice down! Do you want to get me killed?"

Forcing himself to look past the barrel of the gun, Logan saw a skinny, pasty-faced white man only a few years younger than himself, with matted dark hair, an untrimmed beard, and eyes that looked both exhausted and terrified.

"No, Mr. Thompson—I want to help you stay alive."

The hand holding the gun was trembling; Logan realized the man with the weapon was seconds away from blasting him into eternity. . . .

"Until about three months ago, Mr. Thompson," Logan said as calmly as he could manage, "you worked for the NSA, where your supervisor was a very bad egg named Ames White."

Thompson cocked the gun, and the barrel continued to tremble; but Logan knew he'd bought himself some time.

Thompson demanded, "Who are you?"

"My name's Logan Cale. I'm a journalist. I was sent by Eyes Only—I think you should recognize that—"

The barrel waved an invitation. "Get in here!"

Logan did as he was told, and as soon as they were both in the room, Thompson shut and locked and night-latched the door.

The room was a mess—bedclothes scattered, pizza boxes and fast food cartons littering the floor, the scent of stale sweat permeating everything. A portable TV perched on a scratched-up dresser—news on, sound down—a worn-out armchair occupied a corner, and a nightstand next to the bed held a pitiful table lamp that at the moment supplied the only light in the room—even though it was mid-afternoon, the curtains were pulled tight and scant light made it in from outside.

The former NSA agent wore a sleeveless white undershirt, black suit pants, black socks, and no shoes. Logan wondered if the guy had been out of this room at all, since checking in.

Glock at the ready, Thompson peered quickly through the peephole into the hall. Satisfied, he turned back to Logan.

"Clasp your hands behind your head."

"You *will* find a gun," Logan said, as he complied, and Thompson patted him down and found the pistol.

"Since when do reporters go packing?" Thompson asked, an eyebrow raised in the bearded, skeptical mask of his face.

"Since they linked up with Eyes Only," Logan said. "The authorities consider what we do to be cyber terrorism—you should know that . . . you were with the NSA."

Thompson slipped the clip out of Logan's pistol and ejected the shell in the chamber. He stuffed the pistol in his belt; the ammo he slipped in a pants pocket.

Then he pressed the snout of the Glock to Logan's temple,

eyes wild as he said, "How do I know White didn't send you?"

"If White had sent me, you'd probably be dead right now."

"Or *you* would."

Logan—hands still clasped behind him, cold snout of the nine millimeter still kissing his temple—managed to shrug. "Or I would. . . . White does want you dead, right?"

Thompson's mouth dropped open. "Why the hell do you say that?"

"Pieces are falling together. Otto Gottlieb told me—"

The pistol pressed harder into Logan's flesh. "Otto's *one* of them."

"No. He's bolted the NSA too. And anyway, he was never on the inside of White's schemes—he was like you, just a good little NSA soldier. . . . Can I put my arms down?"

"No. But keep talking."

"Gottlieb thinks that what happened to you and your partner—and some other off-kilter things that have been going down—are somehow White's doing."

"A transgenic killed my partner."

"That's the party line, isn't it? Whatever the case, Gottlieb finally realizes White's gone rogue. And part of what White's up to has to do with some . . . some friends of mine, who he's trying to hurt."

Thompson wasn't keeping up. "Rogue? Friends of yours?"

But the Glock had lowered; the bearded former agent had let it slip away from Logan's head. . . .

"Yeah," Logan said. "Several of my friends, actually."

Eyes flashing with the abruptness of it, Thompson changed subjects. "How the fuck did you find me?"

"People hiding under an assumed name often do so under a variant of their real name—helps them fight the loss of identity that comes with going underground."

"Shit," the ex-agent said, knowing.

Logan went on: "I started with your mother's maiden
name, names of people you went to school with, any name
that you'd come in contact with, then I put every anagram of
your name into the computer; after that, I listed synonyms
for 'sage' and fed in Tom and Thomas, under various
spellings, for Thompson . . . and waited for the computer to
spit something out."

Even hotels like the Armbruster had to list their guests
with the government's database; the Travel Security Act
dated back pre-Pulse, one of many repressive laws born out
of a fear of terrorism.

"Shit," Thompson said again.

"Now," Logan said, hands still behind his head, "I have a
question for you."

Thompson—gun in hand but not pointed at Logan—just
looked at him, obviously still pissed at himself for picking a
name that could be traced to him, a pro who should've
known better.

"Why didn't you run?" Logan asked.

"I didn't know, at first."

"That you were set up, you mean."

"Yeah. I mean, I knew I was being railroaded out of the
NSA; but I was healing up from a broken arm—"

"Your file says you took early retirement on full disability
pay."

"That's right . . . which, frankly, made me even more suspicious. It was almost like—"

"You were being paid off."

"Yes! But finally I knew White and his people would be
looking for me, and after I sent my family away, I knew they
would think I ran too. So . . . I didn't."

That made only vague sense to Logan, who said, "Look—
could I put my hands down?"

"Yeah . . . yeah . . . sorry."

"Why don't we sit and talk about this?"

Logan took the chair and a dejected-looking Thompson sat on the bed, the Glock in his hands, draped between his legs. He looked like a man trying to decide whether or not to kill himself.

"Your arm looks like it healed fine," Logan said conversationally.

Flexing his left arm, Thompson said, "It's still sore sometimes." His face changed, curiosity overcoming fear. "Why are you here? Why come looking for me?"

"Surely you know about what's going on at Terminal City?"

Thompson nodded. "About all I do is watch the tube—I see the news. What about it?"

"Those people are the friends I was talking about—and I'm trying to help them. White's putting the squeeze on, to get the federal government to invade and kill all the transgenics. Total genocide."

Thompson shook his head. "Can't help you, then. After what one of those . . . those *freaks* did to my partner, killing 'em *all* is fine by me."

"Are you sure that a transgenic killed your partner?"

Thompson nodded so vigorously he bounced on the edge of the bed. "Listen, Cale—before the NSA, I did time in the Army and was a cop in Los Angeles. I've seen the evil shit that people can do to each other . . . but I've never seen *anything* like what happened to Hankins."

"He wasn't the last, either."

"No—I mean, *skinned*! No normal person could do that—only a monster bred to do atrocities, trained to kill—"

"Bred by the government. Trained to kill by men like Ames White."

"Even so, these transgenics need to be put down—whether it's out of getting even for victims like my partner, or just to put the bastards out of misery—I don't really give a damn. As long as those monsters are wiped out."

"And yet . . . you still believe you were set up by Ames White, right?"

The two men locked eyes, and Thompson said, "We were sent into combat with rubber bullets, Cale. Look—Hankins was a son of a bitch, but he was goddamn good at his job. We were using those new portable thermal imagers—"

Logan held up a hand. "Whoa—I don't know what a . . . thermal imager?"

Thompson nodded.

"I don't know what a thermal imager is."

The agent explained the devices and how they worked; the new devices were under White's personal lock and key. "Anyway, that night last March, in that warehouse—the imager would have shown Cal something if it was working right. Mine too—only it showed nothing."

"Nothing?"

"That's how I got my arm broken! The thing at first gave me a hot reading, then farted out on me. It should have read hot for that homeless guy in that office—he just wouldn't have come up as hot as a transgenic. But it didn't show *shit*! The imagers don't lie, and yet this one told me that room was empty. And Hankins wasn't up against some homeless mook—he was facing a transgenic."

"I'm sorry about your partner," Logan said.

Thompson shrugged. "Thanks. Funny thing is, I never even liked the guy. He really was an asshole . . . but nobody should have to die that way. . . ."

Logan watched the man's face tighten in remembered horror as he relived the moment of discovering his mutilated dead partner.

"Nobody," Thompson repeated, ". . . 'cept maybe Ames White. . . ."

"Do you still have the imager?"

Thompson shook his head. "Company property. Like my gun and my badge. Your buddy Agent Gottlieb took it all when he hauled me to the hospital. Having my partner killed, being injured—plus I shot a civilian—I was put on immediate administrative leave. Last I saw my imager, it was in Otto's hands."

Logan made a mental note to ask Gottlieb about that. "What happened after that?"

"Agent White was livid that one of the imagers had been stolen by the transgenic. He said if the transgenics—and some of them are very smart—figured out the technology, they could also figure out a way to beat it. He expected us to guard those things with our lives. Anyway, after Agent Gottlieb took my gun, my badge, and the imager, I could see the writing on the wall. My career was over."

"How did they manage that? You don't go on full disability for a broken arm."

"They had me talk to an NSA shrink—that was the excuse. I shot that homeless guy, remember. Isn't any of that in the file? That my disability is mental?"

"Not what I saw. But it sounds like you had a free pass—why are you in hiding?"

"That first night, at the hospital—while I was waiting for them to cast my arm—I started thinking about those imagers, and how they couldn't possibly have been working right. Agent Gottlieb had already left—there was no reason for him to babysit me, so he was gone." Thompson sat forward, his eyes haunted. "But the more I thought about it, the more I thought these two imagers were defective and, so, were dangerous . . . and someone else could run into the same fatal snag we did."

"So you called Agent White."

"A few days later, finally I called him. He told me he'd meet me at my house later, to talk about the problem. Then he asked me if I'd talked to anyone else about the defective equipment. When I said no, he said, 'Good,' and then told me not to mention it to anyone until after I talked to him. Man, my hackles rose—him wanting me to meet him, alone. At my house!"

"And you ran instead."

"I ran instead." Thompson shivered. "There was something cold in his voice, almost . . . inhuman. My gut told me that if my family and I didn't bolt, we'd all end up dead."

"You took this extreme action, based on a gut reaction?"

"That, and, well—I believed . . . and I believe right now . . . that the only way those imagers could be defective, both of them, was if White arranged it himself. He sent me, and my partner, into that warehouse, to die."

"Why?"

"I don't know. But I worked with White long enough to know that people around him had a bad habit of dying when they got in his way. And I wasn't about to take any chances with my family."

"When do you plan to join them?"

"When I . . . finish what I have to do."

Suddenly Logan understood. "You're lying low . . . waiting until you think you've dropped off White's personal radar, and then . . ."

"And then I'm going to kill his evil ass."

Logan could well understand the impulse. "Agent Thompson, there's only one problem with your plan . . ."

"Yeah—'Thomas Wisdom.' If you could track me, he'll be able to."

Logan shook his head. "No—a bigger problem than that. White's not just with the government. I can't explain it all now, there really isn't time. But he's involved with a . . . subversive group that is bigger and more dangerous than the government."

"Cale, I don't share your sympathies with the transgenics, nor do I go for Eyes Only's wild-eyed conspiracy theories. I'm a cop—or I used to be. I stick with the facts. And the fact is—Ames White sent me into that building to die. I believe that—but that doesn't make my partner's killer any less a monster."

"White is the monster. Surely you see that."

"I'm not helping you, Cale. We share a common goal where White is concerned, but your transgenics can go to—"

"Forget that," Logan said. "Think about your family's safety. White's operation is not just in this country—his group has operatives everywhere. They'll find your family . . . just like I found you."

"You don't scare me, Cale. I know my family is safe."

Looking into the man's eyes, locking onto them, Logan said, "For now, probably. But White will find them . . . and Kleena Kleene, British Columbia, is so small, he shouldn't have any trouble."

Thompson leaned back on the bed, aghast, springs squeaking. "How . . . ?"

"One of the anagrams my computer spit out—an anagram for your wife's maiden name. She left the night Hankins died and flew to Bella Coola, then rented a car and drove to Firvale. From there she and your kids went through Anahim Lake and took Highway 20 to Kleena Kleene."

All the blood had drained from Thompson's face, making his beard look so dark it seemed black.

"The truth is, Sage—you said it yourself—if I can find that information, so can White."

Thompson brought a hand up to his face; he was trembling, seemed about to weep. "Oh . . . oh Christ. . . ."

"I can have your family out of there within twelve hours and have them safely relocated. Eyes Only has a network White has never been able to penetrate—and never will."

"You're saying . . . ?"

"I can get your wife and children new identities, and you too . . . and eventually you'll even be able to rejoin them."

"But White—"

"A gun is only one way to stop White. A better way is

through Eyes Only—and all you have to do is tell the truth . . . tell what you know about White."

Tears had streaked down to glisten in his beard; there was something strangely beautiful about the effect of it, the teardrops catching the dim light of the lamp. "What do you want me to do?"

"To start with, get your stuff. We're getting out of here right now."

And five minutes later they were in Logan's car; traffic had eased and he was able to speed toward Terminal City, unhindered.

As he drove, Logan phoned Asha. She picked up on the second ring.

"Everything all right?" he asked.

"A-okay."

"Good. I've got the other package."

"Cooperative?"

"Very. Meet me. You know where."

"Half an hour," she said, and the line went dead.

Bobby parked the stolen car near the abandoned building that served as an entrance to the exit tunnel. Once inside, Original Cindy led him down the passage toward where it interesected with the main shaft. Blackness surrounded them, only the thin beam of Bobby's pocket flash piercing the dark.

Cindy thought about running, but the transgenic still held the stun rod in his other hand and she didn't trust her achy body and throbbing skull.

They reached the intersection—to their right lay Terminal City; to the left, Logan's building. Automatically, she turned right.

"Where are you going?" he asked.

She turned back to face him. "Terminal City. Isn't that where you wanna go, Bobby?"

He tossed the beam of the flashlight down the corridor to the left. "What's up there?"

"How should I know?" she asked, her tone bitchy. "Do I look like a freakin' tour guide? You wanna join your brothers and sisters, or what?"

On the ride over, Original Cindy had decided that the best course of action was to simply march this freak into Terminal City and let Max kick his sorry ass.

The bland face stared her down. "I think you're lying to me. I think you know what's down that direction. Do you think I'm stupid?"

She gave him the finger. "I think you should sit and spin."

Bobby took a step closer to her and raised the stun rod. "Would you like to sit and spin on this?"

Though designed to stun, those rods could be lethal—she knew—if application was prolonged. And how long was too long, well, that was an issue she didn't particularly want to research.

She smirked sourly. "Leads to a pad Logan's got."

The kid-on-Christmas-morning smile on Bobby's otherwise blank face told Cindy that she had just revealed the piece of information that Bobby most wanted to learn. . . .

She had to get away from this sick fuck and warn Max, and tell her Logan might be in danger.

So she took the right turn and started running, fleeing into the blackness of the tunnel . . .

. . . making it only a few steps before the pain in her head distorted her balance, and she went down.

She was about to scream for Max when she saw a blue spark in her peripheral vision, and white hot shards of pain shot through her every fiber.

She couldn't talk or move.

Original Cindy just lay there, shaking violently, an epileptic having a hell of a fit, the pain greater than any she'd felt in her whole life. She only hoped that she would die soon.

Eventually, gratefully, she passed out.

When she came to, Original Cindy found herself tied to a straight-back wooden chair in Logan's apartment. Bobby had lashed her wrists and ankles to the chair and run a strip of duct tape over her mouth. She tried to scream, but all that came out was a muffled "Mmmmmm!"

He had placed her so she faced the door that opened to the staircase below. Turning her head as far as she could in either direction, she looked for Bobby but couldn't see him. Either he was gone or he was directly behind her. She listened as closely as she could, but all she heard was the pounding of her own heart.

Trying to break free was useless.

Though she strained against her bonds, she made no progress. Finally giving up, she stared at the doorknob and waited. It didn't take long before she saw the knob turning. She tried, but the tape over her mouth kept her from screaming for help.

Terrible elongated seconds passed before the door opened, and she was surprised to see the federal agent she'd seen at Jam Pony a few weeks ago. She hadn't really caught his name—Gott-something?

Whoever he was, now he stood in the doorway, his hands behind his back, his mouth open in surprise as he saw her rocking from side to side in the chair. Over his shoulder she could just make out Logan's freedom fighter friend, Asha.

They both came into the room, Asha with a pistol drawn and when she saw Original Cindy, the gun seemed to leap up in front of her face, both arms outstretched.

Then Bobby stepped forward from behind Asha. He'd blended into the wall and when Asha turned back to face Original Cindy, he made his move.

Sticking out her chin, gesturing with her eyes, Original Cindy tried to signal Asha that Bobby was behind her . . . but to no avail.

Cindy watched in horror as the stun rod touched Asha's back. The gun leapt from her hand and she wilted to the floor in convulsions. The fed turned and tried to kick out at Bobby, but he succeeded only in providing the transgenic with an easier target. Hitting the agent's leg with the stun rod, Bobby sent him writhing to the floor as well.

Bobby shut the door and dragged the wriggling figures off and out of sight.

And, minutes later, the door opened again.

Logan led the way inside this time, a bearded, wasted-looking man in a black suit trailing behind him. They both froze when they saw her . . .

. . . and again Bobby struck!

He touched the man in the black suit with the stun rod and he went down whimpering, doing the electric dance.

Logan dodged the first thrust of the stun rod and backed into the room, trying to put distance between himself and his attacker. Almost immediately, though, he started talking to Bobby in a cool, calm voice, and Original Cindy was reminded that one of her favorite things about Logan was his courage.

"Whoa—what's the problem here?" Logan held his hands up, palms out in a stop gesture as he backed away.

"I have to remove you."

"Remove me?"

Bobby moved closer but Logan kept backing away, keeping the distance about the same.

"I have to replace you."

"Remove or replace me? . . . Who are you? What did I do to you?"

They wove around furniture in a slow, deadly cat-and-mouse game.

"I'm Bobby Kawasaki, Logan—you used to see me at Jam Pony . . . or maybe you didn't notice me."

"Can't say I ever did. My bad."

"The name they used to call me at Manticore was Kelpy."

"You . . . you're a transgenic?" Logan asked.

Seizing the doubt in the moment, Bobby lunged at him with the stun rod, just missing as Logan pitched to the right, the rod sparking angrily when it banged off a table.

"Bobby—I'm trying to help the transgenics . . ."

"You're not helping me."

"I'm not?"

"No! You stand between me and Max."

Tipping over her chair, Original Cindy fought to get loose. She saw the look of confusion on Logan's face.

"Between you . . . and Max?"

"I need your face!"

"My . . . ?"

Bobby lunged again, and this time Logan tripped on a rug and fell; but it still served the purpose, the stun rod missing him.

"Logan!" someone yelled.

On her side, on the floor, still bound to the chair, Original Cindy turned to see Joshua piling through the door, Alec and Sketchy right behind him. Hope swelled in her chest and she thought that maybe they might get through this all right, after all. . . .

Spinning, Bobby hurled the stun rod at them. Joshua went right, Alec left, and Sketchy stood stock-still as the rod handle hit him in the chest and dropped him to the floor in a quivering mass.

Whirling back, Alec picked up the stun rod and turned toward Bobby. Original Cindy looked back too and felt her newfound hope drain away. Before them stood Logan, and Bobby, who had a knife to Logan's throat, Bobby partially crouched behind him, using the taller man as a shield.

"Move and he dies," Bobby said, his voice raspy with emotion.

"All right," Alec said. "Just stay calm."

Bobby said, "Fuck calm—we're leaving. Try to stop us, he dies."

Motionless on the floor, Original Cindy watched as the transgenic pushed Logan slowly toward the door; something was strange, really weird—Bobby was changing, sort of morphing, but gradually, so subtle you almost didn't notice. . . .

Bobby's back was to her now, as he kept Logan between himself and the others. A trembling Sketchy was sitting up, hands to his chest where the rod had struck. Between the intertwined legs of Logan and Bobby, Original Cindy had the perfect vantage point to see that Sketchy was moving his camera up ever so slowly.

"Can't we talk about this, Bobby?" Alec asked. "We should all be friends—you're our brother. . . ."

His back to the door now, Bobby held Logan tighter, a tiny ribbon of red oozing out from where the point of the large knife touched his throat.

Original Cindy could see Bobby's face clearly now, and to her astonishment, the guy she'd thought had Afro blood in him now looked whiter than Hitler, and his hair seemed sort of spiky and blond.

Shit, if he didn't look something like Logan now!

Joshua had finally roused. "Kelpy—don't do this! Max wouldn't want you to—"

"Max will love me," Bobby said, at the doorway now. "You'll see."

"Kelpy—" Joshua said, moving forward.

"Don't follow me—I see one of you down in that tunnel, I slit Logan's throat, then and there."

Damn, Cindy thought. *Once he's outta here, who's gonna save Logan?*

* * *

A few minutes prior to the confrontation in Logan's apartment, a small council of war was under way.

For what seemed like hours, Max and Mole had been going over contingencies that they hoped would turn their defensive position into an offensive one.

The idea was to turn the disadvantage of being surrounded into an advantage. Their strategy was strikingly simple in nature. When the Army piled through the gates and started going building to building, Max, Mole, and a few others would remain behind to distract them as the rest of the inhabitants took to the tunnels and sewers. As the Army and National Guard came in, they would go out, then come up behind the invaders. Once the tables were turned and it was the Army that was surrounded, maybe they could talk.

When they had gone over the plan for the umpteenth time, Max stretched and said, "All right, break time."

Mole sat back and rolled his head on the column of his neck. "You know, this shit just might work," he said.

She nodded. "Oughta give 'em a hell of goose, anyway. . . . Look, I'm supposed to go meet Logan—he should be back by now."

"Cool," Mole said, and blew a cigar smoke ring. "Young love inspires us all."

"Bite me."

"Have you had your shots?"

"I hang with Joshua, don't I?"

They both laughed—and the levity was a good sign after all the doom and gloom of recent days.

"Go on," Mole said. "We'll hold down the fort."

Then, as she started to walk out, he added, "And see if he got my damn cigars! He forgot last time."

She grinned. "Will do."

Despite Mole's good humor, the atmosphere around the compound remained tense. Max hadn't expected any less.

They were all getting ready for combat now. Her desire to check on Logan—and his efforts to find Sage Thompson—made her want to run; but she forced herself to walk. Behind the broken windows and cracked doors, citizens of Terminal City were watching her.

If she looked cool, maybe they would stay cool, too.

When the National Guard had cut the power to Terminal City, they'd gotten this end of the tunnel too. Dix didn't have it hooked into the grid yet, but it was on the to-do list. In the meantime, she didn't care. Feline DNA made the lights optional anyway.

Max actually enjoyed the darkness—it felt peaceful to her. But the silence that usually accompanied the blanket of blackness was disturbed—somewhere from farther up the tunnel, she could hear something.

Voices?

Trotting ahead, staying silent, she heard Alec's voice from Logan's apartment. "Can't we talk about this, Bobby?"

Then other voices, including Joshua's; but she couldn't make out the words.

Something was wrong. Very wrong. . . .

In seconds she was at the end of the tunnel and silently started up the stairs as she heard another voice.

"Don't follow me. . . ."

This one too was familiar, but she couldn't quite place it.

"I see one of you down in that tunnel," the voice was saying, "I slit Logan's throat, then and there."

At the top of the stairs, she saw someone who looked vaguely like Logan, with an arm around Logan's chest and his other hand out of sight. Without seeing it, she knew the other hand held a knife to Logan's throat.

She still had five steps between her and them.

Normally, taking a guy like this would be no biggie: he had his back to her and all his attention was focused on those in front of him. . . .

Four steps.

The fly in this ointment, though, was Logan. If, in tearing the attacker from him, she somehow accidentally touched Logan, even just brushed her flesh against his in the smallest way, the virus—which Manticore had infected her with, to make her touch deadly to Logan—would kick in, and instead of getting his throat cut, Logan would die at her own fingertips.

Three steps.

The timing had to be perfect, and nothing could go wrong.

Two steps.

One shot, that's all she'd have. Her hand snaked toward the right elbow of the attacker. Just as she was about to grab him, a bright light—a flashbulb—went off in there.

The attacker yowled, and his right hand—the one with the knife—drew away from Logan's neck as the attacker tried to turn away from the strobe. The action of turning had tipped the pair off balance—captor and hostage alike—and they teetered on the brink of tumbling down the stairs on top of Max.

In less than a second she visualized the whole thing: *the three of them tumbling down the stairs, all tangled together, piling up at the bottom, her lying in the one place she longed to be more than any other—in Logan's arms—Logan locked in her deadly embrace, any hope of a life together obliterated by a silly flash of light.*

Then—just as Max clutched the attacker's arm, his skin hot against hers—Alec launched himself at the pair and wrenched Logan from the grasp of the attacker. As Logan and Alec fell back into the apartment, she jerked the attacker's knife arm . . .

. . . and the two of them rolled ass-over-teakettle down the stairs into the black tunnel!

They were both on their feet instantly, he still holding the knife, she circling, looking for an opening. In the apartment, someone hit the switch and the lights in the tunnel came on. The attacker winced at the brightness and gave Max the moment she needed.

She kicked the blade from his grasp, then swiveled and in one fluid motion kicked again, hitting him in the stomach, sending him flying into the stairs, hitting hard.

Max moved in, ready for her opponent to respond; and she got her first good look at him. . . .

He looked almost exactly like Logan!

But an alarming change was in effect: the Logan lookalike was sweating profusely, red sores breaking out on his arms and on his face in a terrible sick blossoming, and he looked at her with shock and confusion in his blue eyes.

"Max," he rasped, slumped against the stairs, a pitiful pile of hive-ridden flesh. "What's happening to me?"

Her hand went to her mouth.

She knew she was witnessing the virus taking full-blown effect—whoever this would-be Logan was, he had taken on much more than just Logan Cale's appearance.

Chapter Twelve
STREAMING FREEDOM VIDEO

Soon everyone was standing around the table in Logan's new quarters, the would-be killer splayed across the table like a ghastly meal. Original Cindy, Otto, and Asha—unbound now—were joined by a revived Thompson, Joshua, and Sketchy, who held an ice pack to his chest where the stun rod had bruised him.

"Fill the bathtub with cold water and ice," Max said, directing the order to no one specifically.

It was Alec and Logan who took off to comply with her command.

"Who is he?" Otto Gottlieb asked.

On the table, shivering, flesh bursting with red sores, this was no longer a fearsome figure—eerily, the resemblance to Logan made this seem like a long-lost Cale brother, in the throes of infirmity.

Joshua said, "Kelpy is his name. He's one of us."

Alec emerged from the bathroom with a plastic bucket in hand, heading to the refrigerator.

Gottlieb eyed Joshua's canine features suspiciously. "You mean . . . transgenic."

"Yes."

Max was wrapping a blanket around the shivering creature, who gazed at her with a sickly, frankly adoring smile.

"Well, his being 'one of us' is not good news," Alec said, at the fridge freezer, filling the bucket with ice. "Bobby or Kelpy or whoever he is, he's our serial killer. . . . So nobody get *too* teary-eyed."

Then Alec went off toward the bathroom with his load of ice.

"The skinner?" Thompson asked, his eyes wide above the dark beard. "This is the son of a bitch who killed my partner?"

Max stepped between Thompson and the prone, blanket-wrapped Kelpy. "And now he's going to die—isn't that enough for you?"

"No."

Turning back to her patient, Max tucked the blanket tighter around Kelpy and, in the process, something fell out of his pocket, rolled off the table, and clunked to the floor, lid popping off, pills bouncing crazily for a second.

"His Tryptophan," Original Cindy said.

Max bent down, picked up a few of the pills. "I don't think so. . . ."

"No, Boo, that's his meds! I saw him at Jam Pony."

Max rose. "Maybe so, but these are the wrong color for Tryptophan." She held one up to her nose. "They don't smell right either." She called: "Logan!"

He emerged from the bathroom, from which the rush of water filling the tub could be heard; Alec trailed after, the empty bucket in hand.

"We're about there," Logan said, jerking a thumb toward the bathroom. Frowning at the sight of her grave expression, he asked, "Something else you need, Max?"

She held up one of the pills. "Do you have the equipment to do a chemical breakdown on these?"

He shook his head. "Don't have that gear in yet—soon."

"Soon won't cut it."

At the freezer, Alec paused in filling his bucket and turned to say, "Dix has got his Frankenstein lab going—unless he's just brewing moonshine."

Joshua corrected his friend: "Dix is doing chemical breakdowns on the biohazard materials in Terminal City, Max. Looking for antigens."

"That could be a break," she said. "I need somebody to take Dix these pills—and tell him we need to know what's in 'em, ASAP."

Stepping forward, Alec handed Logan the ice bucket and took the bottle of meds from Max. "Back in a flash."

Max turned to Joshua. "Put Kelpy in the tub, Big Fella. We need to get his body temperature down."

"Let him fucking suffer," Thompson said.

Stepping over to him, Max said, "Thompson, isn't it? Sage Thompson?"

"I know who you are too," he said, his face edged with contempt.

"Since you love us so much, why exactly are you here?"

Logan said, "He just happens to hate Ames White more than he does transgenics—every alliance starts with a common enemy, Max."

While Joshua lifted his old friend Kelpy into his arms, gentle as a baby, and conveyed the diseased transgenic into the tub of ice and water, Logan gave Max a quick but thorough rundown on Thompson's situation, from his fear of White wanting him dead to the family he'd sent underground.

"Mr. Thompson," Max said, "here's what I want from you, right now—sit down, and shut up. Can you handle that?"

He started to say something but Max's glare silenced him.

"Asha," she said to the blonde freedom fighter, "didn't some members of your S1W group wind up in British Columbia?"

"That's so."

"Will they help us?"

The blonde nodded. "No prob—I'll get 'em headed there right away."

"Thanks," Max said, bestowing her sometime rival a smile.

Thompson—seated at the kitchen table now—shook his head, obviously bewildered. "You're . . . *helping* me?"

"Mr. Thompson, you may be a uniformed, bigoted asshole, fresh from service with a government agency devoted to making my life miscrable . . . but you are also the victim of Ames White . . . which means you and I desire the same damn thing."

"Stopping White," he said softly.

"Stopping White . . . and whatever it takes to make that happen, and soon, is fine by me. If that means helping a transgenic-hating scumbag like you, so be it."

Logan leaned over to Sketchy. "Hey, Jimmy Olsen—you taking notes on this?"

Sketchy's eyes widenend and brightened with something very much like thought. "Pictures too, right?"

Max spun in Sketch's direction. "But no shots with Original Cindy . . . and we need to protect Thompson, and Otto, here."

Gottlieb, who'd stayed quiet on the sidelines, just taking it all in, smirked humorlessly and said, "Hell—go ahead and take my picture. My career's over, anyway."

"Me too," Thompson said. "Fire away, kid—maybe by going public we can keep ourselves alive. Killing us only validates our position."

"Hell of a way to make a point," Gottlieb said wryly.

Sketchy needed no more encouragement, and the flashbulbs started popping.

"Can we get Otto and Thompson on tape telling their stories?" Max asked Logan.

He nodded, and fetched a small minirecorder from his nearby office area, calling back to her, "You talked to Clemente lately? You making any progress?"

"No," she admitted. "Somebody—White maybe—has frozen Clemente out. The feds're jamming all the signals in and out of Terminal City."

"Well, you're outside now," he said. "And if Alec's right, you've got the skinner serial killer in custody."

Original Cindy stepped forward, her complexion pale, sweat running down her face. For a moment Max thought her friend might have caught the virus, too.

"You know, come to think of it," Cindy said. "I think I *saw* the evidence . . . and I know where Bobby left it."

That surprised Max. "You do?"

And Cindy described the patchwork garment. Joshua, returning from the bathroom, reported that he'd also seen it—on a mannequin at Kelpy's apartment, with a picture of Logan attached to the face.

"I think he wanted to have human skin," Joshua said.

The seated Thompson said, "And he would've cut off your boyfriend's face, if he hadn't been stopped."

Max frowned at him and pointed a threatening finger. "Didn't I tell you to shut up? That's your only job. Work hard at it."

"It's not my only job," Thompson said, lower lip trembling, as he summoned some courage and indignation. "You want me to tell my story, and I'm ready to tell it—but don't lie to yourselves. That's a transgenic beast taking that soak in there . . . a monster capable of skinning people and putting their skin on like a suit. Explain *that* away!"

Original Cindy said, "The dude is right, to a point—and I ain't goin' back for that thing alone. I ain't touchin' the motherfucker, you dig?"

Gottlieb stepped forward. "I'll go with her, and collect the evidence."

Max signaled her assent by tilting her head toward the door, and the pair left.

Thompson stood and Max shot him a look; but the agent was just getting his cell phone out, to hand her. "They won't be able to trace this one," he said. "You need to talk to your police contact? Make your call."

She nodded a curt thanks and dialed Clemente's cell number, catching him in the car. She explained the situation in broad strokes.

"You have the skinner," he said. "And the evidence?"

"It's being secured."

"Where do you have this Bobby Kawasaki?"

"Ready for the address?"

"Born ready."

She gave it to him. "Come alone."

"That's outside Terminal City, Max—what happened to our deal?"

"Our deal went on the back burner when the feds took your ass off the front line. You want to wrap this case up and be a hero to both sides? Then you'll just have to trust me . . . and hurry."

Fifteen minutes later Clemente arrived. They gave him a quick overview of the situation, and Max led him into the bathroom.

Kelpy had taken a turn for the worse.

His clothes stripped from him, the sores covered his whole body; he still bore a strong resemblance to Logan—something in the virus seemed to have locked him into the form he'd blended with last. His temperature remained on the rise, though the icy water had slowed its ascent.

Logan sat on the edge of the tub, tending (but careful not to touch) Kelpy. Clemente stood, hovering over the tub, Max framed in the doorway.

Looking down at the pitiful creature, Clemente read him his rights, then asked simply, "Why?"

"To be with Max," Kelpy said with a little cough. "She loved an ordinary—a human . . . Logan. I needed to be Logan."

The detective turned to Max. She kept her face stony, though emotion welled within her, unbidden.

"He worked with us at Jam Pony," Max said. "No one ever paid him much attention. But I guess he was like everybody else—he wanted to be noticed."

Behind her, just outside the bathroom, Joshua said, "Noticed by you, Max. You saved him when Manticore burned. Max . . . he loved you. Not like Joshua loves Max, but like . . . like I loved Annie."

Max felt tears forming—goddamnit!

Clemente was shaking his head. "This is not going to win the people of Seattle over to the side of the Terminal City residents. I mean . . . a transgenic killing people so he can make a *human* suit . . . to woo another transgenic."

Max nodded glumly, glancing at the feverish Kelpy, naked in the tub. He didn't appear to hear any of this, much less understand the trouble he'd caused. The promised Army invasion was less than three hours away, and there was nothing she could do to stop it—they would have to do what Manticore had trained them for, only fighting the country that created them had never been in the plans.

"This couldn't be worse," Clemente was saying, "if Ames White himself designed the scenario."

"Maybe he did!" someone yelled.

Alec.

Popping up next to Joshua just behind Max in the doorway, the handsome X5 said, "Suppose somebody pushed our Chameleon Boy over the edge?"

They all turned, and Joshua stepped back to allow Alec to take center stage in the bathroom doorway.

"Dix just ran a chemical analysis of the pills Kelpy's been popping. They contained Tryptophan, all right . . . but mostly they were a drug Dix had never seen before."

"Shit," Max said. "We have to identify it!"

"Oh, but we have. Dix hacked into one of Uncle Sam's computers and found a reference to the same chemical compound. Seems it's a drug called Cullinasec."

Gottlieb's voice chimed in from the living room: "That's classified information!"

Max and Clemente followed the voice into the living room, where Gottlieb and Original Cindy were back. Cindy was seated at the kitchen table, looking shell-shocked.

Clemente said, "Where's the, uh . . . ?"

"The 'skin suit' is in a big plastic garment bag in my trunk," Gottlieb said, raising an eyebrow. "I don't think I compromised the evidence by moving it from my backseat to my trunk. Better to secure it, considering some of the . . . unusual circumstances surrounding this case."

Clemente was nodding. "I'd have to agree, Agent Gottlieb."

"I hope you don't mind my interrupting this love fest," Max said, stepping between them, directing her attention to the NSA agent. "But what did you mean by calling that drug 'classified information'?"

Gottlieb spoke softly, as if reluctant to even hear the words he spoke himself. "Cullinasec is a psychotropic drug being developed by the NSA for espionage purposes."

Clemente asked, "And no one outside the NSA is supposed to be able to get their hands on this junk?"

Max said, "Maybe no one outside the NSA did."

". . . White?"

Moments later, Max was seated on the edge of the tub. She said to Kelpy, "Where did you get the drugs?"

"A . . . nurse named Betty . . . at Harbor Lights Hospital."

"But then one day she disappeared," Max said.

"How . . . how did you know?"

"It's a long story," Max said.

"And . . . and you don't have time to tell me?"

"No." Max turned to Logan, standing just behind her. "Can you get me a picture of Ames White?"

"Right on it," he said, and was gone.

To Kelpy, Max said, "After the nurse disappeared, where did you get the drugs? Who was your connection?"

"Just . . . some guy. Some guy taking over . . . taking over Betty's clients."

Logan came in with the photo, fresh off the printer, and handed it to Max. She showed it to Kelpy.

"Would this happen to be your dealer?"

"Yes," Kelpy said. "That's . . . that's him."

In the doorway, Clemente said, "Wait, wait. What's going on here?"

Max showed him the picture. "I think you recognize this face."

"Special Agent Ames White. Are you saying . . . ?"

"I'm not saying anything—Kelpy is. Your dying confessed murderer has just identified NSA Agent Ames White as the man who provided him with the drugs that turned him psychotic."

"And why would he . . . ?" And then Clemente answered his own question: "The media war—providing the public with a transgenic boogie man."

"That'd be a big bingo," Max said.

From the hallway, where he'd been listening in, former NSA Agent Otto Gottlieb squeezed into the little room, joining the confab to offer his own informed analysis.

"This whole crisis," Gottlieb said, "has been stage-managed by Agent White. He set Thompson and Hankins up in that warehouse with the bum imagers, providing a psychotic transgenic with two possible victims."

Clemente was frowning. "How could White know what Kelpy would do?"

"He couldn't and he didn't," Gottlieb said. "White just knew it wouldn't be good. That whole human suit routine came from Kelpy's own tortured imagination . . . where it would have remained, if Ames White hadn't turned an already unstable transgenic completely psychotic and set him loose on the city."

"All for a media war," Clemente said, still struggling with the madness of it.

"It's much more than that, Detective," Gottlieb said. "Ames White hates the transgenics—especially her." He nodded to Max. "He wants 452 dead."

"Why?" Clemente asked, eyes like marbles.

"You'd have to ask White. But I do know his desire for her death is why he brought in the snipers to start the shootout at Jam Pony."

Frowning now, Clemente asked, "That pumped-up SWAT team was *government* agents?"

Gottlieb shook his head. "I don't know where White got them—they're sure as hell not feds. I can't find any orders, any requests on file. . . . I can't even find any records of phone calls on White's cell phone, other than the one to the governor."

Still frowning, Clemente asked, "How much can you prove?"

"Damn little," Gottlieb admitted.

From the doorway, the other former NSA agent, Thompson, joined in. "I know my imager didn't work, and Ames White did hand each of us our imagers, personally."

Clemente walked briskly out into the living room, Max and the others following him; Joshua took over the vigil in the bathroom with his old friend Kelpy.

The detective sat down heavily into a chair. "Do we have enough to make a case against White?"

Max realized Logan was at her side; she looked up at him, but his attention was on the detective.

Then she turned to Clemente and said, "The Army will be making their move soon, and it'll be too late."

Clemente pounded his fist into a hand. "We need to get the word out—we can't move through the system in time to stop the slaughter. Shit . . . where the hell is that Eyes Only guy when you need him?"

Several pairs of eyes turned to Logan.

Picking up on it, Clemente turned to him too.

"Something I should know?" the detective asked.

"Well," Logan said, almost shyly, "I sort of have a . . . uh, 'in' with Eyes Only."

"Hell, man!" Clemente said. "Can you reach him? Can he help us?"

"See what I can do. Max—come with me a second, would you?"

Away from the others, they talked quickly, then Max gathered Alec and Sketchy into an impromptu camera crew.

Soon a video camera was set up on a tripod in the bedroom, to be manned by an enthusiastic Sketchy; here were sequestered Clemente, Gottlieb, Thompson, and everyone but Alec and Kelpy . . . in the bathroom with Alec manning another camera on a tripod . . . and Max and Logan, in the latter's computer-and-monitor-arrayed office area.

As far as Clemente, Gottlieb, and Thompson were concerned, Alec was relaying all of this to a secure remote location, where Eyes Only was making broadcast magic. The trio of law enforcement veterans were unaware—or, anyway, so Logan and Max hoped—that the real broadcasting was being done a room away, by the real Eyes Only.

And thus came to pass the first broadcast of Freak Nation TV.

All around the city, TV screens went to static.

The static transformed into a logo depicting a pair of light-colored eyes on a blue background, with the words STREAMING FREEDOM VIDEO rolling by above and below, white letters standing out on a red background.

Then the familiar voice said: *"Do not attempt to adjust*

*your set. This is a Streaming Freedom Video bulletin. This
cable hack could last more than sixty seconds. It still cannot
be traced, it still cannot be stopped, and it remains the only
free voice left in this city . . ."*

In homes, bars, police stations, fire stations, anywhere
there was a television, people's attention turned to the box;
it had been months since they had heard from Seattle's rene-
gade cyber journalist, and the excitement around the city
was palpable.

*"The information you've been given about the transgenic
crisis in Terminal City is tainted and false. Likewise, the
news you've heard about a serial killer skinning police officers has been only part of the story. Tonight, we'll give you
the facts."*

In the family room of the suburban home where he lived
without his family, Ames White went ballistic. It apparently
hadn't done any good, shooting up that asshole Eyes Only's
apartment; right now, Ames White's best efforts seemed only
to have spurred the bastard on. . . .

As the Eyes Only bulletin continued, White dialed the
number of his government office.

"Norton," a voice said.

"The prick's at it again. Start a trace, now!"

"Which prick is at what again, sir?"

"Eyes Only, Eyes Only—turn on the goddamned TV!"

"Trace started, sir," Norton reported.

"Let me know when you get something."

The staticky logo image disappeared and the screen was
filled with a ghostly white man with spiky hair in a bathtub,
red sores pocking his body, floating in water bobbing with
ice cubes. The male form was drenched in sweat and it was
obvious whoever-this-was wasn't going to live out the night.

Was this grotesque crap the best Eyes Only could muster?
White was about to laugh, when the spectral figure spoke.

"My name is Bobby Kawasaki," the voice said, and it was

strangely similar to that of Eyes Only himself. *"I'm a trans-genic. I killed three people. It was a bad and terrible thing—I know that now. What I did was wrong. But I want you to know I did these bad things under the unknowing influence of a powerful drug."*

The picture changed to a still of Ames White . . .

. . . who sat up sharply in his chair in his family room.

Bobby was saying, *"And this is a photo of the man who gave me the tainted drugs. This is the man who turned me into a monster."*

Ames White sat frozen, as if he were the one in icy water, something frigid running through his veins—and in his belly, a million snakes seemed to coil and uncoil.

The picture was now live again, but no longer on the red-splotched ghost in the bathtub. Now the screen showed a room, possibly a bedroom . . . and the face on camera belonged to that fool Otto Gottlieb!

As Otto began telling his part of the sordid tale, Ames White put a hand to his temple.

He was ruined in the NSA. Right now, in front of all Seattle, and no doubt soon, all across the country, he was being outed—all that work to save his cover after the fiasco at Jam Pony, and now it was gone.

White's phone rang and he picked it up on the third ring. "White."

"Norton."

"The trace—"

"I've been instructed to tell you to report to the office immediately."

White hung up the phone.

That idiot Thompson—the guy White had been searching for every spare minute of the last three months—came on next, spewing his self-pitying garbage.

Rising, White picked up his pistol, went upstairs and

quickly filled a suitcase. The conclave would of course see this, and he doubted they would take it lightly either—this could be viewed as nothing but the failure it was. Even he knew that. . . .

The phone rang.

This time he let it ring.

Detective Ramon Clemente was next on screen. *"I would like to personally thank the transgenics of Terminal City, especially Max . . ."*

"Guevara," an off-camera voice prompted.

"Max Guevara," Clemente said, *"who personally, and at great risk to herself, broke this case wide open, and in so doing saved many lives. And when the killer was found, and was a transgenic, Ms. Guevera did not seek to cover it up . . . rather came to me, the police."*

White, gathering some things from his family-room desk, managed not to throw a bookend through the screen.

"As the Seattle police officer assigned to the so-called siege at Terminal City, I make this public plea to the Army: I urge you to reconsider your plans to invade Terminal City. These people—some call them freaks—have done nothing except defend themselves against false accusations, and yet . . . even when overwhelmed by problems of their own . . . still managed to help the police capture a serial killer. In addition, they have helped identify and expose the person manipulating the confessed killer, in an effort to stereotype transgenics as monsters, in a crass and heartless exploitation of the media and the public."

What the fuck office was that detective running for, all of a sudden? God, how White hated that pompous petty nonentity. He picked up the remote and fired it at the picture tube. A minute later he was riding away from the suburban house, leaving the lie of that life behind as quickly as possible, and heading into a precarious future.

On televisions across the city the Streaming Freedom

Video logo returned and that familiar, strangely soothing voice said, *"One man's hatred, one man's fear of things different . . . sometimes that's all that's needed to tip the scales of justice, until they are criminally off-kilter. We hope that those who make decisions are listening. We hope that— unlike Ames White—they will not turn a deaf ear to the cries of those who are different. There is time to stop this madness, this hatred. This has been a Streaming Freedom Video."*

At the end of the broadcast, Max ushered everyone— except Joshua, who was still tending to Bobby—out into the kitchen apartment. No one spoke; a quiet had settled, like ground fog, and they all huddled within it, wondering if their efforts had been for nought.

Max stood, hugging her arms to herself, Logan nearby, his face unreadable. Alec and the three lawmen sat at the table, where Original Cindy remained, apparently still freaked out from the human-skin garment she'd helped retrieve. Sketchy bounced on the periphery, the only one in a good mood; he seemed to be relishing the role of real reporter. . . .

Finally, Clemente's cell phone rang, and he answered so quickly it was almost silly: "Clemente."

Max could hear only one side of the conversation, could read only the detective's somber expression.

"Yes?"

A pause.

"They did?"

Another pause.

"They are? . . . Thank you."

Clemente hit End, rose from the table, and sighed. "That was Colonel Nickerson of the National Guard. . . . The order to attack has been rescinded."

The room erupted in whoops and hollers and applause, and they all took turns hugging each other—except, of course, for Max and Logan.

She approached the detective. "Okay," she said. "I guess I trust you."

His grin was explosive. "That was close."

"Around here, Ramon," she said, putting a hand on his shoulder, "they always are."

Clemente sat back down at the kitchen table and let out an even bigger sigh. "The feds are viewing Kelpy's story as a death-bed confession." He glanced at Gottlieb and then at Thompson. "Nickerson said they want to bring you two in from the cold, *and* they have agents scouring the area looking for Ames White. He's now a wanted felon."

The two former NSA agents grinned at each other like a couple of kids.

Standing nearby, arms folded, Max wasn't grinning. "They won't find White."

Clemente frowned up at her. "You sound sure of that."

"I know him. He's in the wind already." Then she got a little smile on her face.

"What?" the detective asked.

"I was just thinking . . . better him than me."

Max wandered into the bathroom. Joshua rose and made room for her, so she could sit on the edge of the tub.

She took Kelpy's hand in hers. "You know, only Logan was supposed to be able to catch that virus."

The pale red-pocked form shrugged, making waves in the icy water of the tub. "Maybe . . . in a way . . . now I am Logan."

"Maybe."

"Max . . . Max . . . my body hurts."

"I know."

"But my mind . . . it's so clear that . . . it hurts, too."

"Yes."

"I . . . I did bad things."

"Yes."

"Terrible . . . awful . . . monstrous things. . . ."

She squeezed his hand. "But you did good things too. You saved a lot of lives tonight. Every transgenic in Terminal City, and many on the other side of the fence. You saved us all—Joshua, Alec . . . and me."

The smile on the Loganesque face was weak; his blue eyes were hauntingly familiar.

She told him, "I'll always love you for that."

And she kissed his hand.

A splotch of rose came to the pale cheeks, and it wasn't the sickness.

He whispered, "You love Logan, don't you?"

She glanced back.

Logan was in the doorway.

She was looking at Logan as she said to Kelpy, "Yes—yes, I do."

Logan's smile wasn't that big, really; yet the room could barely contain it.

"*He's* human," Kelpy said.

Now she gazed at Kelpy again—at this monster. And yet emotion welled within her.

"But I love you too," she told him. "I'll always love you for what you did for us. . . ."

"I guess that makes me human too," he said. A single tear ran down the chalky cheek; then, with a lurch, he sat forward, almost scaring her, Logan's blue eyes huge in the pale, pale face.

"*Am* I human, Max?" Kelpy asked with terrible urgency.

But he died, his hand in hers, before she had time to answer.

**Look for this explosive novel,
the prequel to the hit television series!**

DARK ANGEL
Book I
Before the Dawn

Los Angeles, 2019. Large sections of Tinseltown are
in Richter-scale ruins in the aftermath of the Pulse
and a devastating earthquake. Surviving among a
ragtag pack of street kids, Max steals from the rich
and gives to Moody, her mentor in crime and leader
of the gang. But with no real family to speak of,
Max longs for her missing "brothers and sisters"
from Manticore, the covert agency with a sinister
history of militaristic manipulation and control. By
chance, Max sees a news story on TV about a dissi-
dent cyberjournalist in Seattle, known to everyone
as "Eyes Only." The police are searching for his
accomplice, a young rebel whose image flashes on
the screen. Max immediately recognizes Seth, one
of her Manticore siblings. She mounts her motorcycle and hightails it north. What she rides into is an
elaborate web of betrayal, greed, revenge, and self-
less heroism that will only further fuel her quest to
uncover the secrets of her past—and seize hope for
the future. . . .

Published by Del Rey Books.
Available wherever books are sold.

Visit www.delreydigital.com— the portal to all the information and resources available from Del Rey Online.

- Read sample chapters of every new book, special features on selected authors and books, news and announcements, readers' reviews, browse Del Rey's complete online catalog, and more.

- Sign up for the Del Rey Internet Newsletter (DRIN), a free monthly publication e-mailed to subscribers, featuring descriptions of new and upcoming books, essays and interviews with authors and editors, announcements and news, special promotional offers, signing/convention calendar for our authors and editors, and much more.

To subscribe to the DRIN: send a blank e-mail to join-ibd-dist@list.randomhouse.com or sign up at www.delreydigital.com

The DRIN is also available at no charge for your PDA devices—go to www.randomhouse.com/partners/avantgo for more information, or visit www.avantgo.com and search for the Books@Random channel.

Questions? E-mail us at delrey@randomhouse.com

 www.delreydigital.com